Anne Elliot
A New Beginning

By Mary Lydon Simonsen

Quail Creek Publishing, LLC

This story was previously published on the Jane Austen Fan Fiction website, A Happy Assembly, www.meryton.com, as *Anne Elliot, I Am Woman*. However, a multitude of changes have been made since it first appeared in 2009, and it is no longer available on line.

Printed in the United States of America

Published by Quail Creek Publishing, LLC
quailcreekpub@hotmail.com
www.marysimonsenfanfiction.blogspot.com
Peoria, Arizona

Cover artwork is an illustration by Charles E. Brock of Jane Austen's *Persuasion* 1909.

Chapter 1

It was official. Anne Elliot was a spinster. During her twenty-third and twenty-fourth years, her father and sisters had frequently stated that if Anne did not find a suitor very quickly, she would die a spinster. Thus it was on the occasion of her twenty-fifth birthday, when friends and family had gathered at Kellynch Hall to celebrate Anne's milestone, that her dear Papa, Sir Walter Elliot, Baronet, had announced that he had abandoned all hope of his middle daughter ever marrying and, therefore, had declared this day of celebration to be the first day of the rest of her unmarried life.

Even though her sister was two years older than Anne, the epithet of "spinster" had never been applied to Elizabeth because she had prospects, whereas Anne had none. It had been eight years since the only man in Anne's life, Frederick Wentworth, had paid any attention to her. With the passage of so much time, only Lady Russell, a family friend, remembered that the two young lovers had once contemplated marriage, and it was Lady Russell who had counseled Anne to end their relationship, pointing out that Frederick had no money and an uncertain future in the navy. The young, shy, non-confrontational nineteen-year old girl had listened to her mother's dearest friend and had regretted doing so every day since that awful morning when Frederick had walked out of her life, but at least Lady Russell recalled their brief romance. She was sure that the two other people who had known of their love affair, her father and her older sister, Elizabeth, had forgotten all about it.

Rather than being downcast or troubled by her new situation in life, Anne found that being a spinster was liberating. All discussions about how she had lost her bloom so early in life had ceased. Comments about how plain her dresses were or the need for her to do something with her hair, likewise, came to an end, and her whereabouts, which had been of little interest to her father and

Elizabeth, became of no interest to them at all. It was as if she was invisible, and people who are invisible can do things that others cannot.

The realization of just how free she was came upon her quite suddenly. On her morning walk, a rabbit had leapt across her path, and without any consideration as to how she looked, Anne started to chase it. As the animal darted back and forth across an open field, so did Anne, and the exercise had exhilarated her. Thus began a daily regimen of vigorous walking, and when the situation presented itself, chasing after small animals. At first her goals were modest, but the distances continued to lengthen until she was walking at a brisk clip for about two miles every morning.

Rising early, before all but the servants were up and about, Anne disappeared into the morning mist, and as soon as she was clear of the house, began her walk. But soon walking was not enough, and she began to run. Then she noticed that if she moved her arms in such a way and if she controlled her breathing, she could run farther and faster and with less fatigue. Soon she had established a pace that brought her to an optimum level of exertion, but it was neither walking nor running and required its own name. If horses could have different names for their gaits, then why not people?

She spent a number of days pondering the perfect name. At first she had called it jigging, but then abandoned it because it sounded like a dance. Jagging lasted only a day, and jugging sounded ridiculous. But jogging, now that was the perfect name, and every day of fair weather Anne went jogging.

Such physical exertion required a change of wardrobe. The first thing to go were her stays—much too constricting. There was also a problem with her frocks as they were too long and inhibited movement and needed to be shortened. However, that problem was soon solved. Because Elizabeth did not observe the tradition of giving her lady's maid her old dresses and kept them all in a drawer, Anne had a dozen frocks from which to choose. This was important because she had found that a jogger worked up a good deal of sweat, and she would need a clean frock every day. Now that she had acquired the necessary raw materials, there was work to be done. Being an expert with a needle, Anne let out the seams and removed the sleeves and all frills so that nothing rubbed against her skin, and after adding a goodly amount of cotton padding to her shoes, she was off and running—or jogging, if you will.

In short order, Anne took to jogging about the countryside, waving to farmers and field workers, who cheered her on as she sped past them and who provided her with tankards of cool water and wet cloths to wipe her face along her route. At the farthest reach of her run, she had made arrangements with Farmer Goodenough to give her a ride back to Kellynch in his wagon so that she might not be missed. The distances she traversed were so great that she decided that her skills needed further classification, and she declared herself to be a long-distance runner. But even that was not enough. She needed a real challenge.

One rainy afternoon, while thumbing her way through the history of Greece, she came upon the legend of the marathon. In 490 B.C., Pheidippides, a Greek messenger, had been sent to Athens to inform the Athenian assembly that the Persians had been defeated at the Battle of Marathon. He had run the entire distance, approximately twenty-six miles, without stopping. Upon his arrival, he had announced to those assembled, "We have won," and collapsed and died. Anne suspected that if his diet had more protein in it, and if he had been properly hydrated, he would not have died. Regardless, Anne found it to be a great story, and the length of the race! Twenty-six miles! That was what had captured her imagination, and she began training for a marathon.

Anne had thought that all this exercise would leave her so tired that she would be unable to see to her duties as the uncredited mistress of the house, but the exact opposite had occurred. She had too much energy, and so on rainy days when she was trapped at Kellynch Hall, she found it impossible to sit still. With the permission of Mr. Allgood, the butler, Anne took to climbing the stairs that were used exclusively by the servants. There were four floors between the servants' hall below and their private quarters above, and these hidden helpers, who kept Kellynch running smoothly on very little money and who loved her, cheered her on.

Because a marathon is a test of endurance, she needed to be stronger, and in order to strengthen her muscles, Mr. Farrier, the stable master, secured pieces of iron from the smithy for her, and Anne began a weight training program.

The changes were dramatic. Her skin, now a beautiful golden-brown, glowed from all the exertion, and under her frock, her muscles rippled. But it was the confidence that she had gained by setting goals and achieving her aims that was the most noticeable thing about her; that is, they were noticeable to those who took note of her. Fortunately, her family did not, and it was only because she was invisible that she was able to accomplish all of these things.

It was on the day she had finally succeeded in running the full twenty-six miles of a marathon that she had learned that everything she had come to value would be denied her. Her father was so hopelessly in debt that it had become necessary for the family to "retrench," and on the advice of the family solicitor, Mr. Shepherd, and with the assistance of Lady Russell, Kellynch Hall was to be let, and the family was to move out of the manor house and into more economical accommodations in Bath, where it would be all but impossible for even one so plain as Anne to remain invisible.

Chapter 2

"Kellynch Hall? Sophia, did I hear you correctly? You and the admiral have taken a lease on Kellynch Hall in Somerset?" Captain Frederick Wentworth of His Majesty's Navy asked his sister, Mrs. Croft.

"Yes, are you acquainted with the Elliot family?"

"I was occasionally a guest in their home before taking command of the *Asp*."

"My goodness! The *Asp*! Your first command. Well, that *was* a long time ago."

"Yes, it was eight very long years ago."

"Well, my dear brother, in the intervening years, it seems that Sir Walter and his family have been living beyond their means, and of necessity, they have been forced to rent the manor house. Does this report not square with what you know of the Elliots?"

"To the contrary, it is exactly as I remember them," Frederick answered with an edge in his voice. "While the middle daughter, Miss Anne, was encouraging economy, the father and eldest daughter were ordering a new carriage," and he shook his head in disgust, thinking of how their spendthrift ways had forced Anne out of the home she loved so dearly. "Since they must quit the property, I assume the family has made other arrangements."

"I have been told by the agent that they are to move to Bath to reduce their expenses and preserve more of their income."

Frederick remembered that Anne hated Bath, but then maybe Anne was no longer an Elliot, having traded her name for another and lived elsewhere. "Have the daughters married?"

"I am sure that the eldest remains unmarried because it was she, along with a family friend, Lady Russell, who negotiated the terms of the lease."

"That the eldest remains unmarried does not surprise me. Both her father and Miss Elliot were of the opinion that no one was good enough for her. She was pretty, like a rose, but was more thorn than flower."

"I did not have time to form an opinion of her," Sophia responded. "It was obvious that she wished to have this unpleasant task put behind her so that she might go to Bath. As for the father, after introductions were made, he left the room, leaving the particulars of the lease to his eldest daughter and Lady Russell. I did learn that one of the two younger daughters has married."

"But you do not know which one? I imagine it must be Anne, being the elder of the two." But Sophia had no answer to her brother's question.

At the mention of Lady Russell's name, Frederick was flooded with a wave of painful memories. It was that meddling lady who had convinced Anne that although he was brilliant, he was also headstrong and with a fearlessness of mind that she did not like, and God forgive him, one of his shortcomings was that he had a taste for wit—no *bon mots* for Lady Russell. It was she who had succeeded in convincing the young Anne that Frederick Wentworth was a man with no future, or if he did have a future, it was in a violent profession which required him to be out-of-doors most of the time, resulting in a rugged, unappealing look that invited comment. Gentlemen did not sport a tan.

He had heard this complaint more than once. "A sailor's face is the color of mahogany—brown, rough and rugged to the last degree, all lines and wrinkles, adding twenty years to a man's true age." But wasn't it these same brown men who had prevented the invasion of Britain by France? Hadn't the Admiralty asked the population of this sceptered isle, "What can England's brown men do for you?" and hadn't they done it? But now that the little Corsican Corporal had been exiled to the Isle of Elba in the Mediterranean Sea, those who had benefited the most from their service wanted these leathery men to go away.

Even if Lady Russell could have seen into the future and had known of the riches he would accumulate as a result of his years on the high seas, or if she had seen him in his glory as a captain in the Royal Navy dressed in all his sartorial splendor: cocked hat, gleaming brass buttons on his navy blue coat, very tight white breeches, and adorable slippers, she would have, with the possible exception of the breeches, remained unmoved and would still have spoken out against the match.

His thoughts were interrupted by his sister. Sophia, who believed that it is a truth universally acknowledged that an unmarried naval officer in possession of a good fortune must be in want of a wife, wanted to know if it was her brother's intention to seek a wife now that the wars with Napoleon had come to an end.

"What else is there to do now that Monsieur Napoleon is no longer a menace on land or at sea, and I am cast upon the shore on half pay? So I shall ask for you to be on the lookout for a woman with a strong mind and sweetness of temper so that I might raise a family. I know what I want in a wife for I have thought on the subject more than most men," and Anne Elliot was still on his mind when he spoke those words.

* * *

Although convinced that it was the right decision to lease Kellynch to Admiral and Mrs. Croft, Lady Russell was concerned about what Anne's reaction might be when she learned that her home had been rented to the sister and brother-in-law of Frederick Wentworth, the great love of her life. To avoid a recurrence of painful memories, Lady Russell invited Anne to take tea with her at her home while the unpleasant business of signing the contract and turning over the keys to Kellynch was taking place at the manor house.

Prior to this day, the subject of Anne and Frederick had never been discussed, but Anne at twenty-seven thought very differently from what she had been made to think at nineteen and refused to avoid the subject.

"Lady Russell, I have never blamed you for your advice regarding Captain Wentworth."

Placing her hand on Anne's, Lady Russell said, "We shall not speak of it, dear. It is best left in the past."

"Shall we not speak of it to spare your feelings or mine?" Anne asked.

"Anne, my thoughts are with you," Lady Russell answered, surprised at her protégé's frankness.

"Then please allow me to speak. Despite your anxiety about Frederick's profession, rank, and ruggedness, I know that I should have been a happier woman if I had kept the engagement than I have been in sacrificing it, but what has been done cannot be undone. I know from the navy lists and the newspapers that the captain has taken many prize ships and has become very rich, and a wealthy, well-established man will want a wife. At some time, probably in the near future, I shall hear news that Captain Wentworth is engaged, and I shall wish him joy. But in the meantime, I have no intention of hiding from him like some frightened mouse. Hopefully, after eight years of separation, both of us can move about the country without embarrassment in the event we should meet, so I shall go up to the house and greet the new residents of Kellynch Hall. If the captain's name should be mentioned, I will be perfectly fine and will be pleased to hear news of him."

"If that is what you want to do and are comfortable in visiting with the Crofts, you should do so. After the Crofts take possession of the house, I assume that you will wish to join your father and Elizabeth in Bath," Lady Russell said, but she was soon to learn that she should not assume anything as far as Anne was concerned.

“Oh, no! I have no intention of going to Bath for several weeks. Mary has sent word that she is unwell and has asked that I come to Uppercross to care for her.”

“Your sister is unwell—again?”

“Not again, but still. I bring her draughts which are little more than honey and some berry juice, but she swears they revive her. However, it only lasts a week or two before her complaints begin anew. This pattern will continue until Charles pays more attention to her, and it is a silly game that must come to an end.”

“Anne, your words… they are so blunt, so unfeeling. It is unlike you. You have changed greatly of late.”

“Yes, Lady Russell, I have changed, and my transformation is ongoing. However, it is not a recent event, but one that has been happening under everyone’s noses for nearly two years and can be dated from my twenty-fifth birthday. And because I have altered, those around me must change as well. The Anne Elliot my family and you knew is no more.”

Chapter 3

Mary's welcome was as expected. "Anne, why did you not come sooner? I have been very ill."

"Didn't I hear Charles say that you and he had dined with the Pooles last evening?"

In preparation for her visit with Mary, Anne had researched her sister's preoccupation with imaginary health issues and had discovered that there was actually a word to describe it: hypochondria. Anne's admiration for the Greeks, who had come up with the terminology, was growing. First, the marathon, and now this. Some medical people associated the condition with the upper abdomen, the hypochondrium, but Anne wasn't buying it. Although slight of build, Mary ate like a horse with no observable adverse effects. Her problems were not in her stomach, but in her head.

"I did eat with the Pooles," Mary said sheepishly. "I was fine until I had to share a carriage with Mr. and Mrs. Musgrove. They take up so much room. We were practically breathing each other's air, and I am sure I became ill as a result of such close contact."

"Mary, as wonderful as your in-laws are, there is more of them to admire every year, so you could not possibly have been surprised to find yourself squashed up when sharing a carriage with two such large people. This could have been avoided if you and Charles had taken your own carriage."

"You are very short today, Anne, and why are you so brown? What have you been doing? You look like a laborer."

Ah! Someone else had noticed. In two days time, Lady Russell and now Mary had picked up on the changes in Anne. If this kept up, then her father might remember that he had three daughters, and not two, and the Elizabeth had two sisters, and not one.

"What have I been doing? The same thing I have been doing for two years. I run every morning from Kellynch to Mr. Goodenough's farm."

"Anne, a lady does not run, and it is not possible for even a man to run such a distance, no less a woman. I do not understand what you are talking about."

"Mary, sit down and allow me to explain," and she waited for her sister to return to her overstuffed chair. "What I meant by my use of the verb 'to run' is exactly what your two sons do every day. I do not walk. I do not skip. I run. This is something I have done every day, weather permitting, for a very long time now, and as a result, I am quite capable of running or, as I prefer to call it, jogging, all the way to Mr. Goodenough's farm."

"Is that why you are so brown? You go out-of-doors without your bonnet?"

"And without my stays as well as they are too confining and interfere with my rhythm. Establishing a rhythm is very important in long-distance running."

Mary stared at her sister as if she were speaking a foreign language—very likely Hindi—since she did not understand a word she was saying. Jogging? Rhythm? Long-distance running?

There was much more to be said, but their conversation was cut short by the sound of laughter coming from Henrietta and Louisa Musgrove, Mary's sisters-in-law, who had come to report on a visit of short duration that they had had with a naval captain who was visiting their brother.

"His name is Captain Frederick Wentworth, and he is so very handsome—quite the handsomest man of our acquaintance and so very tall," Henrietta began with a giggle. "He has come to Uppercross to shoot Charles. I mean to shoot with Charles."

"Captain Wentworth has come to Uppercross?" Anne asked, greatly surprised, and wondered how such a thing had come to be. As far as she knew, Charles and Frederick had had little contact while the Captain was serving in His Majesty's Navy. Therefore, it seemed logical to assume that he had come to Somerset to visit Admiral and Mrs. Croft. She knew that Frederick had a very close relationship with his sister.

"The captain is certainly most agreeable," Louisa remarked. "He says everything with such exquisite grace. It really is too bad that he could not dine with us tonight, but he is to come to supper tomorrow. He promised to do so in the most pleasant manner. Anne, you should hear his voice; it has such resonance," the elder sister said with a sigh. Apparently, Frederick had succeeded in turning the heads of the eligible and well-dowered Musgrove sisters in under an hour. The captain must be aging well.

"I suppose we shall not be invited; that it will be an intimate family affair," Mary said in her most pathetic voice.

"Of course, you are invited, Mary, and Anne as well," Louisa said. "That is why we have come."

"I am not sure we can join you, Louisa," Anne said with a look of regret on her face. "Mary has been unwell, thus the reason for my visit. She asked me to come to Uppercross to see to her care."

"Well, Anne, your presence has already been of great benefit to me," Mary quickly interjected. "So, my dear sisters, please tell your father and mother that we shall be most happy to join them," and Mary gave Anne a great big smile to show her that she was already on the mend.

* * *

As soon as Admiral and Mrs. Croft took possession of the manor house, Frederick had traveled the short distance between Kellynch Hall and Uppercross so that he might pay a call on the couple. Because their sea commands separated them by great distances, Admiral Croft and Captain Wentworth often did not see each other for great lengths of time, but despite that, they enjoyed a friendship that was closer than many who saw each other every day.

"Frederick, come into the drawing room. The Admiral and I were about to have a glass of wine before dinner," Sophie said.

After each had a glass in hand, the Admiral raised his and said, "Let us make a toast to Mr. Bonaparte who was so good as to start a war that has brought both of us such riches," Croft said with a laugh. Frederick's *Laconia* had taken so many prize ships and privateers that it was likely that he was now richer than the Crofts.

"Is this your Madeira or the Elliots'?" Frederick asked.

"Oh definitely not Sir Walter's," Sophie answered. "The wine cabinet was emptied, and I was told by Mr. Allgood that its contents had been sent ahead to Bath, but then he hinted that there was very little to be sent on. This bottle was left for us courtesy of Miss Anne Elliot, who graciously welcomed us to her home and led us on a tour of the house and gardens so that we might immediately feel as if we were in our own home."

So it was not Anne, but Mary, who had married, Frederick thought. But what did it matter? He would not risk having his heart broken again. No, not broken, but pierced a thousand times with tiny arrows. A spear thrust into his chest could not have done more damage. A sword separating the chambers of his heart into quarters would have been a mercy compared to what he had endured as a result of her having rejected him. And, besides, the two Musgrove sisters were pretty and delightful company, and either would serve him well as a wife.

* * *

Anne had been putting the last pin in her hair when she heard the first scream. She hurried downstairs to discover that Little Charles had fallen out of a tree, and it was believed that he had dislocated his collar bone. Mary was running about the yard in a fit of hysteria, and her chicken-without-a-head movements were interfering with a servant carrying the miniature Charles into the house.

It was quickly determined that the injury was not life-threatening, and after Anne popped the bone back into place, she predicted a speedy recovery for the little fellow. Mary was all for sending for the apothecary, but when reminded that she had a dinner engagement, she agreed that the boy would be running around as fit as a fiddle in the morning. But the boy's father disagreed.

"Mary, surely, you will stay with our son. Even if the injury is minor, he will need his mother by his side. It was a frightening experience."

"But there wasn't even any blood spilt!" Mary cried.

Charles quickly left the room refusing to engage his wife in further discussion. There were things that men did, and there were things that women did. Men shot pheasant; women nursed children.

"Mary, I want you to go with Charles," Anne said, after seeing her sister's unhappiness. If Mary did not go, she would whine all night long, and sitting alone with her sister's offspring was better than listening to Mary's complaints. "I will see to the child."

Anne had not been all that keen on going in the first place because she really did not want to see Captain Wentworth, especially since the flirting by the amiable and outgoing Henrietta and Louisa would be considerable. It wasn't because she was concerned that she risked opening old wounds as there were no more tears left to be shed. After Frederick had set sail, she had read copious amounts of maudlin poetry, as well as tales of star-crossed lovers in English, French, and Italian, and without making the effort to search through ancient texts, there was nothing more to be read on the subject. As far as Lady Russell was concerned, she had run out of scenarios for punishing her for her interference. No more thoughts of dungeons and manacles or remote islands with huge bird populations, but no shelter, or a boat cut free from its moorings and left to drift with the ocean's tides. That was all behind her, so why not let Mary meet the captain?

"You really think I should go?" Mary asked, while keeping her eyes on the hallway lest Charles get away without her. "I am not sure that I should."

"Yes, I want you to go, but in return, you must stop pretending to be ill when you are not. You have become a hypochondriac. You act as if you are unwell so Charles will pay attention to you, but it has the reverse effect. He ends up spending even more time away from you. And you really must try to be more positive. You don't want people singing, 'Every party has a pooper that's why we invited Mary.'"

"Oh, that is awful."

"I agree. It isn't the cleverest of ditties."

"I meant that it was awful that they were singing it about me."

"Well, then do something about it," and standing up, she moved Mary in the direction of the front hallway. "You can change your life by thinking positive thoughts and acting on them. Keep to the sunny side of the street."

"Thank you, Anne," Mary said, squeezing her sister's hand. "I will try to be more cheerful. If only Charles would..."

"Off you go or Charles will leave without you."

After seeing the carriage well down the lane, Anne went back into the house to find the younger Musgrove son and his brother, wee Charles, playing with his wooden soldiers using only his left hand. He was doing just fine, and so Anne picked up Mary's knitting to occupy her time. While she stitched one and purled two, she thought how change was possible for everyone, no one knew that better than Anne, but Mary, my goodness, there was a challenge.

Chapter 4

The best way to sum up the Musgroves' visit with Captain Wentworth was "a good time was had by all." The evening had included interesting conversation, music, singing, laughing, and only a passing reference made to Anne by any of the parties.

"The captain is to come by this morning as he and Charles are to go shooting," Mary said, while biting into her third piece of bread smothered in butter. Where did she put it all, Anne wondered?

"Well, now that Little Charles is on the mend, I intend to go for a long walk," Anne said, "so please offer my good wishes to the captain," and she went to retrieve her cloak.

"You may give him your good wishes yourself," Mary said. "He is already here."

From the minute his gorgeous, six-foot frame filled the door of the breakfast room, it was obvious that the captain did not want to see Anne, but being a gentleman, he would not snub anyone—not even an old love who had broken his heart. After interrupting Mary, who was in the process of introducing the two, the captain explained that Anne and he were already acquainted. After that, he said how good it was to see her again—not really—and then mumbled something about not giving Charles the best position for that day's round of killing scores of birds.

Anne, seeing how ill at ease he was, asked if he had found his land legs yet. "I imagine that after walking aboard a ship for all these years that you must find it a challenge to walk on something that does not move beneath you," and she gave him a full smile. She would not be intimidated by his awesomeness or his amazing soulful dark blue eyes, black hair, solid jaw, and broad chest. Unfortunately, the best parts, his trim waist and tight-fitting breeches, were concealed by his long coat, but there were some things one never forgot.

"You are correct, Miss Anne. Now that I am here in Somerset, I do find myself off balance," and he bowed and left the room.

Despite the awkwardness of this their first meeting, Anne was pleased. Finally, they had met, and the worst was over. She had acquitted herself quite well, remaining calm and steady, and being in a very good mood, she happily went outside and walked in the opposite direction to the shooting party so that she might go jogging. After getting clear of the house, she found a place where she could stretch before getting started, and as the muscles in her legs lengthened, she felt all tension leaving her body, and after running in place for a few minutes, she was off.

When she returned to Uppercross, the party pooper was waiting for her. "The captain was not very gallant by you," Mary said as soon as Anne was in the door. "This morning, when Henrietta asked him what he thought of you, he said that you were so altered he should not have known you."

"After eight years, he found me altered? My goodness, what a surprise."

But Anne would not be brought low. She was pretty sure she had turned in one of her best times. If only there was some type of watch—one that she would stop as soon as she had reached the end of her run. In that way, she would have an exact time of how long it took for her to go from start to finish. She decided to visit the watchmaker when she was in Bath to see if such an instrument existed.

* * *

Although an excellent shot, because Frederick had been thinking about Anne Elliot, he had missed another pheasant. There was no doubt that she had used him ill, showing a feebleness of character, weakness, and timidity, which someone with his confident temper could not endure. Except for some natural curiosity, which had been satisfied by their meeting this morning, he had no desire to see her again. Her power over him was gone forever, and it was now his intention to take a wife. Any woman, between eighteen and thirty, with a little beauty, a few smiles, and who uttered some compliments about the navy, could have him for the asking.

Yes, a few smiles—or maybe just one. As he loaded his gun for the next shot, he continued to think about Anne, or at least the Miss Elliot he had left eight years earlier: quiet, circumspect, in awe of his awesomeness. But that was not the Anne he had encountered in the kitchen. That lady was a bronze goddess with a gleaming smile, perky breasts, and arms made of iron. Others might be slow to notice the transformation, but for someone who had made a study of every facet of her being, he immediately noted the changes, especially the aura of confidence that surrounded her.

And she had given him such a warm welcome, as if but a moment in time had passed, and not eight years. But she had greeted him not as a lover, but as a friend. Obviously, she had forgotten him. For what were eight years when measured against her twenty-seven years? Well, actually it was more than a third of her lifetime, which was quite a lot, but that only mattered if she still cared about him.

"Captain, if you do not take better aim," Charles said, trying to get the distracted man to focus, "I shall be able to claim that I shot every one of these birds and you none."

"I apologize, Musgrove. It is just that I spend most of my time with men and away from genteel society, so to be surrounded by so much female beauty, it has quite set me back and I cannot concentrate."

"Yes, Louisa and Henrietta are fine-looking young ladies, and Mary, despite having had the two boys, is still very attractive. And Anne, well, she has never looked better. Of late, there has been such a change in her. It reminds me of why I once made her an offer of marriage."

Frederick had been taking aim when Charles had uttered that remarkable statement, but then stopped and pointed his gun at the ground. "You asked Anne to marry you? When?"

"Oh, I believe you were serving in the East Indies. She did not refuse me outright, but very nicely directed me towards Mary, and I have never forgiven her for that," he said, laughing. "But it was probably for the best. I recall that at the time she had a sadness about her. It was almost as if she were suffering from a broken heart. Got that one," he said blasting another bird.

Why had Anne refused Charles? The man was amiable, not unattractive, had a good income and could have provided her with a comfortable home near Kellynch. Additionally, it would have been a good match for her as well with no objections from the family to deal with, and then he remembered what her family's interference had cost him, and he got a brace of pheasant with one shot.

* * *

That evening at the Musgroves' home, Frederick was to see more of her gleaming smiles at dinner. Anne, sitting at the far end of the table from him, spoke with much animation with Admiral Croft and his sister, paying little attention to the oohs and aahs his adventures were eliciting from Henrietta and Louisa. Such enthusiasm from two women under twenty years of age was to be expected. They hung on his every word and would jump up and consult the naval lists every time he mentioned the name of a ship, but one of his statements regarding his first command had caught the ear of the Admiral.

"Wentworth, you complain of your command of the *Asp.* What nonsense you young fellows talk," Admiral Croft said. "Never was there a better sloop than the *Asp*. You were a lucky fellow to get her—to get anything so soon and at such a young age."

"I felt my luck, Admiral, I assure you," the captain said with a tone that changed from all lightness to one with a seriousness of purpose. "I was well satisfied with my appointment. It was a great object with me at that time to be at sea. I wanted to be doing something. That was in the year six," and he turned his gaze on Anne. That was the year she had rejected him. "Yes, I had much on my mind in the year six, and I was happy to be at sea."

The discussion then turned to the matter of women being allowed on board ship. Mrs. Croft had sailed with her husband on every possible occasion and could boast that she had crossed the Atlantic four times.

"Frederick, last spring, if you had been a week later at Lisbon," the Admiral said, "you would have been asked to give passage to Lady Mary Grierson and her daughters."

"Then I am glad I was not a week later," and all the ladies laughed. "I hate to hear of women on board, and no ship under my command shall ever convey a family of ladies anywhere if I can help it. And before you castigate me, Sophie, please allow me to explain. It is impossible to make the necessary accommodations that women ought to have so they will be comfortable."

But his sister was all over him. "I hate to hear you talking as if women were all fine ladies instead of rational creatures. We none of us expect to be in smooth waters all our days."

To that, Anne added her two pence. "Well said, Mrs. Croft."

"From that response I take it that you approve of women being aboard ship, Miss Anne," the captain said.

"I neither approve nor disapprove, but leave it up to the captain of the ship. Your sister has just shared with us that the only time she was unwell was when she was *not* with the Admiral. Her happiness is tied to that of her husband, and if he has no objection, why should she not sail with him?"

"Sophie has been most fortunate in that she has sailed with Admiral Croft on some very fine vessels. So I would suggest that a lady's happiness on board is very much determined by the quality of the ship," Frederick countered.

"I would say that it is more likely to be determined by the quality of the husband." When everyone burst out laughing, Frederick looked flummoxed. This was not the quiet Anne he had fallen in love with. This Anne was a woman with her own thoughts and one willing to express them.

The evening ended with dancing. Anne offered to play the spinet, and Henrietta and Louisa made the most of her offer and danced one dance after another with the captain. While doing a lively jig, Louisa was heard to remark that Anne no longer danced, and when Anne had stopped playing so that she might find another piece of music, the captain ventured to ask her why she no longer danced.

"I am the designated player. I perform so that others might dance."

"Do you not enjoy dancing? That is not how I remember you at all."

"Oh, I do enjoy dancing, but I also enjoy playing. Besides, it is the young people who should dance."

"Good grief! You are not so old that you must give up dancing."

"Whether I am young or old is in the eye of the beholder. I daresay the elder Mr. Musgrove would declare me to be a youth while his daughters would call me a spinster."

"A spinster? The only spinsters I know are women who have chosen that life or have had it forced upon them because of a lack of offers. In your case, I can say with absolute certainty it was not the latter," he said, looking directly into her eyes.

"There is a third reason, Captain," Anne said, returning his gaze. "There are those ladies who have made unwise decisions in their youth and have had to pay for their errors by living the single life. Now, is there something in particular you wish for me to play for you?"

"Yes, I would like to hear *The Ash Grove*."

"No. I cannot do that. I do not have the music," Anne said. She had not played the tune since he had left her in the year six. Why was he asking for her to play their song? Maybe because it ended with the lovers parting? Often in the years following their breakup, Anne wondered why they had chosen a song with such a sad ending. Was it possible that their separation was preordained?

"You used to know it by heart."

"I haven't played it in a long time," Anne answered, staring straight ahead.

"Play it, Anne. Please play *The Ash Grove*," and he walked away.

Her hands hovered over the spinet, unsure if she could perform. "Well, if he can take it, so can I." Her fingers sought out the keys, and she began to sing.

Down yonder green valley where streamlets meander,
When twilight is fading, I pensively rove,
Or at the bright noontide in solitude wander
Amid the dark shades of the lonely ash grove.

'Twas there while the blackbird was joyfully singing,
I first met my dear one, the joy of my heart.
Around us for gladness the bluebells were ringing,
Ah! Then little thought how soon we should part.

After she had finished, Anne dared not look at Frederick because there were tears in her eyes, and so she began to play a robust tune that caused the Misses Musgrove to pull the captain back onto the dance floor. She ended the evening with a rousing *Rule Britannia* to a round of applause by everyone, including a puzzled Captain Wentworth.

Chapter 5

The next morning, between mouthfuls of ham, Mary asked her sister whether Captain Wentworth would choose Henrietta or Louisa as his wife. Anne was determined to reveal nothing, and so she took a deep breath before answering.

"I confess I do not see much inclination on the captain's part to marry either, but if I must choose, I would say Louisa. She is older and more mature. Although Henrietta enjoys flirting as much as anyone her age, I think she really wants to marry Charles Hayter, and I do not want to hear how much you dislike him because you have never given me one good reason why it should be so. And please do not speak of his taking orders and becoming a lowly curate because when his uncle dies, he will step into very pretty property. The estate at Winthrop has some of the best pastureland in the country and provides its current occupant with a handsome income."

Mary had not heard the second part of Anne's answer because she had been watching Louisa and Henrietta making haste down the lane, and she called after them. When she learned that they were going for a long walk, she insisted on joining them and said that Anne should come as well. It was a beautiful autumn day, and Anne had no objection, although she could not say the same for Henrietta and Louisa as they would have preferred to go without their brother's wife.

Before they had reached the end of the lane, they encountered Captain Wentworth and Charles. The men had taken out a young dog, who had spoiled their sport by chasing away all of the birds, and sent them back home early. Since it was such a beautiful day, they needed little convincing to join the ladies on their walk.

While Louisa and Frederick took the lead, Charles walked between Henrietta and Mary, with Anne bringing up the rear. Louisa's interest in the handsome officer was marked, but for the captain, not as much, or he would not have kept turning around to look at those behind him. In fact, Frederick turned around so frequently that Anne kept looking behind her to see what was drawing his attention, but there was nothing there except woods and pasture.

As for Louisa's part, she did notice that Captain Wentworth was inattentive, and in an effort to engage him, she continued the conversation from the previous evening about women being allowed on board ship. "I should do the same as your sister. If I loved a man, I would always be with him. Nothing should ever separate us."

"Really?" was his only response. "Don't you think we should wait for Anne? She really is falling behind," and he wondered if she was tired from caring for little Charles.

"But that is her preference," Louisa assured him. "She never wishes to be noticed, and do not be surprised if she dashes off the trail, which she has done on a number of occasions while walking with Henrietta and me. She acts no differently than Laddie, our collie, does when he sees a squirrel or a rabbit. One minute she is with us, and the next, she is gone. Captain, please do not worry. I assure you that she will catch up with us. She always does."

The party continued on toward Winthrop, the Hayter estate. It was Charles's intention to call on his cousin, and Henrietta was very keen to see the young curate whom she hoped one day to marry. Once the estate came into view, Mary refused to go one step farther and plunked her bottom down on a rock, but Charles and Henrietta continued on while Louisa and the captain chose a different path.

Anne was now so far behind the party that when she came over a rise, she saw no one but Mary. Because her younger sister was sitting on a rock all by herself, it did not take much guessing on Anne's part to figure out what had happened. But with a blue sky and the autumn colors at their peak, today was a day to rejoice and be glad, not to give comfort to a pouter. Anne, who had spotted an opening in the woods and had discovered a lightly-traveled path, made a dash for it, hoping that Mary would not see her. Mary did not, but the captain did.

"Well, she must have seen a squirrel or a rabbit because there she goes," he said under his breath, watching as Anne emerged from the woods, going at a right good clip.

"Who goes where?" Louisa asked, and the captain just shook his head in puzzlement. Did Anne actually think she could catch a rabbit or squirrel? And what would she do with it if she did?

The couple continued their walk and drew within a few feet of Anne, who waited for them to pass, but not before she had heard the captain describe to Louisa the one attribute he prized above all others: decisiveness.

"Here is a nut," Frederick said, cutting one down from a bough, "which is blessed with its original strength and has outlived all storms. While so many of its brethren have fallen and been trodden under foot, it is still in possession of all the happiness that a hazelnut can be capable of. My first wish for all whom I am interested in is that they should be firm."

Oh, not the nut analogy again, Anne thought. He had used it in their last conversation, and because she could not imagine a hazelnut being happy or unhappy, it had not resonated with her. Instead, she had taken to heart his final words: "No one will ever love you as I do, and I will never love another." But she must think of other things or she would be no better than Mary, dwelling only on the negative.

After being sure that both the captain and his biggest fan had moved on, Anne went and stood where the pair had been because it afforded a lovely view of rolling pasture leading down to the village of Winthrop. Her preference was always to be in the country. She did not want to go to Bath as there were eyes everywhere, just waiting for someone to slip up so that they might criticize them. It would be impossible for her to continue her athletic pursuits while living in town. She had already given up her marathon training, but if she went to Bath, she would not be able to run or even to walk fast because both would invite criticism, and her father and Elizabeth would hear of it and rebuke her for such unladylike behavior. No, she would delay going to Bath, and even though it meant listening to Mary's constant complaining, she would do everything she could to remain in the country.

"Miss Anne, is everything all right?" the captain asked as he came out of the woods.

Anne had been so engrossed in the scene before her that she had not heard Frederick come up from behind her.

"Perfectly so. I was just enjoying the view."

"But you are all alone. It should not be so."

"If you are concerned for my safety, you may come and sit by me, but I am not ready to return to the path," and Anne folded up her shawl, placed it on the grass, and sat down, and the captain, wearing his long coat, sat down beside her.

"I was here a few minutes ago with Louisa."

"Yes, I heard some of your conversation. You were discussing your nuts. I mean hazelnuts—not your nuts. Sorry," she said, blushing.

When the captain saw her reddening, he laughed, and Anne laughed with him for the first time in eight years.

"You always were one for pastoral scenes," the captain said.

"Yes, and autumn is my favorite season, that is, until spring comes."

Frederick nodded in agreement. "I love the sea, but I must admit that it is good to come into port and see trees on their hillside perches. Even if there isn't a leaf left on them, at least you have a real feel for the season, which you cannot get out on the open sea."

"You have done well for yourself on the open sea, Captain Wentworth."

"Which you did not expect to happen."

"No. You are wrong. I had no expectations. When we were together, I lived in the fullness of each day; I had no need of tomorrows. It was others who had expectations."

Frederick looked into her eyes, and as he leaned towards her, he wanted to blot out everything except this beautiful Anne. There was no painful past; no acrimony; no nights spent dreaming, longing, needing his Anne; and, apparently, no privacy either because Louisa was coming up the path calling his name.

"Damn!" he muttered under his breath.

"You should go, Captain, but before you do, please allow me to tell you that Louisa is most amiable and has a kind heart. She will make a fine companion."

"So you will see me married, Miss Anne. Very well." And he got up, and without looking back, he walked towards the sound of Louisa's voice, banging his hat against his leg in frustration.

* * *

When Anne joined the rest of the party, she found the group talking to Admiral and Mrs. Croft, who had come up the road in a gig. All were in good cheer, teasing the Admiral about his unsafe driving, which he vociferously denied, but which his wife confirmed.

"Ah, here at last is Miss Anne," the Admiral said by way of diverting the conversation from his less than stellar driving skills.

"Miss Elliot, I am sure you are tired," cried Mrs. Croft. "Do let us have the pleasure of taking you home. Here there is room for three, and if we were all like you, I believe we might sit four."

"No, thank you, Mrs. Croft. I appreciate the offer, but my preference is to walk," but then Mrs. Croft whispered something to her brother. With everyone insisting that she was too tired to continue, and before she could say no, Frederick, with his arms around her waist, had lifted Anne onto a board that ran behind the seat of the gig. But she was no longer a docile creature who would do as she was told or allow others to make decisions for her, and so she hopped off the gig, right into Frederick's arms, and found herself looking at his chest. All she could manage to say was, "You have very large buttons."

"Yes, so I have been told," he answered, surprised to find his arms around Anne's waist.

Anne looked into his blue eyes and said, "I think we are talking about different things. I was referring to the buttons on your coat."

Embarrassed, Frederick took a step back and turned around to find everyone looking at him—at her—at them. It was an extraordinary display: a man and a woman practically joined at the pelvis, but Anne would not give them time to dwell on the scene and said that she was returning to the house and set such a pace that no one had time to offer to accompany her before she had disappeared into the landscape.

Chapter 6

Following the walk to Winthrop, an embarrassed Anne went to her room for the purpose of collecting her thoughts. What had she been thinking to mention the captain's nuts? She understood why they were in the forefront of her mind. While playing the spinet at the Musgroves, he had come over to speak with her, and with her sitting down and him standing up, her eyes were level with his belt and equipment. That accounted for the dreams she had had on and off throughout the night as well as her morning musings, but she was sure she had put them out of her mind during their walk.

Obviously, Frederick was thinking about them as well or why would he have bragged about the size of his buttons? But she knew a little something about this. After she had read every easily accessible book in the Kellynch library, she had gone looking for other reading material. While standing on the top rung of the library ladder, she had happened upon those writings that had been kept hidden from the children and were long forgotten. Along with some medical texts belonging to her mother, she had also read *Tom Jones*, the Greek and Roman Mythologies, and *A Thousand and One Nights*, and she had come to understand that men spent a lot of time thinking about their manhood. So Frederick's reaction was nothing out of the ordinary. It was her reaction that was unusual because women did not think about such things, or at least she could not find any literature that said they did. But then she had found very little to read about what women thought about anything. Regardless, she would have to clear her mind of such thoughts because the captain was to stay for dinner.

* * *

Anne was correct. Men did spend a good deal of time thinking about their most temperamental member. There was no avoiding it, especially when it was standing at attention, as the captain's was just now. But that was Anne's fault. When she had decided that she would not ride in the gig, she had slid off the board, which had thrust her pelvis forward, making direct contact with his manhood and producing the expected result.

In a flash of memory, he recalled the day that Anne and he had sheltered in an out building at Kellynch after being caught in the open in a summer thunderstorm. They had been enjoying some passionate kissing, when she had pushed off on him. Laughing, she had run out into the rain back to the manor house, and another opportunity for such intimacy never arose. The memory of those precious minutes had served him well on every voyage. But he was a disciplined military man, and he must think of other things because he would be dining with her this evening.

During dinner, the captain regaled his audience with tales of life on the high seas and how to capture a prize ship and board her, and Anne thought, "lucky ship" and smiled to herself. But when she glanced up, she saw that Frederick was looking right at her, and she had no doubt that he knew what she was thinking.

* * *

"What have you got there?" Charles asked Captain Wentworth as he pulled a letter out of his pocket.

"It is a letter from my friend, Captain Harville. He was wounded two years ago and has taken up residence in Lyme with his wife and children."

"Lyme? It is but seventeen miles from here."

"Is it possible to get there and back in one day?" the captain asked.

"Most definitely, especially if it is just you on horseback, but since you would most likely be returning in the dark, you would have to be mindful of the roads—not the best stretch between Uppercross and Lyme."

"But why would you do that?" Louisa asked. She had been hanging on the captain's every word for the whole of the evening and did not like the idea of his going missing even for one day. "Why do we not all go to Lyme? The weather is very mild for November, and I do so love the sea."

When Mary and Henrietta added their voices to Louisa's, the captain was outnumbered, and he held up his hands in mock surrender and agreed to the excursion. Setting out the next morning, the group arrived to find the town quite empty. With the arrival of the cooler weather, most of the lodgers had departed and would not return for another five months. As the carriage descended through the hills, passing orchards and empty boarding houses, the party made its way to the Cobb, a man-made harbor composed of boulders, stones, and pebbles, and Anne pictured herself standing at the very end of the stone wall watching the boats as they churned about the harbor while the sea slashed the shore.

After examining her surroundings, Anne realized that the Cobb was not a good place to run as it was almost always wet, and a thin layer of drifting sand made it too risky to do anything but stroll its length. But on the way into town, she had taken note of how deserted everything was, and if she stayed within the confines of the village, she would be able to go up and down the streets at a good pace. She was pretty sure that with so many navy families living in town and with townspeople who were accustomed to seasonal visitors from all over the British Isles, even the oddest behavior would not trouble them if it might result in the sound of a coin dropping into a till. Yes, until she could get back to the country, this would do quite well.

The travelers immediately proceeded to their accommodations at the Three Cups Inn, and after ordering their dinner, they made their way to the Cobb, leaving Captain Wentworth to go in search of his friend. He soon returned with the news that they had all been invited to visit the Harvilles in their home near the foot of an old pier.

The house was so small that it seemed difficult to imagine a man, his wife, and five children in such a small area, and it gave new meaning to the word "squished." But what the inhabitants of the house lacked in square footage, they made up for in domestic felicity, especially since Harville's hobby was to make toys for his children. There was a smile on every face, but one.

The unsmiling countenance belonged to Captain Benwick, who had fallen in love with Captain Harville's sister, and who had taken up residence at the Harville house. Poor Fanny had died while her betrothed was at sea, and Benwick's grief had quite overtaken him. Sensing a kindred spirit, the sad officer made his way over to Anne. After discovering that they shared a love of poetry, they easily fell into conversation, and as Anne had done in her despair over her loss of Frederick, Benwick was reading excessive amounts of Byron.

"Have you read *Giaour*, Miss Elliot?"

"No, I am not familiar with that one." After having read and reread too much romantic poetry, she had placed a self-imposed moratorium on everything Byron wrote.

"When Byron was in Athens, he became acquainted with the Turkish custom of throwing a woman found guilty of adultery into the sea wrapped in a sack."

Anne cringed at the grotesque subject, but her grimace went unnoticed.

"A *giaour* is Turkish for infidel, and the poem tells the story of Leila, a member of her master Hassan's harem, who loves the *giaour*, but who is killed by being drowned in the sea by Hassan. In revenge, the *giaour* kills him, and then, due to his remorse at his taking a life, he enters a monastery."

"My goodness! Nothing cheery in that one, is there?" Anne felt it was necessary to save the man from himself and recommended a larger allowance of prose in his daily study. In addition, she put forward the works of the best moralists and collections of the finest letters. "May I also suggest Shakespeare? His comedies, I mean," she quickly added. "You should stay away from *Romeo and Juliet* and *Othello*."

After such a depressing conversation, Anne felt the need for fresh air and asked Benwick if he would like to take a walk with her. After telling the others of their plans, all agreed that a stroll would be just the thing, and Louisa quickly ran to the side of Captain Wentworth and stayed there. If this kept up, Louisa might think about buying one of those over-blouses sold in all the shops frequented by tourists saying, "I'm With Him," with an arrow pointing towards the captain.

The salt air and refreshing breeze did nothing to lift the captain's spirits, and he was once again quoting Byron, but Anne decided to steer him in another direction.

"Have you ever thought about running?" and when she was met with a blank expression, she continued. "The exercise is very beneficial to your mental and physical wellbeing. I would advise you to buy yourself a good pair of boots and stuff them with cotton padding and go out running. You should start on a flat surface, but once you get your energy up and your muscles are toned, you might think about running up the many paths that snake through these hills. I must tell you that there will be discomfort, but the more vigorous the exercise, the better you feel. And out of this comes a confidence that makes you think that you can conquer the world—or at least Lyme."

"Is this something you do?" he asked in amazement.

"Every chance I get. I know that sounds odd for a woman to be running about the country, but I, too, had a great loss in my life, and this is the only thing that has come close to bringing closure. It helps if you understand that healing involves a process. First, you are in denial that such a thing could have happened to you, and the pain is palpable. Then you get angry, which is followed by depression. I believe you are pretty much stuck in that phase. But if you can push through, you will be rewarded with acceptance. After that, you pick up the pieces and move on to other things. Because if you do not, you will be miserable, and you will make those around you miserable, and eventually, they will flee your company."

"May I run with you tomorrow morning?"

"Yes, of course," and they fixed a time and place to meet. "You can beat this, Captain Benwick. You will rally."

When Benwick returned to his company, he had a smile on his face, and the Harville children, never having seen him smile, ran away because they were frightened of him.

* * *

When the party arrived back at the lodging house, all went to their separate rooms to dress for dinner, but Frederick asked Anne to remain behind so that he might speak with her.

"I don't know what you said to Captain Benwick, but the Harvilles will be forever in your debt. You see, Fanny Harville died last summer before she and Benwick could be married, and he has been moping about the house ever since. I know his grief is real, but in order to move forward, sometimes it requires that a person look to things other than love to compensate for *his* loss."

Anne took a long look at Frederick, and she could see that he was no longer speaking of Benwick. Was he actually saying that in all these years he had not loved again? She was sure that ladies flew to him like moths to a flame. Just look at what he was doing to Louisa, and he wasn't even trying. Was it possible for a man, who had sailed into exotic ports and had met beautiful women from every continent, had remained constant in his affections to plain old Anne Elliot of Kellynch Hall?

"I agree that someone might engaged in an activity to fill the vacuum left by a lost love, but will you agree with me, sir, that there are some who are better able to put the past behind them?" Anne asked. "It may take a person as long as six years before she can think of other things, and even then, in her quiet hours, she must deal with the magnitude of her loss."

"Anne, if you are talking about me quickly putting the past behind me, I can assure you that…"

"Oh, there you are, Captain Wentworth. I did not hear your footsteps go past my door, so I thought something had happened to you," Louisa said, coming up from behind him. "What are you talking about?" she asked in complete ignorance of what she was interrupting.

"We were speaking of Captain Benwick's devotion to the memory of Fanny Harville, and how his love has not diminished with the passing of time."

"Yes, he is a sweet man who dearly loves poetry. Just before we left Captain Harville's house, Captain Benwick gave me his copy of Shakespeare's sonnets."

Anne smiled. Benwick had not been able to abandon poetry entirely, but at least he had stepped away from Byron. "Yes, he is a dear man," Anne said in agreement.

Unbeknownst to Anne, Frederick had noted the length of her conversation with Benwick, which prompted his retort. "I shall leave the two of you to discuss the good captain, as I see he brings smiles to your faces," and he bowed and went up the stairs.

Louisa, being light of heart and mind, thought that the captain's comment was meant as a compliment to her. "Captain Wentworth likes my smile."

But Anne was seeing something else entirely. Frederick was acting as if he was jealous of Captain Benwick. Was it possible that he still loved her? Tomorrow morning, when they all went for a walk on the Cobb, she would have another opportunity to gauge his interest. Which reminded her that she needed to replace the padding in her boots for her early morning run with Benwick.

Chapter 7

Captain Benwick met Anne on the opposite corner to the inn, and as instructed, he brought two flasks of water for them to drink. Anne pointed to a path that led to Up Lyme, and an enthusiastic Benwick nodded his approval. However, the captain had been idle for too long, his only exercise being short walks near the house, away from the noise and ruckus of the Harville household. He would then stare off into the distance while thinking of his dear Fanny. But pining was not exercise, and by the time they had reached the top, Benwick was gasping for air.

"I can tell that I have slowed you down considerably, Miss Anne, as you show no signs of exertion, while I am soaked through."

"It was the same way with me when I first began, but look what your efforts have yielded," and she pointed to expansive sweeps of the country and the bay below, backed by dark cliffs, making it the happiest spot for watching the flow of the tide and sitting in unwearied contemplation. "This view engages all of the senses. The beautiful vista, the roar of the surf, the feel of the wind on your face, and the smell of the salt in the air."

"And taste, Miss Elliot, you forgot taste."

"Ah, yes. But can't you practically taste the fish we shall have for dinner?" and the captain laughed, and Anne saw that it was good, and they began their descent back to the inn.

* * *

Once the tourist season had ended in Lyme, there was little to do in a seaside town. The bathing machines had been stored away, many of the shops were boarded up in preparation for winter storms, and the street performers had packed up their instruments, balls, and fire sticks and had gone elsewhere or were hibernating for the winter. All that was left to do was to stroll along the Cobb—back and forth—back and forth—and hope that the person walking with you was an agreeable companion and an able conversationalist.

The pairings were as expected: Captain Wentworth and Louisa, Mary and Charles, with Henrietta moving between the two couples, and Anne and Captain Benwick. Everyone took note of Anne and her new friend. Because of the sound of the surf and a stiff breeze, conversation was difficult, and Anne had to stay close to her companion so that she might hear him. They were chatting away as if they had known each other for years, and this, of course, invited comment.

Mary was the first to offer her criticism, stating that it was inappropriate for her sister to be so intimate with a man she had only just met. Also, since Anne and Benwick were the lead couple, they were setting a pace that Mary found unsustainable, and Charles, who was starting to get an ale belly due to a lack of exercise, had to agree. Louisa just wished that Anne and Benwick would slow down because it was hard to look soulfully into another's eyes if you were practically moving along at a trot.

As far as Frederick was concerned, the pace was nothing to him; it was how happy Anne and Benwick looked together that kept him moving along. That morning, while shaving, he had glanced out the window only to see Anne and the captain coming down the hill. When they had reached the bottom, Benwick took Anne's hands in his and came darn close to hugging her. As she walked away, her shawl had slipped off her shoulders, revealing a sleeveless frock, exposing beautiful arms with rippling muscles. And the length of her dress! It was six inches above where it should have been, allowing him to make out the beginning of her long legs. And her gorgeous auburn hair? It was tied back, not in a braid, but in something that reminded him of the tail of a pony. What was going on here?

Since returning from his voyages around the world, he had learned that Charles had made Anne an offer of marriage, and Benwick looked as if he might be heading in that direction. If Anne was comfortable being scantily clad while in the presence of a man so new to her acquaintance, then the possibility existed that the two were forming an attachment. Apparently, while Frederick had been at sea, Anne had become a man magnet.

* * *

During their morning walk, everyone was in favor of a suggestion made by the Harvilles that dinner be a fish bake on the beach followed by roasted potatoes and corn on the Cobb. The ladies would see to the food while the men would gather driftwood for the fire. As they made their way back to the inn, a gentleman bumped into Anne, and by his profuse apologies, she determined that he was a man of exceedingly good manners. Her curiosity being aroused, she thought that she should like to find out who he was, and Frederick was of the same mind. He did not like the way he had looked at Anne, and when he learned that the man was staying at the same inn, he asked the innkeeper who he was and returned to announce to his party that the man's name was Elliot.

All were surprised, but Mary was ecstatic. With hand on her breast, she said, "Bless me! He must be our cousin, William Elliot."

When Charles pointed out that Elliot was not an uncommon name and that there must be hundreds of Elliots in England, Mary insisted she was right. Without a scintilla of evidence to support her claim, she said, "I am convinced that he must be our father's heir. When next we see him, we must seek an introduction."

But Frederick, recalling how he had looked at Anne said, "Putting all these extraordinary circumstances together, his being an Elliot, being in Lyme in November, and bumping into Miss Anne, we must consider it to be the arrangement of Providence that you should *not* be introduced to your cousin, if he is your cousin." After he had finished uttering that sentence, he wondered if it had made any sense at all, which was probably the reason no one had responded.

After Mary and Charles and the Musgrove sisters had returned to their rooms, Anne said to the captain, "Providence must not have a lot to do today if the Deity is concerned with who is introduced to whom."

Frederick gave a hearty laugh. There were so many changes in Anne, but this was not one of them. Fond memories of her sharp wit and subtle humor returned, and he offered to buy her one of the small paintings of Lyme that was sold at the front desk. While he was paying the innkeeper, Mr. Elliot walked in and immediately sought Anne out.

"Please forgive me for being so bold, but when you were out walking, I heard someone call you Miss Elliot. I am William Elliot, heir to the Kellynch estate, and since you have something of the Elliot countenance, I am feeling confident that you and I are cousins."

So this was the man who was to inherit the ancestral home of the Elliots. She had met him several years earlier, but had been unable to recall anything about his appearance. And now she knew why. Except for his two front teeth overlapping and his having an overbite, there was nothing exceptional about his looks. The only reason he would have been considered handsome was because he was exceedingly well dressed in the latest fashion introduced by Beau Brummel, and Anne believed that very often the clothes made the man.

"I am Anne Elliot, the daughter of Sir Walter Elliot, and if you think I have the Elliot countenance, then you are the only one. Everyone thinks I favor my mother's side."

"Then it is true; we are cousins," Mr. Elliot said, ignoring the second part of her statement. "What happy news!"

When Frederick had finished purchasing a watercolor of the Cobb, he turned around to find Anne talking to the stranger they had encountered yesterday morning. He didn't like the man. He had looked at Anne with such familiarity that he had taken offense. Someone who was so presumptuous as to make eye contact with a lady unknown to him was no gentleman, and from the way he was looking at her now, it was obvious that he admired her exceedingly. Frederick went to Anne, and he stood so close to her that their arms were touching. Wentworth was sending a message, and this man better be damned sure he got it because the captain was a big, tall fellow and William Elliot was not.

"Mr. Elliot, this is Captain Wentworth of the Royal Navy. He is a friend of the Musgroves, my sister Mary's in-laws from Uppercross," and for a brief moment, Frederick felt one of those tiny arrows pierce his heart. He was not her friend, but a friend of a friend.

"Captain Wentworth, may I say thank you on behalf of a grateful nation for your service against Bonaparte. My French is a little rusty, and I really wasn't looking forward to brushing up on it."

"What brings you to Lyme at this time of year, Mr. Elliot?"

So much for polite discourse, Anne thought.

"I have come from Sidmouth, and I am going to London by way of Bath."

"Then you have traveled in the wrong direction, Mr. Elliot. From Sidmouth, Bath is northeast, not due east."

This statement was followed by an awkward silence, and so Anne inquired after Mr. Elliot's wife. His marriage to a woman of wealth, but no rank, had been one of the reasons that Sir Walter and his heir had had a falling out many years earlier.

"My wife passed away. I am just out of mourning."

"My condolences, Mr. Elliot. We did not know of your loss," Anne said, embarrassed to learn of his sad news under such circumstances.

"Of course, you did not know. How could you? Relations between your father and me have not been cordial, and because of that, one of the reasons I was going to London was to seek a reconciliation."

"My father is in Bath, Mr. Elliot. He has taken a house in Camden Place, and Papa is rarely in town except for the start of the season."

"Well, then I have stumbled upon a bit of good fortune in meeting you as I would have been in Bath and not have known of your father also being in town."

Frederick doubted it had anything to do with fortune—more likely he had planned this whole thing. He did not like the little twerp, and he harrumphed audibly. And what did "just out of mourning" mean. A year? Six months? More likely a month.

"Miss Anne, would you join me for some tea in the dining room? I would like to discuss some family matters with you," and he emphasized the word "family" so that the captain would know that he was not included in the invitation.

"Yes, of course. If you will excuse us, Captain, I will see you this afternoon."

"I am looking forward to it, and my room is the first one to the right on the second floor."

Anne smiled. Wasn't he adorable—so protective of her, and she felt her heart skip a beat.

After they were seated and the tea served, Mr. Elliot began. "I take this as a good sign that I have met you, Miss Anne. It may give me a head start in repairing the damage done between the two Elliot families by first making amends with one of my cousins."

"I have no quarrel with you, Mr. Elliot," and the gentleman smiled, but then Anne continued. "Of course, my father does. He was quite upset that you had married without consulting him, and as I recall, you made disparaging remarks about the baronetcy, which, I must say, makes you unique. I don't think there is another man in England who cares so little for a title, and I shall warn you that the *Baronetage* is the only book my father reads."

"My only excuse for such actions is that I was feeling my oats," he responded, surprised by her candor. "I am older now and better understand where I gave offense."

"That might be sufficient for my father, but then there is my sister. Everyone thought you would make her an offer of marriage, including Elizabeth, but, of course, you did not."

"Miss Anne, I must say that I am surprised by your directness."

"It saves time, and is it not the truth? These things are known facts, and facts cannot be changed no matter how much one would wish as they are stubborn things. Besides, I think you may receive a warmer reception from my father than you might think. I doubt Papa wishes to continue a quarrel with his heir."

With Anne indicating that she wished to leave, Mr. Elliot pulled the chair out for her. "After meeting you, Miss Anne, I find another reason to hope for a quick reconciliation," and he looked directly into her eyes, which she considered to be an impertinence. Anne gave him a weak smile. If he was flirting with her, he was wasting his time.

Frederick had returned to his room, but his thoughts remained with Anne in the dining room. Then the vision of her from the morning took over, and all the anger he had felt towards her because of the events she had set in motion eight years ago dissolved like melting snow. He loved her, and he would have her, and so he must begin to let her know that she had once again captured his heart—if she had ever really lost it.

Chapter 8

Captain Wentworth was chasing the Harville children through the sand, and the little ones were squealing with delight. Frederick had no idea that Harville had so many children. Obviously, he made good use of his time on shore, and why should he not? His wife was a handsome woman, who was most agreeable and generous to a fault. Who else would have taken in a grieving lover for months on end without complaint? But it seemed as if Benwick's mourning period had come to an end. The captain was sitting on a bench with Anne, and the two were as thick as thieves.

"Louisa told me that you gave her your copy of Shakespeare's sonnets," Anne said. "I was very happy to hear of your selection. They are so beautiful. Who could not read them without their spirits soaring?"

"Exactly, Miss Anne," he said, nodding in agreement. "I have put away my Byron, and I have taken another one of your suggestions, that is, to read more prose. I am now reading *The Travels of Marco Polo*, and it is a ripping good tale."

From that point on, Benwick had control of the conversation, and Anne listened with fascination to the tales of the Occidental Polo meeting the Oriental Kublai Khan. The stories were so fascinating that she failed to notice that Frederick could not take his eyes off of her.

"Damn! At this rate, Anne and Benwick might announce their engagement by the end of the fish bake," Frederick said to himself, and he continued to watch Anne as she smiled and laughed, and at one point, actually clapped her hands as she listened to Benwick. What the devil were they talking about? Benwick, the man with the doleful countenance, had never said a funny thing in his life.

After a few minutes more of absorbing the engrossing tale of Marco Polo's travels, Anne stood up, feeling that she should talk to the others in their party. She was particularly keen to get to know Mrs. Harville better. Despite having only one maid to help her with the children and to run a very busy household, she handled her large brood with cheerfulness and aplomb. But before letting her go, Benwick leaned in toward Anne as if he was telling her a secret, and Frederick could hardly believe it.

"Miss Anne, will you walk with me again tomorrow?" Benwick asked, and when he said the word "walk," he gave her a knowing wink. It was his intention to improve on that morning's performance. If he was not yet ready to run great distances, at least he could pick up the pace, and she smiled, understanding exactly what the wink had implied.

Winking? Oh my God! Frederick thought. They were already at the winking and whispering stage, and he felt another of those tiny arrows shooting into his heart. *Have I lost her again?* It was more than he could bear, and he walked off down the beach by himself. But he wasn't alone for long.

"Captain Wentworth, may I join you?" Louisa asked.

"I do not think it is a good idea, Miss Louisa. It is dark, and if you lose your footing, you will fall and you may get hurt."

"But you are always there to catch me."

"Miss Louisa, you are thinking of our walks at Uppercross, but this is very different from assisting someone who is jumping off a stile onto the soft earth of a pasture. Here, you have the shifting sand exposing all sorts of debris brought in on the tide, and your shoes are inadequate for the task."

But Louisa would not listen and pretended to fall, and as she had hoped, the captain caught her. "See, I told you. You always catch me."

"Always is a word that should be used but rarely," he said in a stern voice. "The sun always rises in the east, and the tides will always be regulated by the moon. But my being able to catch you is not an absolute certainty," and he extended his arm so that he might take her back to her family. Because this young lady was obviously flirting with him, he said nothing as they walked towards the others of their party. He had no intention of encouraging her and pretended to show an interest in the stars, when the only star he cared about was not above him, but in front of him.

Upon their return, Frederick was relieved to find Anne comfortably engaged in a conversation with Mrs. Harville, a woman. *Well, that is a nice change*. But then he saw Benwick make a move to join the ladies, and Frederick's reaction was swift. He jumped over a piece of driftwood, and in three giant steps, landed in front of them. If Benwick wanted Anne, he would have to fight for her because Wentworth was a warrior. From his many engagements on the high seas, he understood how to perform in battle. He knew when he could take a ship merely by maneuvering into position, but he also knew when to use his cannon. His preference was to nudge Benwick out of the way, but if that was not possible, he was prepared to blow him right out of the water.

* * *

The next morning, Anne walked out of the inn and inhaled the sea air and felt a gentle breeze, carrying tiny particles of sand, sweep across her face. Benwick waved to her, and she walked across the road to join him. Today, he was more appropriately dressed as he was wearing boots made of a softer, more flexible leather and less form-fitting pants. She wouldn't be at all surprised to learn that he had some chafing between his legs from the day before. She would have suggested that he apply aloe to the affected areas, but such a thing was not discussed between a man and a woman.

Feeling perfectly comfortable wearing only a chemise and a dress, Anne, along with her partner, happily set off at a quick pace, with the captain imitating Anne's arm motions and attempting to regulate his breathing. However, instead of having the prospect all to themselves, when they got to the top of the rise, they found Captain Wentworth leaning against a rock looking out towards the bay.

"Miss Anne, Benwick, what a surprise to see you," Wentworth said. "I came up here to admire the view."

"You must have walked up here in the dark, Captain Wentworth. The sun is barely over the horizon," Anne noted. What was he doing here? She had tied her shawl around her waist exposing her bare arms, and her hair was pulled back in a pony tail. She looked like the wash woman at the inn.

"But that was my purpose in coming up here, Miss Anne. A brisk walk and to see the sunrise. *Carpe diem* and all that."

Hmmm. If he was out for the exercise, then why was he wearing his finest coat? He couldn't even sit down because he was wearing his best pair of breeches.

"I would think that with all of your voyages, you would have grown tired of sunrises."

"Sunrises on land versus sunrises on the sea, completely different things altogether. But since we are all to return to Uppercross today, it was my only opportunity to view Lyme from this prospect."

"I wish I could convince your party to stay a day or two longer," Benwick said to Anne and the captain. "It has been a long time since I have been in such good spirits, and I would enjoy the company."

"Sorry, but we cannot do that," Frederick answered with a tone that indicated that there was no room for discussion. "Besides, we have seen all there is to see here in Lyme, so we might as well push off. Once we return to the inn, we shall have breakfast, go for a walk on the Cobb, and then be on our way back to Uppercross."

"But, Captain, we are leaving behind our new friends," Anne said, surprised at how easily he had dismissed the captain's suggestion that they remain, and she looked at him with a quizzical expression.

He seemed overly eager to return to Uppercross. But why? There was little to do at this time of year, except to shoot pheasant, and how many birds could you kill before saying "enough?"

"Of course," Frederick acknowledged, "but Benwick is a seafaring man and is used to parting with friends."

"And loved ones," Benwick added. "It was difficult for me to leave my Fanny behind. She would wave to me from the shore, and she always sent me off with a smile," and he smiled as well. "Oh my goodness! That is the first time I have said Fanny's name without crying." Turning to Anne, he said, "You were so right, Miss Anne. I had become a prisoner of my unhappiness—shut away and deprived of all light and hope. I was manacled to my grief, and the key to my chains was just beyond my reach, that is, until now. I am no longer in denial, and I have put aside my anger. I have worked my way through my depression and opened the door to acceptance."

What on earth was he talking about? Frederick asked himself and stared at his fellow officer. If this is what happened to people who read the Romantic poets, he would stick with Walter Scott's *The Battle of Flodden Field* or Henry V addressing his troops before the battle of Agincourt. "We few, we happy few, we band of brothers." Now that stirred the blood. No wonder Benwick took so few prize ships. To be successful on the high seas, you needed to be made of sterner stuff.

Benwick did not notice Frederick's furrowed brow and continued, "I can now go forward and contemplate a life without my Fanny." But then he stopped. "There, I have said her name again! Oh joy! Oh release!"

"Oh, brother!" Frederick mumbled under his breath. But he wondered if all this gibberish about denial, pain, and pushing through his grief was a way of saying that he was over Fanny, and was all this blather about acceptance a prelude to a courtship with Anne?

"Benwick, may I caution you?" he counseled his friend. "Fanny was so special a lady that you need to go slowly in seeking companionship because it hasn't been all that long since she passed away. Small steps are needed here. No rushing into a new relationship. Slow and steady is best. In that way, you will have no regrets later on."

"Captain Wentworth, Miss Harville has been gone for fifteen months," Anne said intervening on Benwick's behalf. She was beginning to suspect that Frederick's interest had more to do with what he wanted than what was best for his friend. "You can hardly accuse Captain Benwick of rushing into another relationship."

"Fifteen months! What is fifteen months?" he said, and then he looked directly at her. "That is merely a blink of an eye when compared, to say, eight years."

Anne made no response other than to suggest that Captain Benwick and she resume their walk and that Captain Wentworth join them.

"Miss Anne, would you mind terribly if I remained behind?" Benwick asked. "Just now, I am flooded with memories—good memories—of Fanny, and I would prefer to stay here awhile and enjoy them."

"Why, of course, I do not mind," and turning to Frederick, Anne asked, "Are you ready to return to the inn or is your preference to remain here in order to make the most of this your only chance for such a view of the bay?"

"I am ready whenever you are, Miss Anne, but do you mind if I take off my coat? If I am to keep pace with you, I will need more freedom of movement."

"You will have no difficulty keeping up with me, sir, which you know very well as you are in shipshape condition."

"You always did favor the pun," he answered with a smile. "As for keeping up with you, I know of no such thing. I watched you as you came up the hill, and I have no wish to be embarrassed by a member of the gentler sex."

He then took off his coat as well as his neck cloth. *Lord, he is handsome and well built, with his muscular arms and broad chest*, and when Anne felt the heat rising in her face, she closed her eyes. But in trying to block out that scene, another appeared. They were behind the stables at Kellynch, and they were clinging to each other. While he whispered that they belonged together and to hell with Lady Russell and her father, she was crying, and with her head upon his chest and her arms about his waist, she had bid him goodbye. Looking at him now, it was almost as if he knew what she was thinking because he took her hand and led her to the path.

"Are we to walk or run, Anne?" he asked in a soft voice as he took her shawl off her shoulders and tied it around her waist.

"I think we should run."

It was but a moment before they had made the necessary adjustments. He shortened his stride while she lengthened hers, and they jogged parallel to the beach without saying a word. When they arrived at the inn, he told her how much he was looking forward to their walk on the Cobb after breakfast. If he had known what was about to happen, he would never have left his room.

Chapter 9

As Frederick and Anne came in view of the inn, they could see Mr. Elliot's carriage with his manservant and driver standing nearby, waiting for their master to emerge from the inn. It seemed that both had been waiting awhile because the driver was whittling a piece of wood and Elliot's man was fidgeting from boredom. But no Mr. Elliot appeared, that is, until Anne did.

"Good morning, Miss Anne," he said, and tipped his hat to the captain. "As you can see I am about to depart."

"I thought you already had," Captain Wentworth said. The two men had met in the reading room the previous evening, and Elliot had mentioned that he would be departing early the next morning.

"I could not possibly leave Lyme without saying goodbye to my dear cousin. Miss Anne, I am on my way to Bath, and I have good news to share. Well, I hope it is good news. Yesterday, I wrote to your father asking if I might call on him. I was not specific as to the reason for my request, but I think the tone of the letter indicates that I am seeking a reconciliation between the two Elliot branches."

"That is wonderful, Mr. Elliot. My father is of a sanguine disposition. He does not like to dwell on the negative, so I anticipate you will receive a warm welcome."

"That is exactly what I had hoped to hear. Of course, I am interested in renewing acquaintances with *all* of my Elliot relations, not just Sir Walter," he said in a voice that made it clear that he was most particularly interested in Anne, and the captain narrowed his eyes.

"I look forward to it," Anne said, and offered Mr. Elliot her hand, "and I shall see you in Bath."

Frederick and Anne stood outside the inn watching as the carriage wove its way through the narrow streets of the village. As far as Anne was concerned, she was saying farewell to her cousin, but the captain was of a different mind.

"He seems to be a nice man," Anne said.

"Yes, he *seems* nice," Frederick answered in a harsh voice. "He is heir to Kellynch, is he not?" Anne nodded, "and will inherit the baronetcy?"

"Yes, the terms of my grandfather's will were very specific as to whom should inherit. Without a male heir, the estate passes in its entirety to Mr. William Elliot."

"And his wife will be Lady Elliot?"

Anne finally caught the captain's tone of voice, and after looking off into the distance as Mr. Elliot's carriage disappeared from view, she turned her gaze on Frederick. Now, she understood the reason for his harshness and the look on his face.

"Oh, I see how it is," she said, with an edge in her voice. "An Elliot daughter marrying Mr. Elliot will unite the two branches and heal old wounds, and because that is what is good for the family as a whole, I shall be the sacrificial offering." Anne then stepped in front of the captain so that she might look into his eyes. "Henrietta told Mary of a remark you made concerning me, Captain Wentworth, and Mary could hardly wait to repeat it. You said that I had altered so much that you would not have known me. Well, that comment was correct because I have changed. The mouse you left eight years ago is no more. People may have their expectations, but I shall do what I think is best for me. I only have this one life, and as limited as it is by society and my own family, it is mine to live as I see fit," and she turned and walked into the inn without looking back.

* * *

After performing her morning toilette, Anne did not go down to the dining room for breakfast as she had no appetite. She had never spoken with such anger before, but how wrong of Frederick to assume that she would marry Mr. Elliot in order to end a schism between the two families. And what point was he trying to make when he had made reference to the baronetcy? She had little interest in titles. As for the rift between Mr. Elliot and her father, she had had nothing to do with it. All she knew was that the young William had not been sufficiently grateful for what he was to inherit, and because of one's pride and the other's arrogance, it was presumed that she would marry a man she did not love to repair old wounds.

And what about Elizabeth? It had always been understood that if Mr. Elliot married a daughter of Sir Walter of Kellynch, it would be Elizabeth, the oldest, and so let Elizabeth have him.

Besides, she had options which Elizabeth did not have. Her mother, fully realizing her father's lack of discipline with regard to money and the spending of it, had set aside a trust fund for the children that Anne began to draw on when she was twenty-one. In the intervening six years, she had invested wisely, and her fortune had grown. That was not the case with Elizabeth. She had burned through her inheritance like a fire in a cloth manufactory. But that was Elizabeth's problem, not hers. Her resources were sufficient so that she could live comfortably and independently without having to turn to others for assistance.

Anne let out a huge sigh. What a disappointing end to a morning that had held such promise. Her heart had soared when she saw Frederick sitting on that rock, and contrary to his assertions, he did not just happen to be in that spot for the purpose of watching the sunrise. He had obviously planned the whole thing, and she must assume that his reason for doing so was to separate her from Captain Benwick. That, in itself, was laughable. Mr. Benwick was a decent man, but there was no romantic interest there, on either's part. He simply needed an understanding person to lift him out of the well of despair he had fallen into as a result of the loss of Miss Harville, but she had no desire to replace her in Captain Benwick's affections.

Their run along the trails above Lyme had been so enjoyable. As the pair had drawn closer to the inn, they had altered their pace from running to walking. Frederick had just started to say something about their return to Uppercross when Mr. Elliot had appeared, and his mood had soured immediately.

Anne banged the bed in frustration. What was he going to say to her before they had been interrupted? Was he on the verge of asking permission to court her? She suspected as much, but she had doused that possibility with a large bucket of anger. How stupid of her! But all was not lost. She had been given a second chance, and she would not risk losing Frederick again because of Mr. Elliot, a man she barely knew and did not care a whit about. If it truly was her cousin's intention to request permission to court her, he would be disappointed because she would never marry him. It was Frederick or no one.

* * *

Damn, damn, and damn again! Had there ever been a time in Wentworth's life when he had made a bigger fool of himself? Anne was still in love with him; he had no doubt of that. But you would not have known that from his actions. In the pre-dawn darkness, he had made his way up the hill so that he would be there before Benwick and Anne. If that behavior wasn't immature enough, he had acted like a jealous adolescent because of Mr. Elliot, a man Anne had no interest in.

It was just so damn frustrating. Even though eight years had lapsed since their separation, Anne still loved him, and he still loved her with a passion that left him trembling inside and, apparently, addled in the brain. But how had he rewarded her devotion and constancy? With a display of jealousy and temper.

But considering their history, wouldn't anyone's temper flare? First, Sir Walter, Lady Russell, and Elizabeth had succeeding in separating them, and now when things looked as if they might actually work out, her piss ant of a cousin had showed up in Lyme. Very suspicious to his mind. And then there was Louisa. He did not want to hurt the young lady's feelings, but she was sticking to him like a wet wool blanket. All he wanted to do was throw her off.

But Louisa's excessive interest was his own fault. He had paid too much attention to her during his time at Uppercross, and she had interpreted his actions as any twenty-year old woman would: he had a romantic interest in her. But he did not, and he would have to make that clear to her today because when they got back to Uppercross, Frederick was going at Anne full tilt and nothing or no one was going to get in his way.

* * *

Frederick was waiting outside the inn, hoping that Anne would come downstairs before the others. Instead, everyone but Anne came down.

"Is Miss Anne not joining us?" Frederick asked Mary.

"Oh, she is already out and about. Captain Benwick came by for her earlier, and Henrietta decided to join them. But Louisa wanted to stay with me. They said that they would meet us at Captain Harville's house."

"Very good. Then shall we go?" the captain asked, offering Mrs. Musgrove his arm.

No it was not "very good," but it was what he deserved. No matter. He had a plan, and neither hell nor high water would keep him from asking Anne if he could call on her when they returned to Uppercross. Unfortunately, the captain had allowed only for acts of God and not the actions of a love-struck young woman.

Chapter 10

As Mary and Charles Musgrove and Captain Wentworth were walking in the direction of Captain Harville's house, Anne, Henrietta, the Harvilles, and Benwick were making their way toward the inn. When Henrietta saw Louisa, she ran to her sister as if she hadn't seen her in a week. Both Musgrove sisters had perky personalities, but Henrietta was darn near giddy in her enthusiasm for just about everything, which would make her a very interesting helpmeet for the dour Mr. Hayter. As expected, Louisa was walking next to Captain Wentworth, but Henrietta pulled her aside long enough for Frederick to have a word with Anne.

"Other than it being a bit windy, it is a lovely morning for a walk," he said.

"It is nearly noon, Captain. The morning has got away from you."

"That may be a good thing," and his face showed how much he regretted his earlier remarks.

"There are few days when everything is absolutely perfect. A storm now and then is to be expected, and when it passes, there is usually no harm done, and the air has cleared."

Frederick smiled at Anne in such a way to let her know that he felt like a complete fool. She would have provided further assurances of no hard feelings, but Louisa had managed to break free of Henrietta, who had been trying to interest her sister in something she had seen on the shore.

Time was growing short for the Musgrove party as they must leave for Uppercross within the hour or they would be traveling in the dark. After Louisa's persistent requests, it was agreed that there was enough time for one more walk along the Cobb. However, some friends would have to take their leave.

"We must say goodbye now," Mrs. Harville said, as we have a house full of hungry children to see to," and they departed after much thanks from their guests.

The wind was picking up, and so Benwick suggested that they go down the steps, known locally as Granny's Teeth because of their irregular shapes, to the lower part of the Cobb. The steps were quite steep, and because of their dainty footwear, Mary, Anne, and Henrietta required the assistance of Captain Wentworth, but Louisa refused, insisting that she would jump down. After safely landing on the pavement with Wentworth's assistance, he spoke in a very firm voice telling her that she should not do it again.

But Louisa was determined to show off, and this time she went higher up the steps. In her haste to repeat her feat, she lost her footing and went flying through the air landing at an awkward angle into the arms of Captain Wentworth. The thrust of her weight had pushed him to the ground, and there was the dull thud of his head hitting the pavement followed by the sound of her head hitting it as well. The captain was momentarily dazed, but Louisa lay beside him unconscious.

All stood staring in shock until Henrietta started screaming, followed by Mary, whose caterwauling was even louder than Henrietta's. When Charles and Benwick made a motion to move Louisa, Anne cried out, "Stop! Do not touch her. You may injure her further. Captain Wentworth, stay where you are. You may experience some dizziness and possibly pitch forward and hurt yourself or someone else. Captain Benwick, go to the Harville house and see if you can find something—a door or anything that will enable us to carry Louisa back to their home. Charles, you must hold her head quite still, keeping the head, neck, and spine in a straight line. I shall go for the surgeon as I know exactly where his surgery is, but while I am gone, *do not move her*."

Without further ado, Anne hiked up her skirts and took off, and mouths dropped at the sight of Anne Elliot of Kellynch, the daughter of a baronet, running full out, so much so that her bonnet flew off her head, but nothing so unimportant as a hat would stop her. If it weren't for poor Louisa lying at their feet, Anne's performance would have been the most surprising sight of the day.

By the time Anne returned with the surgeon, the Harvilles had arrived with a door that they had removed from its hinges, and under the surgeon's instructions, Louisa was placed on it. Mrs. Harville immediately went to see how Captain Wentworth was. Although his injury was not serious, it was causing some dizziness, and every time he attempted to rise, he fell back.

With the surgeon being advanced in years, there were only three men, Charles, Benwick, and Harville, to carry the injured girl. Harville was about to call out for assistance from one of the fishermen, when Anne assured them that she was perfectly capable of carrying Louisa the short distance to the Harville home, and she directed each man to a corner of the door.

"On the count of three, we all lift together. Steady as you go, please," and upon hearing the word "three," the men and Anne lifted the door. Once again, mouths fell open and eyes widened, but Henrietta and Mary immediately stopped crying. Thus, the sight of Anne's exceptional strength restored order to the scene.

After seeing to the injured Miss Musgrove, Anne went back to Frederick so that Mrs. Harville could help the surgeon with Louisa. The captain's wife was an experienced nurse and a source of calm, which was much needed, what with Henrietta and Mary's sobbing. When Anne got back to the captain, she found that Frederick had crawled his way over to the steps, and using them for support, had lifted himself up and was sitting on one of the steps holding a handkerchief to his head. He was all alone as the curious crowd had left him to gather outside the Harville house.

"How is she? Is she alive?" Frederick asked in an anguished voice.

"The surgeon is with her now, and I did see her open her eyes."

"Thank God!"

"Let me have a look at your head."

"It is nothing," he insisted.

"Can you see the back of your head, Frederick? I didn't think you could, so may I have a look?" After taking the bloody handkerchief from his hand, she stanched the bleeding with another that she had obtained from Mrs. Harville's nursery maid. "Head wounds bleed profusely, but once we get it to stop, you will have a nasty bump, but it should be no more than that. Are you still dizzy?"

"No, it has passed, and I have had worse injuries, I can assure you."

"I know. I saw one the other day when you removed your neck cloth. Something very sharp came close to the vein in your neck. God was with you that day."

Frederick took Anne's hands in his, ignoring her concern for his wound. "This is entirely my fault."

"It is not your fault, Frederick," Anne said emphatically. "You told her in no uncertain terms that she should not jump. She disregarded your instructions, slipped, and fell. How is that your fault?"

"I encouraged her on walks at Uppercross to jump off the stiles."

"And because you did something with her on a walk in the country that should not have been attempted on this hard surface, you are responsible for her accident?"

Frederick said nothing, but buried his face in his hands, and the consequences of what had just happened came down on Anne like a brick wall. Because he believed that he was responsible for the accident, if Louisa had any permanent injuries, Frederick would be obligated to remain with her, and she thought that she would be ill.

"Take my arm, Captain Wentworth, so that we may walk back to the house where your wound may be properly dressed," Anne said with tears in her eyes, but in a voice that gave little hint of the agony she was experiencing.

After wrapping her arm around his, they began to walk, but then Wentworth stopped. "Anne, once we had returned to Uppercross, it was my intention to..."

But Anne would not let him finish. "Don't say anything else. There is no point as everything has changed."

There would be no courtship at Uppercross—at least not for her. Louisa had seen to that.

Chapter 11

When Anne and the captain entered the Harville home, they found a house in mourning. With Mrs. Harville and the surgeon seeing to Louisa in the Harvilles' bedroom and Captain Harville tending to his children, the others had been left to their own devices. Charles was sitting in a chair with his head back and his eyes closed, seemingly incapable of movement, and Henrietta and Mary were once again sobbing. It was as if Louisa had already died.

Anne walked past the three and entered the room where Louisa lay unconscious and spoke with the surgeon.

"There are no injuries to her limbs, but the head has a severe contusion. However, she is very young, I have seen people recover from worse injuries. I am by no mean hopeless."

When Anne shared this news with the three Musgroves and Frederick, there was a sigh of relief from all, and Mary went into the room to be with Louisa. Once his wife was gone, Wentworth pointed out to Charles that a plan of action was required, and the two men soon came up with one.

"Then it is settled. Charles, you will stay here, and I shall take your wife and sister home," and then he turned to Anne, "I hope that you will agree to stay. There is no one so proper, so capable, of caring for Louisa than you."

Anne nodded in agreement. Beyond a doubt, she was the most capable as she had cared for her mother when she was little more than a girl and had seen to the ailments and minor injuries of the family and servants, and since she had started running, she had developed an interest in anatomy. She knew how the muscles moved the skeleton, how to avoid injuring them, and how to keep them healthy. "Yes, I will stay."

But when Mary was advised of the plan, she launched a verbal assault on those who had come up with the scheme. She insisted that Anne was nothing to Louisa, and with Henrietta returning to Uppercross, she had the best claim on staying in Henrietta's stead. All eyes were now on Anne.

"I do not think anything should be decided today. It is far too late for anyone to go to Uppercross. It would be unfair to Mr. and Mrs. Musgrove to receive such news about their daughter just as they are about to retire, and Henrietta is emotionally exhausted." She then turned to address Mary. "If you are to remain and care for Louisa, then there is much to learn as you must see to all her physical needs, including things that you have never done before, not even for your own children." Anne waited for a sign that Mary understood what would be expected of her. What went unsaid was that bodily functions did not cease just because a person was unconscious. Mary's eyes widened when she realized what was being asked of her, but then a look of resolution came over her.

"Anne, I will try," and through her tears, she added, "If you and Mrs. Harville will show me what to do, I promise that I will do my best." Anne looked at her long and hard. It was almost as if she could see into her very being, and she knew that Mary was sincere.

"Very well. After I see to Captain Wentworth's head wound, you and I will go into Louisa's room, and I will show you what needs to be done."

Anne went to the cupboard where Mrs. Harville kept all of her medical supplies. She had five rambunctious children, and the shelves, lined with bandages, ointments, and balms, were proof of how frequently the children had scrapes and bruises.

After cleaning the wound on the back of his head, Anne told the captain, "You have a good-sized lump, but if you do not touch it, it will heal quickly." At that moment, a wave of fatigue washed over her, and she rested her hands on the captain's shoulders. Incapable of words, Frederick reached up and took one of her hands, and for a moment, Anne rested her head against his. But to linger would only make matters worse, and so she left him and went in search of Mary.

* * *

Between caring for Louisa and instructing Mary in what was required to care for her sister-in-law, all the while keeping an eye on her brood, Mrs. Harville was exhausted, and because all of this was so new to Mary, all her energy was spent as well. Anne insisted that both retire because she would be leaving in the morning with Henrietta and would be able to rest on the ride to Uppercross.

"Both of you must go to bed or you will not be able to provide Louisa with the proper care because you will be too tired. Now off you go," Anne said in a voice that left no room for argument.

Mrs. Harville had provided Louisa with such excellent care that there was little for Anne to do. After moving her arms and legs so that her muscles would not atrophy, she sat down and closed her eyes, but it was merely a moment before the captain came in.

"I thought you could use some company," Frederick said. "I know how tedious a long watch can be."

"Thank you. It has been quite a day," and she gestured for him to be seated. "I shall share with you that there is reason to hope that all will be well. Louisa is moving her arms and legs, and at one point, she actually made a sound. They are small things, but I think in a day or two, she will open her eyes and surprise everyone."

"Pray God that it is so and that there is no injury to her brain."

"If I did not believe that she would recover quickly, I would not leave her, no matter how strident Mary's protests."

Because the room was so small, the two chairs that were next to Louisa's bedside touched each other, and Anne could have easily put her head on Frederick's shoulder. Instead, she rested it against the wall, and in doing so, she was able to study his face. What she saw was a man of integrity who would do his duty. In this case, his duty was to care for Louisa, and since she could not talk about something so painful, she was thinking of something to say when he began speaking.

"You are quite a runner, Anne. I am sure that what I saw yesterday and today was merely a hint of your talents. When did you start running?"

"Two years ago, after being declared a spinster by my family, I stepped back and examined my life, and I did not like what I found. So I started to go for long walks, which turned into running, which became long-distance running. I just wish I had better boots. Even though they were custom-made for me in London by a fine bootmaker, I know they slow me down, and I have problems with blistering."

"What bootmaker did you use?" and when Anne told him, he shook his head. "No, don't go to him. I had a pair of boots from Mr. Cleat, and I was not pleased. I shall give you the name of my bootmaker. No one is better. When you go, mention my name and tell Mr. Hightop to put your boots on my account."

"Thank you, Captain, but it is not necessary that you pay for my boots. I have my own money. Yes, I see that you doubt it, but I do have money left to me by my mother and an annuity from my Grandfather Stevenson. I have taken those funds and invested them wisely, and I have received handsome returns as a result."

"May I ask what you invested in?"

"No, I shall not tell you. You might try to buy up all the shares and pressure me into selling at a lower price." Unsure of whether or not she was kidding, he looked at her with a most quizzical expression, but because he was taking her seriously, Anne changed the conversation back to running. "When you are onboard ship, do you ever have cause to time anything?"

"I don't understand. What do what you mean by 'time?'" and he made air quotes with his fingers.

"For example, exactly how long does it take for a sailor to go from the deck to the crow's nest?"

"With a lieutenant's boot in his butt, not very long at all."

Anne laughed, and despite everything, Frederick smiled. "Please be serious," she asked.

"I am being serious."

"Well, I am sure a boot in a sailor's butt is not required on every occasion," and Frederick had to keep from laughing out loud at Anne repeating a vulgar phrase. "Truly, is there anything you do on a ship that requires knowing exactly how long it takes to do it, right down to the very minute?"

"Like how long to cook a soft-boiled egg?"

"Captain, please," and she gave him a stern look.

"I can't think of anything that needs such a precise accounting. What needs to be done must be done correctly in as little time as possible as lives depend upon it. So if you are asking if there is a timepiece which can give such accurate readings, unfortunately, the answer is 'no.' If such an instrument did exist, the Royal Navy would have it as we love gadgets," and to prove his point, he took out his own pocket watch. "This was made by Mr. Chimes, the head master watchmaker at the Worshipful Company of Clockmakers in London, whose motto you would appreciate, 'Time commands all things.'" The instrument looked much more complicated than her father's pocket watch.

"I did not think so," she said disappointed. "You see, I have worked so hard to improve my running skills, but there is no true measurement of how quickly I get from where I start to where I finish. I have trained so hard that if an opportunity ever arose to compare my time to that of another, I would like to do so, if only I knew what it was."

"I have no doubt that you would have the best time. There are few who run as fast as you do."

"You could not pay me a higher compliment, Captain."

"Anne, must you call me captain? Are we no longer to be Frederick and Anne?"

Anne shook her head. "In the future, there will be few opportunities where it would be possible for me to call you by your Christian name, so it would be best to address you as Captain Wentworth from this time forward."

Frederick closed his eyes. For the few minutes he had been with Anne, some light had come back into his life, but with Louisa there as a reminder of what awaited him, the darkness returned.

"Anne, you and I are star-crossed lovers."

"Yes, but we are also victims of persuasion. I was persuaded too easily, and you cannot be persuaded at all."

"But Louisa lies there because of me," he said, pointing to the bed. "If it had not been for me, she would never have jumped."

"Of course, she wouldn't have. She did it to keep your attention on her." But Anne said nothing more; there was no point. "I can see that you are resolved to act in one way, and nothing I say shall change your mind because you think to do otherwise would be dishonorable. So we shall speak no more about it. Now, it is very late, and I must ask you to leave because the nursery maid will be here shortly to relieve me. There are things I must do for Louisa that you cannot see."

But when Anne went to stand up, Frederick took her hand and held it to his face. "And what of you, Anne? What will become of you?"

"Do not worry about me," she said with authority and conviction. "In the last two years I have learned many things, but, perhaps, the most important lesson is that I am the only one responsible for my own happiness. If I am unhappy, there is no one to blame but me, and I refuse to be brought low. I have spent too much of my life living in the doldrums. For the past two years, I have had the wind in my sails, and I intend to keep it that way."

Since this might be the last time that they would be together as lovers, Anne placed her hands on both sides of Frederick's face and bent over and kissed him. Knowing that such a thing would not happen again, he stood up without their lips parting, and he put his arms around her and drew her to him.

"I love you, Anne" he said, clinging to her in much the same way as he had before they had parted eight years earlier.

"And I love you, Frederick," and putting her finger to his lips, she whispered, "but that must be our secret."

Chapter 12

Even though Henrietta fell asleep in the Musgrove carriage two miles outside of Lyme, little was said by Frederick or Anne. For her part, she made a half-hearted attempt at conversation by asking about Mrs. Croft and the captain's brother, Edward Wentworth, the Vicar of Monkford, but at that moment, Frederick cared little about his relations. He was like an injured animal that wanted to crawl into the bushes to lick his wounds. He just wanted to be left alone with his thoughts.

When they arrived at Uppercross, Frederick was witness to the most heart-wrenching scene of Louisa's mother crying uncontrollably for her daughter and her father's struggle to keep from doing the same. After Anne had provided reassurances that Louisa was already somewhat better, some calm returned to the house, and feeling that he had nothing more to contribute, Wentworth was saying goodbye to Mr. and Mrs. Musgrove when interrupted by Henrietta.

"Captain, you cannot go without receiving our thanks. Mama, Papa, the good captain had cautioned Louisa not to jump off the steps, but she did not heed him as she was in very high spirits that day. If he had not caught her, the sound we heard would not have been a thud, but a crack. We would now be talking about a serious concussion instead of a contusion."

Anne had to hide a smile. Henrietta was parroting the surgeon's words, and she doubted very much that Henrietta knew the definition of either contusion or concussion.

As soon as this intelligence was digested, Mr. Musgrove shook the captain's hand as if working a pump, and Mrs. Musgrove pulled him to her bosom as if he were her own son. This display of thanks intensified the captain's need to be gone, and he refused all pleas that he join them for their midday meal.

Anne walked with him to the carriage. "It would be a kindness if you stayed as they want to be near the man who saved their daughter."

"Even if such praise was deserved, do you think I am made of stone? If I remain an hour longer, I will abandon my duty and remain with you."

"Stay or go. It is your decision, but if you expect to receive support from me for your decision, you will not get it," Anne said in extreme frustration. "You are blameless in all this, and, yet, you will bind yourself to a woman you do not love. And what do you know of her? What books does she read? What are her interests? You don't even know that she has motion sickness."

"Louisa gets carriage sick? Is that why the driver pulled over on the way to Lyme?"

Anne nodded. "We tried to make it appear as if it was a call of nature, but in truth, she parted with her breakfast."

Frederick looked lost. It seemed as if all the Fates were against him. Not only would he have to marry a woman he did not love, but now it appeared that she was unfit for service as a navy wife because she would be susceptible to seasickness. There would be no sailing the high seas together, tasting the salt water, braving storms, outrunning the enemy. She wouldn't even be able to get in a dinghy to meet the ship when it came into port, and although he did not actually approve of any woman, except Anne, being on board the *Laconia*, it was just the idea of not having that option that was distressing.

"Frederick, don't look so forlorn. If this is what you must do, you will do it well, and you will come to love her because she is a good girl and worthy of your affection." Anne stepped back from the carriage. "I am sorry to have kept you. I wish you Godspeed," and she quickly went away.

"Anne, Anne," he called after her, and she returned to his side. "You are right about one thing. If I must do this, I will do it well, but as for loving Louisa as a man loves a wife, that is not possible. In order to do that you must have a heart, but I have already given mine away—to you.

* * *

When Wentworth returned to Lyme, Mrs. Harville greeted him with good news. "There is more movement in Louisa's arms and legs, and she has opened her eyes several times now," and she directed him towards the invalid's room.

Louisa was propped up on three pillows, but looked little different to him, and when she did open her eyes, they kept rolling back in her head. Rather than reassuring the captain, it depressed him. But before leaving the room, she seemed to raise her hand in greeting, and he felt somewhat better, but not enough to linger.

"Mrs. Harville, I have decided to stay with my brother, Edward, who is the Vicar of Monkford. If my presence is required, I can be in Lyme in a little more than three hours. May I ask that you keep me apprised of Louisa's progress by letter? It would be a great consolation to me," and he handed the lady enough money to pay the post.

"I will be glad to do so, Captain, and I believe I will have something to write to you very soon. You are not trained as I am, but I do see progress," Mrs. Harville said in a reassuring voice.

Frederick could not get to Monkford fast enough, but even though he was no longer a witness to the constant reminders of Louisa's condition, it was less than satisfactory. Although he loved his brother dearly, he found him to be rather tedious with little or no curiosity about the wider world that Frederick had seen in his years in the navy.

Edward lived a sheltered life ministering to the smallest and oldest congregation Frederick had ever seen, and as entertainment, he and his wife, along with some ancient parishioners, played a Bible version of charades. Without rising from his chair, ninety-year old Mr. Frost succeeded in acting out Methuselah, and while Edward always seemed to draw Samson, his wife, Margaret, managed to pick Delilah, which seemed to please the other guests immensely. Acting out the roles of two of the Bible's most overtly sexual characters might possibly be an indication that their time together behind closed doors was more interesting than their public faces. He certainly hoped so. As for his part, he was tired of acting out John the Baptist eating locusts or hiding under a table pretending to be Jonah sloshing around the inside the belly of a whale.

After a week spent chopping wood and making every possible repair at the parsonage, he got on his horse and went to Kellynch to see Sophie and the Admiral. His brother-in-law had been at sea from the time he was a young lad and had risen through the ranks. Polite conversation was not his strong suit.

"You have a strange way of making love, Frederick. Breaking the lady's head! But it certainly got her attention. I daresay she will listen to you in the future, which will serve you well when you marry."

Such remarks, and being an observer of the domestic felicity of the Crofts, did nothing to lighten his mood, and so back to Monkford he went.

For the next two weeks, Frederick did little except walk into the village to check the post, but the inactivity was driving him to distraction. There had to be something he could do to pass the time, and then he thought of Anne. "I shall start running."

How long was a marathon? He remembered from his World History class that it was upwards of twenty miles. It was difficult for him to imagine that his petite Anne could undertake so grueling a regimen, and he smiled when he pictured her with her beautiful brown hair with its auburn streaks pulled back in a pony tail. And was there a more pleasant sight than watching her wipe the sweat from underneath her bodice with a handkerchief? To paraphrase Romeo, "If I were but a hankie so that I might touch thy breast." Oh, blast, this wasn't doing him any good.

When he got back to the parsonage, he told his brother that he was going up to London for at least a week to see his bootmaker. "I need a pair of running shoes."

Edward, aware of the situation in Lyme, nodded in understanding at his brother's need to get away, but what did Frederick mean by running shoes?

Chapter 13

Three days after Anne's return to Uppercross, Charles Musgrove arrived with the good news that Louisa was sitting up in a chair. With hope in their hearts, her parents immediately departed for Lyme to see their beloved daughter, leaving Henrietta and Anne to care for the two Musgrove boys. Subsequent news received from Mrs. Harville was very promising. She had hired an in-home physical therapist. Part of Louisa's rehab focused on improving her fine motor skills, and the two were working on the hand motions to the "Teensy Weensy Spider." They were hoping to start on "I'm a Little Teapot" in the coming week. Better yet, Louisa was getting out of doors and taking short walks on the arm of Captain Benwick, who was reading her Cowper and Marlowe, with an occasional Byron thrown in to satiate his appetite for the maudlin.

Each morning, Anne arose early so that she might go jogging and was back at the manor house in time to eat breakfast with Henrietta and her young nephews. Even with chillier temperatures and an almost daily rain, Anne loved being in the country. After the tragedy in Lyme and the heartbreak of watching Frederick walk away—again, the fresh air and the bucolic landscape had lifted her spirits.

But Anne knew that this idyll must come to an end, and it did when Lady Russell's carriage pulled up to the entrance of Uppercross. Because Anne had been ignoring letters from Elizabeth, her older sister had written to Lady Russell asking that she go to Uppercross and make Anne come to Bath. Although Elizabeth enjoyed all the advantages of being Miss Elliot, mistress of Kellynch and now Camden Place, she detested the day-to-day management required to run a household. That was Anne's job, and the servants were happy to have it so.

"You are missed in Bath, my dear," Lady Russell began.

"I am sure my management skills are missed, but as for me, Elizabeth has Papa and Mrs. Clay," Anne answered. Mrs. Clay was the daughter of the family solicitor, Mr. Shepherd, who had taken up residence at Camden Place, and because she was supremely sycophantic, Elizabeth found her to be a valuable companion.

"And now they have Mr. Elliot as well."

"So Mr. Elliot did go to Bath to speak with Papa. I actually encountered the gentleman in Lyme. We were staying at the same inn, and upon hearing someone mention my name, he introduced himself."

"How odd! Considering the time of year, it is a curious thing for him to be in Lyme at exactly the same time that you were."

"I thought so as well. But it might prove to be fortuitous as he expressed an interest in reconciling with Papa."

"Because you did not read your sister's letters," Lady Russell said with a hint of disapproval in her voice, "you do not know that he has succeeded. I had a long letter from Elizabeth, and other than discussing her friend, Mrs. Clay, she had little to write that did not involve Mr. Elliot as he calls daily at Camden Place. For my part, I have no wish to see him. His declining to be on cordial terms with the head of his family has left a strong impression in his disfavor with me."

"Maybe once you are reacquainted with the gentleman, you will change your mind. When we spoke in Lyme, Mr. Elliot attributed his thoughtlessness to his youth, and I am willing to believe him. People should be given second chances as we alter so much as we grow older."

Anne looked at Lady Russell to see if she understood her meaning, but she did not. She still thought that Anne would follow her advice in all things. To her mind, if Lady Russell did not like Mr. Elliot, neither should her young friend.

The next day Charles and Mary returned to their home, confident that Louisa was well enough to remain in the care of Mrs. Harville and her parents. However, it was necessary for her to stay in Lyme so that she could continue with her rehabilitation.

"Mrs. Harville was a great help to me in nursing Louisa, but since she had to spend so much time with her children, the bulk of the work fell to me," Mary complained before providing Anne and Lady Russell with a detailed description of a typical day spent caring for Louisa. If only one-quarter of what Mary said was actually true, then Anne was satisfied that her sister had been of some help to Mrs. Harville. However, Mary's good mood soon soured when she learned that Anne and Lady Russell were to leave for Bath.

"Why should you go to Bath, Anne? You have not been laboring for weeks at the bedside of a convalescent as I have done. It is I who should go."

Before Anne could say, "Who's stopping you?" her husband piped up.

"We are not going to Bath, Mary. I intend to sleep in my own bed for a fortnight before I venture anywhere," and despite howls of protest, Charles would not yield. So it happened that Anne and Lady Russell went to Bath without Mary. As the carriage made its way through the town from Old Bridge to Camden Place, Anne could hear the sounds of the city: the heavy rumble of carts, the bawling of newsmen, muffin-men and milk-men, and the dash of the other carriages wending their way through the crowded streets. Lady Russell, who had tired of the country, perked up at the sights and sounds of Bath, but Anne most definitely did not share her enthusiasm. Before the carriage had stopped in front of the residence of the Elliots, formerly of Kellynch Hall, she was already thinking of how soon she might leave it.

* * *

Anne received a warmer welcome than she had expected from her father and sister, and a good deal of this could be attributed to Mr. Elliot's being in Bath. Upon his arrival in town, he had called at

Camden Place, and by such openness of conduct and such readiness to apologize for the past so that he might be received as a relation again, their former good understanding was completely reestablished. They had not a fault to find in him.

But Anne was puzzled. After an interval of so many years, why was Mr. Elliot so eager to seek forgiveness? Absent moral turpitude, whether or not Mr. Elliot was in the good graces of Sir Walter Elliot, he would inherit Kellynch, so why all this solicitousness? Perhaps, it had something to do with Elizabeth, who was pretty, well-bred, elegant in manners, and someone who had kept her true nature successfully hidden from the heir to the Elliot estate. So it must be that he wished to marry the eldest daughter and once again unite the two branches of the family.

The gentleman was staying with his friend, Colonel Wallis, and his wife, in Marlborough Buildings, but Anne had learned from Patsy, her lady's maid, that Mr. Elliot was such a frequent visitor to Camden Place that he might have been mistaken for a resident.

That evening, the prodigal cousin put in an appearance, and after expressing a desire to become better acquainted with Miss Anne, he engaged her at length in conversation and complimented her profusely on the scope of her knowledge as a result of her extensive reading. Elizabeth, in an attempt to control the conversation, told the tale of Louisa Musgrove's accident, even though she had only just heard of it from Lady Russell, who had heard it from Henrietta Musgrove, and the fact that much of what she had said was incorrect (Louisa had not lost the use of her legs), did not bother her a bit.

Mr. Elliot asked numerous questions about the accident. He lauded Anne for her role in assisting Louisa back to the Harville house and mentioned how much she must have suffered in witnessing such a tragedy.

"Mr. Elliot, I was only one of several who acted quickly in securing help for Miss Musgrove. Your praise for my role is excessive, with the unfortunate result being that it shifts the emphasis away from the injured party."

But Mr. Elliot would not listen and attributed her words to a praiseworthy sense of modesty. It was only when Anne asked to be excused that the acclamations stopped. She found this whole matter with Mr. Elliot to be very odd, and she sensed that there was something amiss. She would keep her ears and eyes open and learn everything she could about her cousin because something was rotten in the City of Bath.

Chapter 14

Anne soon found herself pulled into the vortex that was Bath society. She did everything that one did in the city: attended concerts and dances, strolled the pleasure gardens, went to the theater, listened to lectures, visited the pump room, patronized the shops, and paraded about the public rooms so that she might be seen. And she was seen—by Mr. Elliot. His constant hovering was getting on her nerves, and she found it necessary to point out that she was not the eldest Elliot daughter and asked if his time might not be better spent with Elizabeth. And then it all came out.

Mr. Elliot had been in Bath for a number of weeks before Anne had arrived, and in that time, he had been able to take Elizabeth's true measure. He had witnessed her cattiness in a conversation with Mrs. Clay in which the two had torn apart the very plain Miss Kneedy and had heard her sharp tongue lacerating a servant and a clerk in the draper's shop. He confessed to Anne that if he was ever to remarry, the lady must be of an amiable temperament. However, since his wife would someday be Lady Elliot, she must also possess an awareness of her responsibilities as the wife of a baronet, including being very careful as to those whom she admitted into her circle of friends. There was no doubt that that statement was directed at Mrs. Clay, and it was then that Anne realized that Mr. Elliot felt threatened by Elizabeth's friend. If Sir Walter married Mrs. Clay, he could still father a son, and Mr. Elliot would no longer be the heir to Kellynch. Anne chuckled to herself at the idea of her father falling in love with anyone. Other than Elizabeth, there was only one person he truly loved, and he looked at him every morning in the mirror.

Anne was determined to break free of Mr. Elliot, and when she learned that her former governess, Mrs. Smith, was in Bath, she immediately set out to visit her and learned that she was now a widow who had been impoverished by her husband's poor business dealings.

In addition to these troubles, she was afflicted with a severe rheumatic fever which had settled in her legs, but neither sickness nor sorrow seemed to have ruined her spirits.

One of the reasons she was able to avoid falling into depression was Mrs. Rooke, the sister of her landlady, and a nurse as well, who provided, not only excellent medical care, but who was her conduit to the outside world. In other words, Mrs. Rooke loved to gossip, and Mrs. Smith loved to listen to it.

A friendship quickly developed among the three ladies, and Anne visited as often as her obligations at home would allow. Because Mrs. Smith's ailment had left her legs very weak, Anne asked her former governess if she could show her some exercises that would strengthen her muscles. The invalid was most agreeable, and in little more than a week, Mrs. Smith and Anne were walking about the room, arm in arm, and venturing up and down the sidewalk in front of her building, much to the approval of Mrs. Rooke.

It was during one of these walks that Anne saw Mr. Elliot walk by, which was puzzling, because this was a poorer part of town—not an area where one would expect to see a future baronet, and he was in a great hurry.

"Do you know that gentleman?" Mrs. Rooke asked Anne after taking note of her interest in the scurrying male.

Anne nodded. "He is my cousin. Even so, I do not know him very well," and after weeks of frequent interaction, Anne felt as if she knew him less, not more.

"He is staying with Colonel Wallis. I am the nurse to his wife, who has entered her confinement."

Anne detected a note of disapproval in Mrs. Rooke's tone and asked if that was the case.

Mrs. Rooke nodded. "The colonel pays little attention to his wife and spends most of his time with Mr. Elliot. She's so lonely that she told her husband that she needed a nurse as the baby was coming soon. Truth to tell, that baby won't be born for another month."

From Mrs. Rooke's look, Anne knew that there was more to be said, and it took little effort to coax it out of her.

"Mrs. Wallis don't like Mr. Elliot, even though she can't say why. She just thinks he's sneaky."

"Have you seen him in this part of town before?"

"All the time, but where he goes, I don't know."

What was Mr. Elliot doing so far from Marlborough Buildings and in a rundown part of Bath? Anne had no answer, but she was determined to find out.

* * *

Two days later, at approximately the same time as she had seen Mr. Elliot, Anne went to visit Mrs. Smith. She was wearing the street clothes of her maid, Patsy, who was the sweetest lady's maid anyone could ever hope for. Along with a borrowed dress and cloak, Anne had purchased a poke bonnet with the biggest brim of any hat she had ever seen. The clerk explained that it was worn by those ladies who could not be exposed to the sun even for short periods of time because of skin rashes, and because of the width of the brim, Anne's face was completely hidden.

As soon as Anne saw Mr. Elliot go past, she was after him, bobbing and weaving between the carriages and scooting from one building to the next, at one point, hiding behind a pillar and another time pretending to knock on a stranger's door. She was enjoying the thrill of the chase when a street urchin jumped in front of her.

"I been tailing you for the last ten minutes, and if that toff had looked back but one time, he would have made you."

"Do you mean that the gentleman would have known that I was following him?" Anne asked the lad, whom she guessed to be no more than ten or eleven.

"If he didn't know, he'd be the only one."

Anne sighed. "But now I have lost him."

"No you ain't. I know where he's going, but I ain't in the habit of giving anything away for free."

"Oh, of course," and Anne reached into her purse and took out a coin and placed it in the boy's palm.

"That coin better have a friend or I'm out of here."

"Sorry," and Anne took out another coin. "I am new at this."

"Really? You could have fooled me," and he looked down at the second coin and made a face. "I'll accept this pittance this one time. You may consider it an introductory offer—not to be repeated—just so you get an idea of the quality of my services."

"And what is your name?"

"Swoosh."

"Swoosh? Is that your Christian name?"

"Don't nobody use my Christian name unless they want two black eyes and a broken nose. Swoosh is my street name."

Although she did not smile, she was amused by the belligerence of so young a lad. "Very well, Swoosh. Where did that man go?"

"There's a gaming house down on Baker Street where they play for high stakes only. The first time it cost you a monkey just to get in the door. You know what I'm talking about, right?" And seeing that she didn't, he continued, "A monkey—five hundred pound."

“Five hundred pounds! Just so one might participate? Good grief!”

“Me and my brother knows everybody what comes into this part of town because it’s my brother’s turf. He’s a runner for Blackjack Cleaver.”

“He is a runner? Really? So am I!” Anne said with real excitement. “Does he run hereabouts?”

“I think you and me we’re talking about two different things. My brother’s name is Moves, and he goes back and forth between the different houses, or if a gent is in need of female company, my brother knows where to take him. Mind you, he don’t get involved in the business end of it. It’s just a courtesy service Blackjack offers.”

“Oh, I see,” but Anne really didn’t understand, and her next sentence proved it. “Females are permitted to play at games of chance as well. I mean as long as they have the monkey.”

“You don’t get out much, do you?” Swoosh said, shaking his head at her ignorance of women who, for the right amount, put their all into entertaining gents. “Listen, I can get Moves to keep an eye on your toff, and I can get word to you. Then we’ll meet up, and I’ll dish the dirt, but for more than what you give me today or you get nothing.”

Swoosh suggested a sum, which Anne refused, thinking she already had enough dirt on her toff to alert her family to his true nature. When an amount was finally agreed upon, Swoosh told Anne where to look for him, but added that he would only be there if he had something to report. Then the young rascal spit into the palm of his hand and held it out for Anne to shake. Without any hesitation, she spit into her own palm and clasped his hand in agreement.

As Anne walked back to Mrs. Smith’s, her heart was pounding. What she had learned about Mr. Elliot was very disconcerting. On the other hand, her interaction with Swoosh had been truly exciting. It was similar to the rush she got when she went jogging, and Anne thought: I can do anything. I am a woman!

Chapter 15

Anne was getting cabin fever, and her cabin included all of Bath. She needed to get out into the country and breathe. Being thus confined resulted in an edgy Anne who said what was on her mind, and her father was the first to hear from her. When she had returned to Camden Place after her first meeting with Swoosh, Sir Walter had announced that they were all to play cards with Lady Dalrymple that evening at Laura Place.

"I have a previous engagement, Papa, and I will not be able to join you," and she explained that she had reconnected with Mrs. Smith, her former governess, and that she was to go to Westgate Buildings that evening.

Her response elicited a hissy fit from her father with Elizabeth chiming in. "We are to dine with members of the aristocracy, but that is not good enough for you, Anne. You are to visit Mrs. Smith, who is nothing to Lady Dalrymple and Miss Carteret."

"I make no claims for Mrs. Smith being anything other than my friend, and since I have told her that I shall visit her, that is what I intend to do."

Despite the vitriol heaped upon her, Anne refused to alter her plans. The next day, with both father and sister giving her the cold shoulder, Lady Russell made an appearance—hardly a coincidence. It was obvious that she had been told of Anne's refusal to dine with Lady Dalrymple and daughter.

"Anne, connections are important. That is how we make our way in the world."

"But it is not how I make my way in the world, and since I have been declared to be a spinster with no hope of marriage, these connections you speak of are of no benefit to me."

"But things have changed greatly since Mr. Elliot was welcomed with open arms by his Kellynch relations, and, Anne, pardon my interference, but his interest in you cannot be mistaken."

"You would encourage me to marry Mr. Elliot?"

"Yes, of course. He is to be the master of Kellynch."

Anne was not surprised. Lady Russell had taken Anne's advice and had given Mr. Elliot a second chance, so much so that she was lapping up everything he was feeding her.

"Along with being a very handsome man who cuts a dashing figure, he has many fine qualities," Lady Russell continued. "And let us not forget that a marriage between Mr. Elliot and you will serve to repair any fracture within the Elliot family."

"Like plaster of Paris."

Lady Russell's eyes widened. Of late, there had been an unfortunate change in Anne's tone and an increase in sarcastic comments. This was especially painful because Lady Russell was her mother's oldest and dearest friend, and because of this brashness, she thought Anne was in need of correction.

"Anne, that remark does not do you credit. I have made note of many changes in your attitude, but none more obvious than how you interact with your family and friends. If your family wishes to attend a private party, you say that you will go to the theater. When I offer my carriage, you say that you will walk."

"Lady Russell, with all due respect, I am twenty-seven years of age. Am I not entitled to some independence of thought and movement, and considering the mess my father and sister have made of things, is it wrong of me to feel that I can do better without their help?"

"I cannot argue with that statement about the unfortunate state of your family's finances. However, I have done my best to fill your mother's shoes and have offered those opinions which I believe your mother would have given as well. I hope you have found some value in the guidance I have provided."

"Of course, I have," Anne said, taking Lady Russell's hand, "but none of us is perfect."

"How have I failed you?" she asked surprised at the appendage to Anne's statement.

"Most of your advice is excellent, and I am grateful for the affection and care you have shown me. However, when it comes to matters of the heart, your record is not the best. I do not think there were two people who had less in common than my father and mother, but the match was promoted by you because my mother had a handsome dowry and my father had a title. Papa was happy with the match; Mama was not.

"As for me, you said that I should not marry Captain Wentworth, whose attributes and chances for success went unrecognized by all, including me, or I could not have been persuaded to let him go. And, now, after being so opposed to any contact with Mr. Elliot, you have changed your mind about him, saying that he is a fine gentleman and would make a good husband. Unfortunately, Lady Russell, you were wrong about Captain Wentworth, and your estimation of Mr. Elliot is even further off the mark. If all goes as planned, I will be able to prove the defects of Mr. Elliot's character, and as far as the captain is concerned, his record of achievements speaks for itself."

* * *

The next morning, Anne left Camden Place earlier than usual. In that way, with most people still abed, she would be able to walk at a quick pace without drawing anyone's attention. She desperately needed to clear her mind. The conversation with Lady Russell had been unpleasant, the proximity to her vain father and mean-spirited sister was a major irritant, and Mr. Elliot's constant attention left the same impression as that of a dog drooling over his supper. And now she had learned that Mary, Charles, Henrietta, and Mr. and Mrs. Musgrove would be arriving in Bath the next day. All were welcome, but their presence would make it more difficult for her to go out alone.

"Oh, whereforth art thou, Swoosh?" Anne thought as she left the townhouse, expecting another disappointment after three days of nothing from the boy. But there, with his saucy grin, was Swoosh leaning on a lamppost. She could tell by Swoosh's posture that he had "come up with the goods."

"My brother's got the inside scoop that your friend is going to meet someone near Baker Street at 4:00 today. You still up for this?"

"Oh, most definitely. As agreed, I shall meet you at the first lamppost inside your brother's territory at 3:30, but before we part, may I ask a favor?" Anne said after handing Swoosh a five-pound note.

"For a fiver, I'll give up my granny," but then he smiled, and under all that dirt was an adorable boy with beautiful sky-blue eyes and a button nose.

"May I have a street name like yours? You must call me something and shouting out my real name is highly inadvisable."

Swoosh could see the logic in this and stepped back and studied Anne, and after giving it careful thought, he said, "You says you're a runner, so how does 'Flash' sound? Like a flash of lightning."

"Oh, I like that very much," Anne answered, truly pleased with her street name.

"By the way, Flash, speaking of running, it is 'highly inadvisable' for you to be running between carriages. You're supposed to cross the street at the lamppost with the green dots on them. You know, 'cross at the green, not in between.' And another thing, didn't your mother ever teach you about 'stranger danger.' You don't know me from Adam, but still you followed me clear acrost town. You have to be on the lookout for cutpurses because they'll separate you from your pretty little reticule in the blink of an eye, and there's those who will take the hand with the purse if that's what they have to do."

Anne nodded in understanding at the dangers she might encounter in pursuing Mr. Elliot. "In my enthusiasm for the chase, I did act precipitously. You see, except for walking within the boundaries of our own area of Bath, ladies such as I do not go out without a family member or a friend of the family. I promise not to do that again. Thank you for your concern."

"Don't make nothing out of it. I don't want to lose a customer is all. 3:30 then. Be there or be square," and Swoosh disappeared into the crowd.

* * *

Anne was on pins and needles waiting for the hallway clock to chime 3:00 so that she could get dressed in Patsy's clothes. Her heart was all aflutter at the idea of finding out what Mr. Elliot was really up to. By 3:30, she was at the appointed place, but looking around, she could not locate Swoosh. She should have looked behind her.

"Flash, if you're gonna keep on in this line of work," he said, chastising her, "there are a few things you need to know, like making sure your back is covered. Not everything is right in front of you. But at least, you've got your purse tucked away. Come on, Moves is waiting."

The pair quickly made their way deeper into Moves's territory by way of back alleys filled with trash and vagabonds sleeping it off before emerging onto Baker Street. Leaning against a tree was a stretched-out version of Swoosh. Although he was about fifteen years old, there was nothing of the boy left in Moves. Apparently, in order to hone his skills, he had voluntarily served an apprenticeship in London with the "Don't Mess Around with Jim Jenkins" gang. Compared to the mean streets of that city, Bath was a picnic.

"Who's she?" Moves asked in a tone that let his brother know he wasn't pleased.

"This is Flash."

"Flash? She ain't no Flash. She's a toff's dame."

"Excuse me, Mr. Moves, but you are mistaken," Anne said in a confident voice. "I am no toff's dame. I am my own person. I am lovable and capable and have unlimited potential—something your brother immediately recognized, and I have hired your brother in order to learn more about Mr. Elliot."

"Listen, Moves. She's all right. She give me a fiver."

"Oh, hell, you should of said that in the first place. Money gets my attention and respect."

"Would you please acquaint me with Mr. Elliot's perambulations and the reason you think he is frequenting this part of town?" Anne asked Moves.

When Moves looked confused, Swoosh interpreted for his brother. "Flash wants to know where the toff's been going and why?"

"His arse is in the wringer because he's into Big Bill Blowhard for a couple thousand nicker. The reason he come down here all the time is to give him some bar and smacker to keep him off his back, but he don't have the bread and honey to pay it off."

Swoosh now turned to Anne to fill her in. "Your toff is in trouble because he owes Big Bill a lot of money and has been unable to make any payment on the actual principal. He comes down here every couple of days to pay off some of the interest, but with interest compounding daily, he's in a world of hurt."

Moves smiled at his brother in approval. "He runs the money side of our partnership."

Then Mr. Elliot's whole scheme became apparent to Anne. Obviously, he didn't know the financial situation of her family. He was assuming that in addition to being rich in land, his relations were wealthy in liquid assets as well. She suspected that it was widely known around Bath that he would inherit a baronetcy, and trading on his expectations, he had been able to get credit at the gaming establishments. Now that he was deeply in debt, he believed that if he married Anne he would be able to cover his losses, or at least pay off some of the interest with hard cash or by mortgaging the property. Unfortunately for Mr. Elliot, there was no ready money, and the manor house was already mortgaged.

"Don't look now, Flash, but your toff just turned the corner," and Anne had to fight the urge to turn around.

There was no need to worry that she would "be made." Mr. Elliot was unaware of anything going on around him. His mind was on one thing only: meeting Big Bill or his representative so that he could keep his arse out of the wringer for at least one more day. The three watched as Mr. Elliot met with a man who was standing across the street from the Baker gaming house.

"That's Ben Scofflaw, Big Bill's enforcer," Moves said.

"I wish I knew what they were saying," Anne said, never taking her eyes off her cousin.

"If you keep your head down, you can walk right by them," Moves told her, and Swoosh added that if she dragged her leg as if she was a cripple, she could walk slower and hear more of what they were talking about.

Anne could almost hear the sound of her heart beating as she limped across the street. As she drew nearer to Mr. Elliot, her gimp became more pronounced, and she was practically crawling as she walked by them. After re-crossing the street, she joined Moves and Swoosh who were waiting for her to give them the lowdown.

"This is what Mr. Elliot said: 'I am going as fast as I can, but *she* is dragging things out. I will vigorously press my suit this week, and if Big Bill can give me a little more time, I will have the money for him.'"

"He's got you pegged as his future mattress mate," Moves explained, "and after you're wedded and bedded, he's gonna gobble up all your bread and honey. In the meantime, he'll be after you for a steady stream of bar and smacker to keep Big Bill from rearranging his face."

Anne merely nodded, but could not speak. Now she understood why he just happened to be in Lyme exactly at the same time as she was. He had followed her there in hopes of getting into her nicker. It was truly distressing to find out that Mr. Elliot was so very bad, but she had to stay strong because she was sure her cousin was determined to wed and bed an Elliot. If Anne refused him, then he would turn his attention to Elizabeth.

After giving Moves a sovereign and her thanks, she started walking back to Camden Place with Swoosh at her side. When they reached the boundary of Toff Town, Anne assured her young friend that she would be able to go on alone, but Swoosh could see how affected she was by what she had just witnessed. Her gait was slower, and her shoulders were hunched down.

"Listen, Flash, if you need me, all you have to do is whistle. I'm always around and about. So keep your head up, your eyes open, your mouth shut, and watch your back, and everything will be aces."

Taking Swoosh's hand, she said, "You have been of more help to me than you will ever know, and I appreciate your kindness and patience."

Anne started to walk away, but Swoosh, with a worried look, called after her. "Hey Flash, you do know how to whistle, don't you?"

Anne nodded and put her thumb and forefinger in her mouth, and let loose with an ear-piercing sound that had heads turning.

"At one time, I had a nearly deaf dog," she said by way of explanation, and Swoosh nodded his approval at her unexpected talent and range.

"All right then. I'll see ya when I see ya," and he disappeared into the crowds.

* * *

Anne's mind was racing as she tried to take a full account of what she had just witnessed. Mr. Elliot had got himself hopelessly into debt and wanted to marry her for the sole purpose of getting at the Elliot fortune. Her family needed to be warned, but who would believe the fantastic tale she had to tell about their evil cousin? No, the weight of this matter fell squarely upon her shoulders. She must give Mr. Elliot enough encouragement so that he would continue his addresses to her while she built up a case against him.

As she made her way back to Camden Place, she forgot the most important rule that Swoosh had taught her: watch your back. If she had turned around, she would have discovered that she was being followed. Captain Wentworth had come to Bath for the purpose of telling Anne that Miss Louisa Musgrove was to marry Captain Benwick and that he was once again a free man.

Chapter 16

After making sure that Anne had returned safely to Camden Place, Captain Wentworth did a U-turn and tried to find the scrawny, dirt-encrusted youngster who had guided Anne from that part of Bath where the privileged few lived, past the more modest accommodations leased by tradesmen, officers, and shopkeepers, through the area that housed the work force that kept Bath going, and, lastly, to the other Bath—the one few visitors saw—where the poorest of the poor lived side by side with a criminal element that grew like a fast-spreading mold in a town where unsuspecting out-of-towners came on holiday and where the bad boys hoped to part them from their spare change. But the lad had disappeared.

There had to be a logical explanation for Anne being on the wrong side of town accompanied by a jackanapes. Obviously, she had engaged the boy for purposes of following Mr. Elliot. But why? During their many weeks of separation, and devoid of all hope of their ever coming together, had she become so enamored of the heir to Kellynch that she had taken to tracking his every movement? And what were her thoughts when she had seen her cousin standing across the street from a gaming establishment talking to a man who was a villain if ever there was one.

This was a completely different Anne from the one he had left eight years ago. That Anne would never have gone anywhere without a male escort or invested her own money in a financial scheme or bought shares on the exchange. She most definitely would not have run about the countryside with her hair flowing freely and outfitted in a frock that was too short and sleeveless and with sweat glistening from the tiny beads that had formed on her bosom. Damn! Now he had an erection. But then he thought about that pipsqueak, William Elliot, and anger quickly displaced passion.

Frederick needed a plan, and so he went to the assembly hall to see what events were scheduled for the evening. After scanning all that was being offered, he decided that if Anne was in a position to chose, she would attend a performance by an Italian soprano in the Octagon Room. When they had been a couple, Anne, who had a lovely soprano voice, would sing an aria until she reached, or more accurately, failed to reach the highest notes. She would then dissolve into giggles, delighting him with her contagious laugh. The sound of her laughter was better than any music, and despite being unsettled by her inexplicable behavior, he found himself smiling at the memory.

* * *

After pinching her cheeks and biting her lips to add color, and after taking one last look in the mirror, Anne went downstairs to join her father and sister. She had taken extra care with her toilette and had surprised Patsy when she had asked for pearl pins to be put in her hair and for some of her curls to be allowed to fall freely on her neck. Another surprise was when she chose to wear her most recent purchase, a pale green muslin gown, cut lower than any dress she had worn since Frederick had sailed off into the sunset. But if she was to play the role of *female fatale*, she must dress the part.

"My goodness, Anne! You look lovely," her father said genuinely surprised. "You don't look at all like a spinster this evening!"

"High praise, Papa," she said, laughing at her father's left-handed compliments, but Elizabeth said nothing. As always, Mrs. Clay followed her sister's lead and remained silent.

As soon as Anne entered the lower rooms of the assembly hall, Mr. Elliot crossed the expanse and was on her like a duck on a June bug.

"Miss Anne, there are no words to describe how positively beautiful you look tonight."

"Oh, do try," Anne said, clearly encouraging him.

Without a moment's hesitation, he began, "alluring, charming, dazzling, enticing, graceful, pleasing, radiant, stunning, sublime."

"Well done, Mr. Elliot, and in alphabetical order!"

"You mock me when I am in earnest."

"I *am* teasing you," she told him and then pulled out a fan and covered her face, revealing only her eyes.

"I am bewitched, bothered, and bewildered."

"And the evening is still young," she said, tapping him on his sleeve with her fan.

At that moment, Viscountess Dalrymple and Miss Carteret arrived to great fanfare. The noble one stood in front of the crowd, like a female Moses before the Red Sea, and by her mere presence, she was able to separate the crush of people into two equal parts. The elegantly-dressed ladies walked slowly so that all could bask in their glow, and Anne's outrageous flirting was placed on hold. She had met the Viscountess and her daughter at a tea the previous day. Both were pleasant, but uninterested in any subject that didn't circle around to them. She actually pitied Miss Carteret, whose ignorance of anything that did not have to do with those of her immediate entourage was glaring. She was unaware of the subject that everyone in England was talking about: Napoleon's escape from Elba and his march north to Paris.

"I thought they had put him on an island. How can you escape from an island?" Miss Carteret asked genuinely befuddled.

"By boat," Anne suggested.

This information seemed to unsettle Miss Carteret, and with a befuddled expression, she stated, "I hope once he gets to Paris he will not march on London."

"Unless he's an apostle capable of walking on water, I think he must stop at the Channel," Anne said, trying to reassure her with a little humor.

"But you said he had a boat."

"He would need more than one boat to get an Army across the Channel to conquer England, and we would notice all the preparations required for such an enormous undertaking."

Anne changed the subject as the young lady was clearly distressed at the idea of Napoleon possibly standing on the beach at Calais looking out at England's green landscape while his men went looking for boats.

At the first opportunity, she detached herself from Miss Carteret and moved in on her prey. In an effort to establish a climate of intimacy, before the concert began, Anne offered to translate the selections for Mr. Elliot. The lyrics for *Che ė Amore*, a popular Neapolitan ballad, were in the program, but in Italian, a language that was Greek to Mr. Elliot.

"And since it is Italian, it must be about love," he purred.

"Of course," and leaning towards him, she translated the song and whispered the last two words in his ear, "*That's amore*."

"*Amore*, so beautiful," he said looking into her eyes, but before she could say anything else, Signora Culogrande, was introduced and performed so magnificently that for a moment Anne was able to stop thinking about the moral bankrupt sitting next to her.

During intermission, before Anne could utter a word, Elizabeth nearly leapt over a chair in order to get to Mr. Elliot. But her sister, bless her, led the conversation exactly where Anne wanted it to go.

"Please do share with us what you have been doing these last few days, my dear Mr. Elliot," Elizabeth said, batting her eyelashes.

"Do you mean other than admiring all the beautiful women?" which Mr. Elliot practically crooned, which caused Elizabeth to nearly swoon.

"I agree that Bath does have its share of attractive women, but beautiful, Mr. Elliot?" Elizabeth said, surprised by Mr. Elliot's excessive praise of Bath's female population. "I think there are very few who meet that definition, and being among them, I would know."

Elizabeth was not one to hide her light under a bushel, and that was the wonder of Elizabeth. She was so sure that she was practically perfect in every way that it never occurred to her that other people might see her "tooting her own horn" as being conceited and self-serving.

As much as she would have liked to have left Elizabeth and Elliot to their own devices, Anne had a job to do, and her sister was interfering with her mission to strip William Elliot bare so that all might see what a deceitful, conniving piece of work he was.

"Have you seen much of Bath itself, sir?" Anne asked her cousin. "I have gone no farther than Popinjay Street. Have you ever walked beyond the apothecary's shop?"

"Miss Anne, beyond the apothecary's shop?" he asked, truly astonished. "I should say, 'No, indeed, I have not.' There are only the lowliest forms of people in that part of town. No better than thugs, if you ask me."

"Oh, I had no idea. I am sure your knowledge of the particulars about that part of town must have been gained by talking to others since you have never been there yourself."

"Exactly," Mr. Elliot said as he pulled at his neckcloth.

Anne was enjoying his discomfort, but she was soon to experience her own. All the while she had been speaking to Mr. Elliot, Captain Wentworth had been watching her from the back of the hall. As soon as they made eye contact, the captain bowed and moved towards the door, but Anne was quick enough to catch him before he could leave.

"I did not know you were in Bath, Captain."

"Obviously," he said in a voice that was somewhere between pain and anger. "I only arrived last evening."

"How is Louisa? Does her recovery proceed satisfactorily?"

"More than satisfactory. She is nearly completely recovered."

Anne let out a sigh, and not just because the young lady had sustained no permanent injuries. With Louisa's recovery, Frederick would no longer be under any obligation to marry her.

"Oh, I am very pleased to hear it. We have had little news from either Mary or the Musgroves about her. I know they have been very busy, but even so, they are poor correspondents."

"I would imagine you would have little time to spend on correspondence since your days appear to be so full."

Before she could answer, Mr. Elliot came and stood next to her, and with barely a nod to Wentworth, encouraged Anne to return to her seat as Signora Culogrande was about to sing a song about a farmer and his cucumbers.

"I shall be there momentarily, Mr. Elliot."

"You should go," Captain Wentworth said. "You would not want to keep that particular gentleman waiting."

"Why do you say 'that particular gentlemen?'"

"Is it not obvious?"

"No, it is not. Please explain."

"You two were sharing so intimate a conversation that I assumed that you had come to an understanding about a future together."

"Oh, I see. Again, you will have me married to Mr. Elliot."

"Is there another conclusion to be drawn?"

Anne could see out of the corner of her eye that Mr. Elliot was returning.

"Mr. Elliot, I said that I would be with you in a moment. Please go sit down," she answered, waving him off as if swatting a gnat.

"You should return to your partner," the captain said with acid dripping from his tongue.

"And you to yours," she answered, turning away.

But he stepped in front of her. "And who would that be?"

"Louisa Musgrove."

"Did you not hear? She is engaged to Captain Benwick."

"What?" Anne asked, her mouth dropping open. "Captain Benwick? Are you saying that James Benwick was able to take Louisa away from you?"

"Not exactly," he said, insulted by her remark. "Because of the possibility of Louisa and I being united, I did not think it proper to remain with the Harvilles, so I visited at length with my brother in Monkford and my sister at Kellynch before going up to London."

"And while you were gone, Louisa did a complete about face and chose Captain Benwick over you?" This information stunned her. Louisa had walked away from one of the most handsome, virile men of her acquaintance, a man of wit, grace, and charm, to hitch her wagon to a man who usually wore the doleful look of a basset hound? "What could she possibly have been thinking?"

For a brief moment, Frederick smiled. “Apparently, he won her heart by reading poetry to her, something I never did.”

“No, you were never one for poetry, except, of course, Homer’s *Iliad*, with all its gory battles.”

“Not all of it was about battles. There was the love story of Helen and Paris and do not forget Helen’s lamentation over the loss of Hector.”

Wherefore I wail alike for thee
And for my hapless self with grief at heart;
For no longer have I anyone beside in broad Troy
That is gentle to me or kind.

She understood that the captain was not referring to Helen and Hector, but to Frederick and Anne.

“Frederick, you must trust me. Do not go away in anger. It is not as it seems.” She wanted to touch him so badly, but she dared not.

“Say no more,” he said, cautioning her. “Mr. Elliot is coming.”

“He is so annoying,” she said completely exasperated, “but to remain any longer would invite suspicion.”

So this time, when Mr. Elliot offered his arm, Anne took it and, for effect, appeared to go off in a huff.

“I think you dislike Captain Wentworth very much,” Mr. Elliot said as soon as they were seated. “I certainly have a low opinion of him. He was nothing short of rude while we were in Lyme, but to my mind, he is guilty of a much more serious offense. He has clearly upset you.”

“Mr. Elliot, there are few people I truly dislike. I limit those to deceitful, lying, low-down, lily-livered, thieving, traitorous pond scum.”

“Do you know such a person?” he asked aghast at her description. When she did not answer, he prompted her. “Do you?”

“Hold on. I am thinking.”

Chapter 17

Wentworth needed a drink, and so he went into The Sitting Duck and ordered an ale and chaser. Taking his drinks to a back corner, he sat in the shadows and drank the chaser first and nursed the ale. "What the devil was going on with Anne?" and he pounded the table so hard that the glasses jumped.

There was only one other time when he had been this frustrated, and, of course, that was the day he had been forced to walk away from Anne. In the intervening years, he had sailed the Seven Seas and had fought battles on most of them. He had very nearly lost his life in ferocious hand-to-hand fighting on the *Asp*, and during his recovery, he had staved off boredom in a naval hospital in Portsmouth, mostly thinking about his only love.

Seeing Anne brought back memories of that first day at Kellynch. He had arrived at the estate during pheasant season as a last minute replacement for one of the guns who had dropped out. When Frederick had arrived at the manor house, he had been met by a beautiful young lady with black hair that contrasted with her fair complexion and dazzling blue eyes. She was short, but well proportioned, and had enough of a bust to hold his interest and that invited one's eyes to follow the contours of her body. A slight smile on the lady's lips had let him know that she had found him to be attractive as well. He was just beginning to think how fortuitous it had been for him to have been invited to Uppercross by Charles Musgrove when Elizabeth Elliot opened her mouth.

When Musgrove had introduced him as a naval officer, Miss Elliot had backed away from him. Although it was only one step, a great divide had opened up between them.

"A naval officer? But who are your parents? What are your connections?" And that was all Wentworth needed to hear, and he was only sorry that his horse had been taken to the stable or he would have got on his mount and ridden right back to Uppercross. Fortunately, he didn't. While walking in the parkland later that afternoon, he had seen three young girls running about, squealing with delight, as a young lady, little more than a girl herself, had tried to catch them. When she saw Frederick, she had stopped chasing Mary, Louisa, and Henrietta and had stepped out from the shade of a chestnut tree into the sunlight, and for the first time, his eyes were rewarded with the sight of Miss Anne Elliot.

His first impression was that she was not as pretty as her older sister, but that had lasted but a moment, and when she smiled, his heart had melted. After introductions were made, and in direct contrast to her sister, she had thanked him for his service to England in keeping Napoleon far away from its shores. For the next few days, they had sought each other out at every opportunity, and in the weeks that followed, he had found himself a frequent guest at Kellynch.

They had managed to spend so much time together only because Elizabeth and Sir Walter were so self-absorbed that they paid little attention to anything that did not affect or benefit them. However, all that changed when Lady Russell came for a visit. Unfortunately, being so enamored of each other, and thus oblivious to everything and everyone around them, they did not realize that they were being watched.

On his next visit to Kellynch, the young officer was immediately directed to the study by Mr. Allgood, whose face said it all. Something very bad was about to happen. As soon as he entered the room, Frederick saw them, the killers of his dreams: the Master of Kellynch, Miss Elliot, and Lady Russell. His request for permission to marry Anne was summarily dismissed with a wave of the baronet's hand. Although Sir Walter had done most of the talking, the words coming out of his mouth were those of Lady Russell. He was informed that a decision had been made, in concert with Anne, and that their "little romance" must come to an end. He was then directed to the garden where Anne was waiting for him and was told that he needed to say goodbye as he would not be coming back to Kellynch.

That had been eight years ago. In all that time, why hadn't he gone back to Somerset to try to win her heart again? He knew the answer. It was his damnable pride that had kept him from writing to her. Now that he knew she had never stopped loving him, he was in physical pain because of what that decision had cost him, and the bile rose in his throat.

When he had first seen Anne in the Musgrove kitchen after so much time had elapsed, he had tried to act as if he didn't care, but the sound of her voice and her smile began the process of removing the armor he had been wearing for eight years. On the walk to Winthrop with Anne and the Musgroves, he had shed one piece of armor after another as if he was molting metal. In the process, he had laid bare his heart, and without her even knowing it, she had touched it and he loved again. And when she had jumped off the back of the Crofts' gig and they had been joined at the pelvis as a husband and wife would be, he was so overwhelmed with love—lust as well—but it was because of his love that he was lusting, that he wanted to take her right then and there.

Once the decision had been made to go to Lyme, he was determined to let Anne know that he wished to begin courting her again. But then Louisa had cracked her cranium, and he had very nearly been forced to marry a woman he could never love. When he had returned to the Harville house from Monkford to check on Louisa's progress, an unexplained tension hung in the air, and he believed the reason was that Mrs. Harville had been overly optimistic about Louisa's recovery. Instead, he had been told that Captain Benwick and Louisa were to marry. The news had catapulted him out of his chair, and he had run from the house because it was too small to contain his joy. Benwick had followed him and had found his fellow officer jumping up and down, punching the air with his fists. Believing Wentworth to be distraught, Benwick tried to explain the series of events which had led to their falling in love, but Frederick had quickly disabused his fellow officer of the notion that he had been dealt with in a less than an honorable way.

"No, no, no. I have not been ill treated," Wentworth insisted. "Please take her and love her and be fruitful and multiply and don't give another thought to me. Not one thought. Time for me to move on, old boy. I have learned something from watching you in your mourning for Miss Harville, and so I am going to skip the earlier stages of grief and move right on to acceptance."

Freed of his shackles, Frederick had quickly returned to Monkford, and after one final game of Bible charades with the over-the-hill gang, he had hired a carriage, loaded up his locker, had his best uniform cleaned, and his hardware polished, and was off to Bath. Strutting into the Assembly, he looked awesome and better than any officer in His Majesty's Navy. With his captain's hat on, there was no way Anne would not see him. But before she did, he had found her, and what he saw had shocked him. She was openly flirting with Mr. Elliot, and he thought he would be ill.

When she ran after him outside the Octagon Room, acting as if nothing was amiss, he did not feel one of her thousand tiny arrows, but a huge shaft splitting his spleen. What did she want from him? An engagement present? Well, he had one for her. It was in his pocket—something he had gone to the trouble of having custom made in London to his exact specifications just for her. He had intended to give it to her after she had accepted his offer of marriage.

But something was wrong with this picture. By the time the pubtender had brought him his third ale, he was positive that Anne was up to something, and it somehow involved the young whippersnapper who had led her through the streets of Bath. He suspected that she believed that Wee Willie Elliot was not what he appeared to be. What he needed to do was to find that boy.

* * *

Swoosh was leaning against the lamppost outside Camden Place hoping that Flash would appear. When he had left her two days earlier, he could tell how upset she was, and he wanted to know if there was anything he could do to help her. But when Flash emerged from her posh townhouse, she was also in the middle of a gaggle of giggling women, and he could not approach her without drawing attention to himself, and so he waited. He was so preoccupied with his task that he did not notice that Captain Wentworth had come up from behind him, and when he tried to bolt, the captain grabbed him by his arm.

"I mean you no harm, boy. I am in need of your services, and I will pay for them," Wentworth said, trying to reassure the lad.

"What do you want? If it's a woman, I don't do that."

"No, I don't want a woman, but it is about a woman—Miss Elliot."

"Never heard of her. Sorry. I've got push off now."

"I know that you two are acquainted because I saw you with her two days ago. You guided her through the streets of Bath and brought her back here to her home."

"Oh, you mean Flash?" Seeing his quizzical brow, Swoosh explained that Flash was her street name. "I didn't know her real name. To learn it was highly inadvisable as it would have put her at risk," he told the captain with some pride at his expanding vocabulary.

Wentworth pulled out a one-pound note, and seeing the gleam in the boy's eye, he believed that he would do whatever was asked of him. "Why did Flash need your services?" the captain asked. "Why was she following Mr. Elliot?"

"Oh, he's her brother? I didn't know that."

"No, Mr. Elliot is not her brother, but her cousin."

"Well, it don't matter—brother or cousin. I can't help you 'cause it ain't good for business to ask too many questions of my clients. So I took her where she wanted to be taken, and then I took her back. That's all."

Wentworth smiled, "You are fond of her, aren't you?" The boy was obviously lying, and he was trying to protect Anne by pleading ignorance.

"It was a business arrangement. That's all. Don't make nothing out of it, and I ain't taking your money because I don't know nothing."

"What if I told you that Mr. Elliot wants to marry Flash? Would you help me then?"

Swoosh shook his head in dismay. "This cousin marrying cousin business don't sit right with me. A friend of mine breeds hounds for an earl, Lord Got His Nose Up His Arse, and he won't breed dogs that close."

"They are not first cousins, and we are getting off topic. I am convinced Mr. Elliot is a bad man. Miss Elliot senses that as well, and if provided with sufficient evidence, she will expose him."

"So you call her by her Christian name, do ya?" he said with a devilish grin. The toff was in love with Flash. How adorable. "What's she to you?" When Wentworth said nothing, Swoosh pressed him. "Give me one good reason why I should answer your questions."

The captain hesitated. Here was a boy who most likely had been abandoned by both parents on the streets of Bath at a tender age. What did he know of love? The captain studied Swoosh and believed that under all that dirt was a good lad, and so he answered him.

"Miss Anne Elliot is the love of my life."

"Yeah, is that right?" he asked skeptically. "She ain't no spring chicken, so where ya been?"

"At sea, both literally and figuratively."

And then it was Swoosh's turn to study the captain. He was a handsome bloke, sharp dresser, big buttons, probably had a lot of money because of the war, and someone who could have any unmarried lady in Bath, but, instead, he wanted Flash.

"All right then. If you pay all my out-of-pocket expenses, we'll call it even steven." Swoosh spit into the palm of his hand, and the captain did the same, and they shook on it. “I done the same thing with Flash.”

Wentworth laughed. “I am not surprised. Nothing about Anne, I mean Flash, surprises me anymore. She is fearless. Even so, there are things ladies cannot do, so let us do them for her and find out what Mr. Elliot is up to.”

Chapter 18

Anne had little time to think about Frederick because the next day the Musgrove tribe descended: Mama, Papa, Mary, Charles, and Henrietta. The only one missing was Louisa, and she had gone with Captain Benwick to visit with his family in Deal and would join them in a week to pick out the material for her wedding dress. But it wasn't only news about Louisa that was being shared. Mr. Hayter had asked the Musgroves if he might call on Henrietta upon her return from Bath. It was nearly a certainty that an offer would be made.

"I have always like Mr. Hayter very much," Henrietta told Anne after pulling her into a corner away from the crowd. "He has been most kind and attentive to me, and I feel very comfortable in his company. The only thing I do not like is that my married name will be Henrietta Hayter. It sounds self-loathing. But Mr. Hayter told me in confidence that when he inherits Winthrop, he will take the name of the estate. He agrees that Hayter is not the best name, especially for a curate."

While they had been talking, Anne noticed that Mary was wearing a red glass pin in the shape of a cross on her bodice and asked Henrietta about it.

"Oh, that is Mary's red cross pin. She had it custom made by a jeweler in Exeter. It is a symbol of the Christian charity she exhibited in nursing Louisa back to health," Henrietta explained. "I will tell you how it came about. The day after you left with Lady Russell for Bath, Charles slashed his hand with a kitchen knife, and it was gushing blood. And my brother said, 'Where is Anne when you need her?' but Mary said, 'Who needs Anne? Mrs. Harville and the surgeon showed me how to clean and bandage a wound, and I practiced on some of the fishermen. So I can do it better than my sister because I have more experience.' And that's exactly what she did. She cleaned the nasty thing, applied some salve, bandaged it, without gagging I might add, and cleaned it every day until it scabbed over. Well, that was the start of it."

"The start of what?"

"Mary becoming a rapid responder, but she prefers be called an angel of mercy. First, Charles and she went to Exeter where she bought bandages, poultices, salves, antiseptics, and so many other things, and when she got back home, she cleaned out several shelves in the pantry to make way for all of these medical supplies. Then she paid a visit to Dr. Gurgling and told him that since he lives so far from the village that she would be able to see to the care of any minor injuries without his having to make the trip, and he was most agreeable to the plan. After that, she told the vicar that she was now a trained medical assistant, and he announced it from the pulpit. Mrs. Cutlet, the butcher's wife, was the first to use her services, and she was so pleased that she has been telling everyone about Mary. So when a rider comes with word that she is needed, John, one of our grooms, takes Mary in the gig with her medical bag to attend to her patient. She has two friends covering for her while she is in Bath."

Anne was all amazement. When she had left Uppercross a month ago, Mary was whining about not being able to go to Bath, and now she had transformed herself into an angel of mercy.

"*Brava* for Mary," Anne said. "I am pleased to hear she is making good use of her time, but what of Charles and the boys?"

"You would think that with all these added responsibilities that she would have less time for the family, but, instead, it has energized her. The boys are listening to her most of the time, and Charles is paying more attention to her." Henrietta hesitated before continuing. "I confess I frequently found it difficult to talk to Mary, but not now. She tells me the most interesting things about medicine in a most erudite fashion, and she has enlisted the help of a few ladies from the church, Miss Barton and Miss Nightingale, to roll bandages and the like. When she goes to church on Sunday, she pins a piece of paper to her coat which says, 'Ask me about fighting infection.' She is quite a different person."

Anne could not have been more pleased. By becoming an angel of mercy, Mary was experiencing the same freedom her sister had achieved with her jogging because she was mining unknown depths within herself. Now, if only Elizabeth could have a similar awakening.

But with Louisa to be married in a few weeks' time, the conversation quickly turned to the future bride and groom. Anne confided in Mrs. Musgrove that she was amazed by the turn of events between Louisa and the captain, and Mrs. Musgrove confessed that she had been equally surprised when Captain Benwick came to ask their permission to court Louisa.

"At first, we thought it was because she got a knot on her noggin and wasn't thinking straight," Mrs. Musgrove began. "Then Mr. Musgrove thought it might be more out of gratitude than love, seeing how Captain Benwick came to read to her, hour after hour, day after day. I had no idea how long *The Rise and Fall of the Roman Empire* was. But then we saw the change with our own eyes. The only thing we feared was that Captain Wentworth would take it badly, but that was not the case at all. He said that if Louisa preferred Benwick, he would withdraw, and that is exactly what he did. After congratulating the pair, he was out of the house in a flash, but to where I do not know."

"He is here in Bath, Mrs. Musgrove. I saw him last night at a concert."

But she had not seen him since that time. Nor would she. While Anne had been shopping with Henrietta or playing cards with her family or being required to pay homage to Lady Dalrymple, Captain Wentworth and Swoosh had been planning how best to smoke out Mr. Elliot and expose his true nature to the world.

* * *

With another day of shopping planned by the ladies, Anne excused herself so that she might visit Mrs. Smith. Despite her poverty and ailments, the former governess tried to look on the bright side, and with her heated exchange with Frederick fresh in her mind, Anne was in need of cheerful company.

After Mrs. Rooke brought their visitor a cup of tea, Anne described all the hubbub at Camden Place. "While Henrietta and Mrs. Musgrove shop for satin and lace, Mary is at the Army and Navy Surplus store buying up all of their medical supplies. Mrs. Clay is still joined at the hip with Elizabeth, which is fine with my sister since she relishes having someone hanging on her every word. As for Papa, he is thrilled to be one of Lady Dalrymple and Miss Carteret's favorites, and although nothing of substance is exchanged among the three, they talk for hours, mostly about cosmetics and fountain of youth creams."

What went unsaid was all the attention Mr. Elliot was paying her. She was truly disgusted with him. While they had been playing cards the previous evening, he had rubbed his foot against hers, and although she continued to smile, once they were away from the table, she had hit him so hard on his hand with her fan that she had left a red mark. His response: "Grrrrr" and then made snapping noises with his teeth. Mr. Elliot was the last thing Anne wanted to talk about, but it was not to be.

After beating around the bush for several minutes, Mrs. Rooke casually mentioned that she had heard that Anne and Mr. Elliot would soon have an announcement to make.

"We understand that you are to marry Mr. Elliot, and that you will become Lady Elliot, just like your mother," Mrs. Smith added.

Anne shook her head vigorously before saying, "You will never hear such an announcement. I will never marry Mr. Elliot. Not only do I not love him, I do not even like him."

Mrs. Smith and Mrs. Rooke let out a huge sigh of relief. "We are very glad to hear it, because we know him to be a very bad man."

"Please tell me what you know." Anne asked eagerly.

"Do you know a Mr. Silas Warner?"

"Yes, he is my financial advisor. Why do you ask?"

"Do you know his partner, Mr. Brothers?"

"I have met him in passing while in their offices, but I do not know him."

"Mr. Brothers is Mr. Elliot's financial advisor." That statement alone raised Anne's suspicions. Another coincidence? Just like his appearance in Lyme? No, she did not think so, and she waited to hear more. "Apparently, when he first approached Mr. Brothers about retaining him as his advisor, he had asked for a history of some of his clients and their successes. It seems Mr. Brothers told Mr. Elliot that he had assisted another member of the Elliot family, namely you, and when questioned, he revealed that he had taken your small fortune and had turned it into one of a goodly size. Mrs. Rooke learned this from Mrs. Wallis, who heard Mr. Elliot bragging about it to her husband.

"My dear Anne," Mrs. Smith continued, "the only thing I know of your fortune is that you share some of it with an old friend, and I am very grateful to you for your assistance. But if it is true that you do have a fortune, then it is also true that Mr. Elliot knows of it."

Anne felt a wave of disgust come over her. Now all was revealed. His purpose in paying all this attention to her was not to marry her so that he could have access to the supposed Elliot fortune, but because he was so deeply in debt, he needed ready money, and he knew from Mr. Brothers that she had it. She had been his target all along.

"But how do I expose him?" Anne asked.

Without revealing Mrs. Wallis and Mrs. Rooke's role, there was no proof that Mr. Elliot wanted to marry her for her money, and with Elizabeth and Papa thrilled at the reconciliation between the two branches of the family, they would believe him before they believed her.

Neither Mrs. Rooke nor Mrs. Smith could answer Anne's question, and Anne left Westgate Buildings frustrated, angry, and feeling very alone. The only thing she could think to do was to contact Swoosh. Who else could possibly help her? If she had only known that Swoosh and the captain had already devised a plan of attack, she would not have returned to Camden Place with such a heavy heart.

Chapter 19

When Anne returned to Camden Place, she found the drawing room to be a beehive of activity. Sir Walter, who had purchased a large tub of night cream at a lotions and notions shop, was educating Charles Musgrove on the necessity of caring for one's skin in order to prevent premature aging and liver spots and examined Charles's skin through his monocle.

While Elizabeth and Henrietta were displaying the beautiful accessories they had bought to wear to Louisa's wedding, Mary was showing Mr. and Mrs. Musgrove her latest acquisitions from the Army and Navy surplus store: scissors, bandages, bandage clips, a neck brace, and more. One of Mary's purchases was a bundle of about two hundred facecloths. Whatever was she going to do with all of them, Anne wondered?

"Allow me to explain," Mary said, directing Anne to the sofa. "I have been reading a great deal about why some wounds become infected while others do not. Basically, it is a matter of sanitation. Using the same rag over and over while treating an oozing mass almost guarantees the onset of infection. The cloths are for one-time use only and are to be burnt in the fire once they are soiled."

That made perfect sense to Anne, and it was something she had done instinctively in all her years of nursing family members and the servants. But with the enthusiasm of a convert, Mary wanted to educate others about the necessity of maintaining as sterile a work area as possible when caring for the sick and injured. It was her hope to organize other ladies into chapters so that they might go into every corner of Somerset and beyond, and she had ordered two dozen additional red cross pins for her army of volunteers as a sign of their commitment to providing quality medical care for everyone regardless of their ability to pay.

"Anne, I want you to know that I would never have considered doing any such thing if it had not been for your inspiration."

"I inspired you?" Anne asked, greatly surprised. "But we have never spoken on the subject. How did all of this come about?"

"Do you remember the day I asked you why you were so brown, and you told me it was because you had become a long-distance runner?" and Anne nodded. "Well, during the many quiet hours I spent in Louisa's room, I had ample time to think about a great many things because Louisa wasn't holding up her end of the conversation." When her sister said nothing, Mary added, "That was a joke. Louisa was unconscious most of the time."

Anne chuckled. This was the amusing Mary that she had known when they were both young girls, and it was a pleasure to be in her company once again.

"As I was saying, one of the things I had time to think about was the change in you. No offense, but you really were so easy to take advantage of, and so we all did. But your running gave you a confidence that you never had before, and you became the mouse that roared and then a mouse no more. You say what needs to be said, including telling me that I had become a hypochondriac. Yes, I looked up the word, and I did not like its meaning.

"Anne, I do not want to be a hypochondriac nor do I want to be the party pooper, and I most certainly do not want Charles coming up with every possible excuse to get away from me." Taking Anne's hands in hers, she added, "I am so grateful to you. By your example, you have showed me that I have the power to take charge of my life and to make a difference in the lives of others."

Anne was nearly reduced to tears. It was only the many years of training in hiding her true feelings that enabled her to avoid opening a floodgate. Was it actually possible that Mary and she could have a mature sisterly relationship? She would like to think so.

"Now, we must work on Elizabeth and Papa," Mary said, nudging her sister with her elbow. "With those two, we shall have our work cut out for us," and the two sisters laughed out loud.

* * *

Wentworth looked at Swoosh, who was walking as fast as his short legs could carry him so that he might keep up with the long strides of the six-foot captain. They were headed back to Wentworth's rooms at the Admiral's Club where, Swoosh insisted, the captain had to shed his uniform for street clothes. If not, once they met up with Moves, everyone would be looking at them and asking, "Which one of these doesn't belong here?" and their cover would be blown.

"Don't get me wrong, Cap'n, but who was the bright light what thought about putting a fighting man in white britches? And while we're at it, what's with that hat? You're on a ship with a hundred Frogs shooting at you, and you wear the mother of all hats. It practically screams, 'Shoot me! Come on, just try and shoot me!' That's what got Lord Nelson a ticket to the beyond at Trafalgar."

Without being condescending, Wentworth smiled. He liked the half pint's sense of bravado. He would have made a fine sailor.

"I am the captain of the *Laconia*, and my men must be able to find me quickly, especially when we are in battle. The hat certainly helps."

"Well, you ain't exactly a shrimp. Even without the hat, you're six foot. I bet there's not another officer on your ship who's that tall, so, trust me, those swabs will find you with or without the hat." Because he liked the captain, Swoosh wasn't letting this go. Not only did the hat act as a bullet magnet, it looked stupid. "It's just a suggestion, but one I think you should take."

While Wentworth was changing into his street clothes, he thought he would take the opportunity to get to know his partner a little better.

"Exactly how old are you, Swoosh?"

"Exactly? I couldn't say exactly on account of I'd have to ask my mother. Only I don't know where she is. Last time I seen her, she was getting on the London coach blowing kisses at me."

The captain nodded, indicating he understood that his mother had abandoned him and that he had made his own way in the world. When Wentworth said nothing, Swoosh asked him, "So you're not gonna feel sorry for me? 'Boo hoo, poor lad. No mother. Lives on the streets,' and all that rot."

"No. I have lads on my ship who are younger than I think you are."

"What do you make me for?"

"Looking at you, I would say eleven, but listening to you, I would wager that you are coming up on thirteen years."

And Swoosh burst out laughing. You're the only one that ever guessed right. I could tell just by the way Flash looked at me that she had me pegged for someone just out of his nappies. If I let her, she'd of taken me home with her, washed my face, fed me a bowl of soup, and bought me new clothes. Then she'd try to reform me so that I could have a better life. After that, she'd make me go to church with all them toffs. No thanks."

"Miss Elliot has no experience with lads who have to do the work of a man. I do. But it looks as if you are doing all right for yourself."

After acknowledging the compliment, Swoosh said, "Which reminds me, we have work to do, but we need to go over a few rules before we get going. (1) Don't look at nobody in the eyes because that means you're looking for a fight, and you'll get one. You can beat the crap out of most men, but that's not what we're here for. And, besides, they'll gang up on you. (2) Lose the cockiness. Just from the way you walk, you'll have everyone looking at you. Keep your eyes down, like you're looking for a stray coin. (3) Do what I says, when I says it. That's cause I'll find Elliot before you do, and I don't want to blow this whole thing because you stood out like a Christmas gift in June.

“Last, but not least, I ain’t gonna call you captain nor mister neither. If an officer is in my part of town, that’s ’cause he’s looking for action or a woman, and anyone who is called ‘mister’ is the mark or the target. So we got to come up with a street name for you. “How about Fish? Shark? Mast? Skipper?”

But the captain shook his head after each suggestion. “No nautical references, please.”

“Brass? Rocks? Cannon?”

“No, they all have sexual connotations.”

“Ain’t that the point?”

“Using a name to establish that I am well endowed is unnecessary. I am a manly man, and I am confident in my own sexuality and do not need any such crutches.”

“Got it,” Swoosh said, but actually he didn’t. The captain had been blessed with big buttons, so why not show off a little bit with a studly name. When he reached puberty, Swoosh was certainly hoping that he would fill out his pants, and he would want everyone to know what he had going for him.

“Warrior?” The captain shook his head. “Dash?” he said smiling. “You and Miss Elliot could be Flash and Dash. That would be real cute.”

“I don’t do cute.” And after every one of Swoosh’s suggestions, Wentworth shook his head ‘no.’

“I’m guessing it don’t take you this long to make a decision when you’re out on the Atlantic fighting the Frogs,” Swoosh said, giving the captain his most annoyed look, but that didn’t stop Wentworth from rejecting another half dozen suggestions.

“Why can’t we use one of my real names?” Wentworth asked.

“*One* of your real names? How many you got?”

"I was christened Frederick Charles David Alexander Wentworth."

"Did your mother give you all those names because she didn't think she'd have any more kids?"

"I was named after my grandfather, my father, and my two godfathers."

"Right. You and the Prince Regent," Swoosh said, mumbling to himself. "Let's keep this simple. We'll call you Rick," and after the captain agreed, Swoosh said, "We're ready now, so let's get after it."

But the captain hesitated. "Swoosh, before we go, as a sign of your trust in me, may I ask you what your *real* name is?"

Swoosh hadn't been called by his real name in so long, he had to think what it was. "Unlike you, Frederick David Goliath Alexander the Great Wentworth, I only got the two names. My Pop's name was Reno, and my mum called me Louie after the French king what got his head whacked off. That didn't sit right with her, her being a monarchist and all. Now, if we could quit jawing, we've got a job to do."

"All right, Louie," and putting his hand around the lad's shoulder, he said, "I predict that this day marks the beginning of a beautiful friendship."

The pair quickly made their way through the seediest parts of Bath until they had arrived at the rendezvous point with Moves. After a brief introduction, Swoosh's brother gave his report.

"Mr. E. come up with all the bar and smacker what he owed Blackjack Cleaver and paid him off last night."

"How the hell did he do that?" Swoosh asked.

"You won't be seeing that particular toff riding around in his bad and black carriage on account of Blackjack has got himself a new set of wheels with a big gold "E" on its side."

Swoosh and Moves did a high five. They loved to see how far the high and mighty could fall.

"Blackjack told him he never wanted to see his ugly mug again, so, of course, Mr. E. went back home and took up reading the Bible," and the brothers doubled over laughing. "I got everything I needed from listening to the toff run off at the mouth. He's been bragging that he'll be knee deep in coin once he marries his rich cousin."

"But she is not rich," the captain interjected. "She receives a modest annuity, but it can, in no way, pay off all of Elliot's debts."

"Whatever," Moves said. "And that part don't matter. What Mr. E. was saying was that this dame took the money what comes from her mother's side and bought shares in a private shipbuilding yard in Dartmouth."

"In Dartmouth? Why that's where the *Laconia* was built," the captain said, amazed at the coincidence.

"That part don't matter neither," Moves said in a voice that showed his growing impatience with the captain's high distractibility. "Mr. E. says she's got the Midol touch…"

"You mean the Midas touch." the captain said, correcting him.

"Whatever! If I may continue, puhleeze," he said with his voice growing louder. "He says she bought them shares low and sold them high, and on account of the war, she's a rich lady."

Wentworth could hardly take it all in. Because of the rapid expansion of the Royal Navy during the wars with France, it had been impossible for the Royal shipyards to build all the ships necessary to fight the French on the broad expanses of the Atlantic, the North Sea, and in the Mediterranean as well, and handsome contracts had been awarded to private merchant shipbuilders with yards all along the coast of England and on up into Scotland. He smiled at the thought that Anne was a wealthy woman as a result of her having invested in the construction of the very ship that had brought him such riches.

“Where’s Mr. E. at now?” Swoosh asked.

“Shooting pool at McCoy’s,” Moves said, shaking his head at the toff’s total lack of judgment. “He’s gone from the frying pan into the fire. Willie McCoy’s a bad one from Bristol. Back home they call him Slim, but Slice would be a better name ’cause he carries a dirk in his boot, and he’ll have you sliced and diced and served up for supper before you know what hit you. But Slim’s doing his usual act. Let the mark win for a while, and then bring in a ringer and clean his clock. Last I heard, he was up about one-hundred pound, which is about as much as Slim will let him win before he turns it around.”

Turning to the captain, Swoosh asked, “How do you want to play this, Rick?”

“If we are ever to convince the family that the heir to Kellynch is a duplicitous, devious, double-dealing, fallacious knave, we must have hard evidence or the Elliots will never believe it.”

“What did he say?” Moves asked his brother.

“He said we’ve got to come up with something what proves Mr. E. is as big a bastard as we’re making him out to be or the toff walks.”

“Then why don’t he just say that instead of him using all them big words?” Moves asked.

“On account of toffs talk toff talk, which is a good thing, ’cause it makes it easy to pick ’em out of a crowd. Anyone can play dress up and wear nice clothes, but that toff talk, you’re gotta be born with that.” Because Swoosh knew more about Toff Town, his brother would not challenge him. “Moves, you keep a tail on him while me and Rick figure out what to do.”

After the captain gave Swoosh’s brother a one-pound note, he disappeared into the crowd heading for Willie McCoy’s.

As the two conspirators made their way to the Admiral’s club, they went through a dozen scenarios, but all lacked the *coup d’ grace* they needed in order to convince Sir Walter that his heir was a turd. As they approached the shopping district, they had to make way for a traveling troupe. While jugglers, fire-eaters, acrobats, and men on stilts paraded down the street, a few entertainers remained behind to amuse the crowds that had gathered to witness the spectacle. Clowns pulled coins out of the ears of children, a magician produced a rabbit from his top hat, and a quick sketch artist drew pictures of the ladies.

The solution to their problem hit both Rick and Swoosh at the same time, and they pushed their way through the crowd until they were standing next to the artist.

"You interested in earning some real money?" Swoosh asked.

"That depends on what you want. I am not going to gaol for anyone. Been there; done that."

Rick produced a pound note. "You can earn more of these, and you won't have to do anything illegal," and he explained what was required.

"Done," he quickly answered. He took his work-in-progress off his easel, handed it to the lady, and asked her to remove her bottom from his collapsible stool. "Now, where is the gent you want me to sketch?"

Chapter 20

Wentworth returned to the Admiral's Club alone. His young partner had informed him that until he had something to report, the captain was to sit tight and wait to hear from him. In the meantime, Swoosh had scheduled a meeting with his brother and the artist to formulate a plan as how best to capture Elliot's shenanigans when he again came into Tough Town.

When Wentworth went into the lobby, he saw a familiar face, and his old friend from Lyme, Captain Harville, called out a greeting.

"Wentworth, it was not more than an hour ago that I had a conversation with Admiral Croft and your sister right here in the lobby, but they said nothing of your being in Bath."

"They did not know of my arrival. I have only been here a few days, but Sophie had written to say that the Admiral and she would be taking the waters. I am afraid the quiet life of a country gentleman does not suit my brother-in-law at all. He writes that the quiet keeps him up at night."

"That is easy enough to understand," Harville replied, laughing. "The Admiral craves action and watching the grass grow and the cows eat it does not satisfy. He mentioned that he hopes this business with Napoleon will result in his being recalled by the Admiralty."

"Don't we all," Wentworth said. "I have some personal matters to attend to here in Bath, but then I am hoping to be back in action on the *Laconia* engaging the French. There are still fortunes to be made, and I plan to make the most of it while it lasts," and the two men nodded their heads in agreement. "I have an idea, Harville. Why don't we discuss the riches that are there for the taking over a pint of ale?

The first one is on me." And the two men soon found themselves quenching their thirst in a nearby public house.

"What brings you to Bath?" Wentworth asked his fellow captain.

Taking a small box out of his pocket, Harville explained, "I have been asked by James Benwick to have this painting properly set for Miss Musgrove," and he showed Wentworth a miniature of the captain. "Benwick had it sketched at the Cape for my sister, Fanny, but now it is to go to another. Truthfully, I have little stomach for the task."

"Then allow me to do it for you," Wentworth immediately offered. "However, I would hope that you would find it in your heart to be happy for Miss Musgrove and Benwick. Since you have had the good fortune to secure the love and devotion of a wonderful woman, you would not wish to deny it to a fellow officer who will soon sail from Portsmouth. Surely, you have not forgotten that it is in the quiet hours between darkness and dawn that our thoughts turn to those whom we love best, and during those long voyages, it is the memory of our times together that keeps us whole until we may return home to them."

"No, of course I have not forgotten," he answered. "You speak eloquently of an institution you do not support."

Wentworth sat up in his chair. "You should not assume that because I have not married, I have not loved. I can assure you that that is not the case. I gave my heart to a young lady many years ago, but she gave it back to me. And there has been no other since that time."

"So sorry, Wentworth," Harville said embarrassed. "It was presumptuous of me to assume... I had no idea. You play your cards close to your vest."

"No worries, Harville," he said, standing up. After throwing a few coins on the table, he told the captain, "I am to meet a party of friends on Milsom Street, but I am sure I will see you later in the day."

"That is very possible as your sister has invited me to join her at the Musgrove residence this afternoon. If you are in that part of town, why don't you meet me there as the jeweler who is to make the frame is nearby?"

"Agreed," and Frederick quickly took his leave. In that way, he would not have time to dwell on the eight years of memories lost to him because Anne had refused his offer of marriage.

* * *

As Anne left Camden Place, she scanned the street hoping for some sign of Swoosh. It had been three days since she had seen Frederick at the concert, and she was beginning to think that she had failed in convincing him that she had no interest in Mr. Elliot. If she could just make contact with Swoosh, then, possibly, the little rascal could find Frederick and tell him what they had learned about the heir to Kellynch as well as their plans, as Swoosh put it, "to take him down." But there was no Swoosh to be found, and so she did what she had done nearly every day since her arrival in Bath. She went shopping with one of her sisters.

Mary was out with the Musgroves driving up and down the streets of Bath. While Mr. and Mrs. Musgrove and Henrietta admired the sights, Mary was looking for some poor afflicted person in need of her nursing skills. With her bag stuffed to the brim with medical supplies, she was hoping to pick out a person in the crowd who required bandaging. Surely, someone, somewhere, must be oozing. She hit pay dirt when she saw the green grocer's son who was covered from head to toe with sores from the chicken pox. He had been scratching them, and as a result, most of the sores were infected. After consulting with the boy's father, Mary told the Musgroves to return for her in about a half hour, and with her red cross pin, identifying her as an angel of mercy, shining on her blue cape, she took the lad to the family's living quarters and got after it.

With Mary otherwise engaged, Anne was stuck with Mrs. Clay and Elizabeth, but after two hours of watching them shop, she had had enough and told the ladies that she was going into the circulating library to view their new titles. Unfortunately, they too had tired of going from shop to shop and had followed her in. Worse yet, Mr. Elliot had seen the trio go in to the library and had decided to join them.

"Ladies, it has begun to rain outside, but with such beauty as I have before me, the sun continues to shine indoors," Mr. Elliot gushed.

While Mrs. Clay smiled and Elizabeth cooed at his statement, behind his back, Anne was ready to gag, and in order to avoid actually doing so, she walked to the far end of the library. But Wee Willie followed her.

"Apparently, Lady Dalrymple saw the three of you come in here, and she has sent for her carriage," Mr. Elliot whispered. Of all the annoying things he did, and they were legion, that was the most annoying. She could feel his breath on her ear, and it made her want to swat him like a bug. "Unfortunately, Elizabeth pointed out that not all of you could fit comfortably in the carriage, so your sister decided you were the one to remain behind."

"What a surprise."

"However, this series of events is fortuitous as it allows me to walk you home while sharing an umbrella," and he arched his eyebrows several times indicating that he was looking forward to being glued to her side during the walk to Camden Place. She wanted to tell him what he could do with his umbrella, but instead she smiled because she had not yet come up with a plan that would expose him, and until such a plan was in place, she had to continue to give him encouragement.

"Oh, goodie. Lucky me," she said. But while she clapped her hands, she was actually imagining her elbow connecting with his jaw.

"Once I have seen your sister and Mrs. Clay to Lady Dalrymple's carriage, I shall return."

"Please do not hurry on my account. You need to make sure that they are all comfy and want for nothing," and she wiggled her fingers at him in goodbye.

At that moment, there was a commotion at the entrance to the shop as a number of people were taking refuge from the rain. A large party had entered, and towering above them all was Captain Frederick Wentworth.

"Miss Anne," he said, bowing, "are you not going to Camden Place with your sister? The Dalrymple carriage is outside."

"No, there is not enough room for me."

"Then please allow me to walk with you back to your townhouse. Although I came only a few short days ago, I have equipped myself properly for Bath," and he pretended to use his umbrella as a sword to fight off the rain, and his levity did more to reassure her than any utterance could have.

"You have come too late, Captain. Mr. Elliot has already offered to see me home, and it would be rude to go with you after accepting his offer."

"I see that Mr. Elliot has attached himself to you once again," Frederick said in a voice indicating his displeasure.

"Yes, just like a tumor and about as welcome."

The captain laughed so loudly that it invited attention from his party, but when they resumed their conversation, Frederick and Anne could hear what was being said and so, without shame, they listened in.

"One can guess what will happen there," one of the ladies said, "Mr. Elliot is always with her; he half lives with the family."

"Anne Elliot is very pretty, I think," said another. "It is not the fashion to say so, but I confess I admire her more than her sister."

"But the men are all wild after her older sister. Anne Elliot is too delicate for them," the first one said, while the second and third nodded in agreement.

The captain took Anne by the elbow and walked with her behind a bookshelf so that they would be neither seen nor heard.

"I think if those ladies had seen you running for the surgeon or lifting Louisa on a door, they would not describe you as being delicate."

"I am sure they mean it as a compliment, but I was never delicate. As a child, I was very much a tomboy."

"That does not surprise me at all, and if the word, 'delicate,' ever did apply to you, it no longer does."

Anne recognized that as a compliment and thanked him. "What have you been doing since we last met at the concert?"

"Oh, quite a lot actually. It seems that you and I have a friend in common who lives here in Bath."

"Who might that be?" she asked truly puzzled because she knew that the captain had never before been to Bath.

"Oh, he stands about so high," and he held his hand below chest level, "and goes by the name of..."

"Swoosh," Anne said, finishing his sentence. "You have met my partner in crime."

"Yes, Flash," he said, emphasizing her street name, and this caused Anne to smile, "and he has told me all about Mr. Elliot and his love of gambling and his extensive debts."

"Frederick, then you *do* understand what happened at the concert the other night and why I was so attentive to him?" she asked with her eyes searching his own. "You see, he must be exposed because if I refuse him, he will turn to Elizabeth."

"I disagree. Your sister lacks her own fortune and that is what he is after."

"You know that I have money?"

Frederick then explained all the information that Moves had gleaned from eavesdropping on Elliot's conversations. "I suspect his plan is to marry you and use the law to gain control over your finances."

"Undoubtedly. He really is a cur."

"No, he is a Piglet or so he has been christened by Moves and Swoosh."

Anne covered her mouth with her hand to stifle a laugh.

"Granted, it is not as clever name as Flash, but accurate nonetheless," the captain continued. "By the way, I too have a street name. It is Rick. I know it is rather boring, but you should have heard some of the suggestions Swoosh made. I cannot imagine someone shouting 'Cock-a-doodle' or 'Masthead' at an officer in His Majesty's Navy. Such a possibility would make me hide as no bullet ever did."

And the two of them laughed at the ridiculousness of a daughter of a baronet and a naval officer having street names.

"Was Cannon suggested as a possible street name?" Anne asked. "I think that would have suited you."

"Miss Anne, you will make me blush."

But, instead, Anne blushed. "Do you know how I made my fortune?" Anne quickly asked embarrassed by her question. First, while at Uppercross, she had mentioned his nuts, and now his cannon. He would think she had cannon envy, and thinking about his hardware had brought on that familiar sensation, the one she experienced only when she was with him. Seeing the change in her, Frederick placed his hand on her shoulder and ran it down her arm until he was holding her hand, and he cherished the moment because he had thought that the opportunity to do so would forever be denied him because of the events in Lyme.

"Moves learned from eavesdropping on Piglet's conversations with Blackjack Cleaver's enforcer that you had invested in a merchant shipyard that built ships for the Royal Navy," he said, reluctantly releasing her hand. "But how could you possibly have known that I would be given the command of the *Laconia*? Do you have a spy at the War Office?"

"Not at present, but I am working on it," she said, chuckling. "Seriously, there was no way for me to know such a thing. I chose Dartmouth because my financial advisor said that they had the best safety record of all the yards in the south of England, and their ships tended to stay afloat. I found that to be an important factor in making my decision, but I did not rely exclusively on my advisor. Instead, I visited the yard myself, and they had a huge banner which said, '96 days since our last fatal accident.' I thought any yard that paid so much attention to worker safety would build a good ship. As for your vessel, all I could do was pray that the safety record of the yard that had built your ship would be as committed to safety as Dartmouth was."

By that time, the captain's party had found them, and with Miss Atkinson motioning for him to join them, he indicated that he must leave.

"Now, Miss Anne, please allow me to call a cab for you."

"Frederick, I mean Rick," she said and winked at him, "as you know, I run every morning by myself. I hardly need to travel by cab for what is no more than a five-minute walk."

"I do not like the idea of you running by yourself." It was one thing for her to be jogging about the countryside near Kellynch and Uppercross, but quite another to be doing the same in a town as large as Bath.

With her chin jutting out, she said, "Well, you will have to get used to it."

"And so I shall," he said, knowing that he would have to accept this new Anne, whom he liked very much. All evidence of the feebleness of character, weakness, and timidity that she had exhibited at the time of their parting had disappeared. "I will be at the Musgroves later this afternoon. Will you be there?"

"I think I can arrange it."

Wentworth handed her his umbrella and said, "That's to make sure that you do come. I will want that back."

* * *

Lurking nearby throughout the exchange was William Elliot. Although he could not hear what was being said, it seemed as if Captain Wentworth might be making a move on Anne. He was so close to winning his cousin's affections, and he was not about to throw it all away, not even for someone with such big buttons. After Anne had turned the corner, he approached Wentworth as he exited the shop.

"You seem to be quite friendly with Miss Anne Elliot," Elliot began.

"Yes, I am a friend of hers of long standing."

"And I am her cousin. We are family. I have known her all my life."

"I understand that there were some lengthy gaps in your relationship—years in fact."

"That is a family matter and of no concern to you. May I ask the purpose of your coming to Bath?"

"No, you may not. It is none of your business."

"I might make it my business," Elliot answered in a threatening voice.

Wentworth took his hat, which he had been holding under his arm, and placed it on his head. With the captain's hat on, he now gave the appearance of being a giant, and he was well aware of his awesomeness, especially while standing next to the shorter and slightly-built Elliot.

"Mr. Elliot, you are addressing someone who commanded a frigate at the Battle of Lissa in the Adriatic. As the French bore down on us, we fought under the raised banner of 'Remember Nelson.' By the time we had finished with them, we had sunk the French flagship, captured two others, and scattered the remainder of the squadron to the four winds." After allowing all of this to sink in, he concluded, "Now, do you have anything else to say to me before you leave?"

Elliot said nothing, he had been out-hatted and he knew it, and touching the brim of his top hat, he quickly made his way down the street. After Elliot was out of sight, Wentworth heard a sharp whistle, and turning to his right, he saw Swoosh, who was grinning from ear to ear.

"I heard everything you said to him. You told him to go 'frig it,'" Swoosh said, obviously very pleased with the captain's manly display. "You were like a cock strutting around the farmyard with his chest all puffed out, or in your case, with your big hat on and your buttons all polished."

"I did not tell him to go 'frig it.' I am an officer and a gentlemen. I would never use such language anywhere near the presence of a lady."

Swoosh did not pursue it, but he knew what he had heard. The captain had said "frig it."

"Do you have news for me?" Wentworth asked his young friend.

"The best news there is. Can you meet me at 9:00 out in front of the Admiral's Club? Why, you ask? It's on account of we're about to take Piglet down? By this time tomorrow, he'll have his hooves up in the air in surrender," and Swoosh laughed so hard his side ached.

A very pleased Wentworth reached into his pocket for a coin as a way of thanking him, but Swoosh stopped him. "She's my friend, too, you know. This one's on me."

Chapter 21

After parting from Rick, Anne was experiencing a lightness of heart that she had not felt in years. As she walked past the White Hart, she saw Mrs. Musgrove and Henrietta alighting from a carriage. The two ladies were carrying bundles of wrapped goods, proof of a successful day spent shopping, and she quickly crossed the street to join them.

"Oh, Anne, you must come and see what we have bought for Louisa's wedding," Mrs. Musgrove said.

"Mrs. Musgrove, I was planning to visit you this afternoon to view your treasure. May this wait until that time?" Anne asked, gesturing for the lady to go ahead of her to get out of the rain.

"Oh, you are just like Mr. Musgrove, Miss Anne. He has no interest in shopping and abandoned us early in the day."

"Is Mr. Musgrove within?"

"No, he went to retrieve Mary from the greengrocer's home." Mrs. Musgrove explained how Mary had come to be there. "Once in the family's residence, she found that there were three other children who were all suffering from the chicken pox. The mother had thought it best to expose them all at the same time, but what a handful to have four children with sores all over their bodies. We offered to help her, but Mary said that it was her 'calling' and that she would see to the little ones herself.

"As we were leaving, the man responsible for the containment of disease within Bath, a Mr. Blight, was paying a call on the Kales, the greengrocer, that is. Mary was delighted because she was now able to converse with someone whose expertise was in the same field as her own. When we left, they were discussing the necessity of Mary having all her patients sign a document that is meant to protect their privacy. She did not know she had to do that, but it didn't seem to bother her. She teased Mr. Blight about filling out all this extra paperwork so that they might keep the bureaucrats on the city council fully employed.

"My word, she is a different person," Mrs. Musgrove continued. "Nothing bothers her; nothing is an inconvenience. It is quite a remarkable change, and Charles is as happy as I have ever seen him. They laugh and giggle like newlyweds. I just wonder if it will result in another grandchild."

They talked for several more minutes before Anne was allowed to continue on to Camden Place. She believed that in the next few days she would be rid of Mr. Elliot, and her relationship with Rick could be brought out into the open. She had little doubt that the captain would act with great speed to secure her father's permission for them to marry. Finally, at long last, she was to receive her fair share of happiness. As far as she was concerned nothing could dampen her spirits; that is, until Mrs. Rooke intercepted her at the front door to the Camden Place townhouse.

* * *

When Anne saw Mrs. Rooke, she felt her chest tighten. Surely it must be that her friend, Mrs. Smith, had died. What other reason could there be for the nurse to have come so far?

"Mrs. Rooke, is there something wrong?" Anne asked, trying to keep the quiver out of her voice.

"Mrs. Smith sent me. She's been going back and forth, back and forth, as to whether or not to tell you something."

"Tell me what? Is her ailment terminal? Is she at death's door?"

"Oh, no. She's fine. Those exercises you gave her have made a world of difference. We were running in place in the kitchen this morning," and she pulled on her dress and turned so that Anne could see her in profile. “I think I’m losing weight because of it. But never mind me. I’m here with a message from Mrs. Smith. She wants to make sure that you know just what slime Mr. Elliot is.”

“Oh, my goodness,” Anne said relieved, “no worries there. He is such a lowdown varmint that he could crawl under the belly of an ant. That, in a nutshell, is my opinion of Mr. Elliot.”

“That’s good to hear because she’s got something important to tell you.”

The story that the former Miss Hamilton had to share with her friend was as pathetic as Mrs. Smith had been when Anne had first encountered her in Bath.

“Mr. Elliot is a man without heart or conscience; a designing, cold-blooded being, who thinks only of himself; who is guilty of cruelty and treachery. He is totally beyond the reach of any sentiment of justice or compassion.” And the words flowed in a torrent from the lips of Mrs. Smith.

“Yes, I agree with everything you are saying, but what exactly did he do? Why was I summoned at this particular time?” she asked eagerly, waiting for Mrs. Smith to add to her growing case against William Elliot.

“My late husband, my poor, dear Charles, who had the finest, most generous spirit in the world, would have divided his last farthing with Mr. Elliot, shared his last bowl of broth, taken the shirt off his back. Our home, our bed, our cupboard, our purse were all open to him whenever he needed it because of my husband’s deep affection for that man.”

“I am sure Mr. Smith was kindness itself, but what exactly did Mr. Elliot do to deserve such disapprobation?”

“While we were living in London, my husband formed an acquaintance with Mr. Elliot, his true nature unknown to him. As a result of my sweet Charles’s regard for the gentleman, Mr. Elliot and I developed a friendship, and he took me into his confidence. He told me that he did not want to marry your sister as it did not give him immediate access to ready money. He needed cash, and he did not want to wait for his inheritance, especially since he believed your father ate a healthy diet, avoided direct sunlight, and would not die young. So he was determined to make his fortune by marriage, and that is why he married Phoebe Welling-Dowd."

"Well, I guessed as much. I am sure even my father guessed that he married her for her dowry, and Papa's not very good at guessing. You should see him play charades. When he is on my team, I know that we shall lose," and Anne rolled her eyes. "But is there anything more substantive to report other than he did not wish to marry Elizabeth?"

"Mrs. Rooke has learned through Mrs. Wallis that he is involved in some kind of conspiracy with Mrs. Clay."

"Mrs. Clay!" Anne said in complete astonishment. To her mind, Mrs. Clay wasn't very bright. After months of residing in Bath, she still got lost nearly every day, and she pictured an unpacked crate in Mrs. Clay's room that said "this side up," except that it was upside down. "Well, Mr. Elliot and Mrs. Clay may conspire all they wish. It will not do them any good. My father thinks of no one other than Elizabeth and himself."

"I am sure I can think of something more substantive," and a furrowed brow appeared, and after a few minutes, she finally thought of something. "Mr. Elliot frequently spoke to me about Kellynch, and he said that all the honor of the estate was as cheap as dirt to him. He declared that if baronetcies were saleable, anybody should have his for £50, arms and motto, name and livery included. Do you need additional proof that he is black at heart?"

"Actually, I do. What you are saying is hearsay and would not be inadmissible in court."

"I do have a letter from Mr. Elliot to my husband ridiculing your father. Would seeing these statements in writing help?"

"Of course," Anne said eagerly. After Mrs. Smith handed her the letter, she quickly scanned it until her eyes settled on the following:

> *Give me joy: I have got rid of Sir Walter and Miss Elliot. They are gone back to Kellynch and almost made me swear to visit them this summer, but my first visit to Kellynch will be with a surveyor to tell him how to bring it with best advantage to the hammer. The baronet is not likely to marry again; he is quite fool enough. I wish I had any name but Elliot. I am sick of it. The name of Walter I can drop, thank God!*

The letter was perfect. It showed a degree of disrespect for the head of the Elliot family that almost surprised her.

"At the time that letter was written, Charles and I were very young, and we associated only with the young. We were a thoughtless, gay set, without any strict rules of conduct and lived for enjoyment. I think differently now. Time, sickness, and sorrow have given me other notions, but at that period, I must own that I saw nothing reprehensible in what Mr. Elliot was doing. That would come later—when I saw his unbridled avarice in pursuing Miss Welling-Dowd. Money and more money was all he wanted. Her father was a grazier, her grandfather a butcher, but that was all nothing, and not a difficulty or a scruple was there on his side with respect to her birth. All his caution was spent in being secured of the real amount of her fortune before he committed himself to the marriage."

Her cousin's rapaciousness was of no surprise to Anne nor was his determination to marry Miss Welling-Dowd for her money alone, but it was hard for Anne to think of Miss Hamilton/Mrs. Smith as being without any strict rules of conduct, but she must take her at her word. Who would admit to such a thing if it were not true?

"One last thing, I must share," Mrs. Smith continued. "Mr. Elliot was also named executor of my husband's estate, but he would not take up his duty. I have some property in the West Indies, which might be recoverable by proper measures and make me independent of all charity, but I haven't a clue as to how to start such an action. If it requires the involvement of a solicitor, I have not the funds."

Anne assured her friend that she would immediately put her in touch with the Elliot family solicitor to resolve the property issue. But there was so much else to think about, and she mulled over some of the things her former governess had shared. Mrs. Smith just so happened to be married to a close friend of Mr. Elliot's, and even when she realized what a scoundrel Elliot was, she did not warn her husband because she was only nineteen years old, something of a party animal, and had no idea that a friend could rake you over the coals. She had also learned that Mrs. Clay was acting in concert with Mr. Elliot.

"Does the letter help, Anne?"

"Oh, yes. Even allowing for Mr. Elliot's youth at the time he wrote that letter, his cruel words are unpardonable. I would mention to Papa his reprehensible behavior to you in particular, but my father is much too self-centered to care."

"Yes, I know. Remember, he was my employer."

Anne kissed Mrs. Smith goodbye, and with the letter tucked in her reticule, she quickly departed. It was important that Lady Russell know of these things as she would need an ally in convincing her father that his heir was a cur—correction—a piglet.

All the happiness that Anne had felt upon seeing Rick was gone, now to be replaced by a feeling of emptiness and sadness that such unkindness could exist in the world. Even as awful as the letter was, would it be enough for her father to begin proceedings to disinherit Mr. Elliot?

As Anne departed Westgate Buildings, she thought she heard someone whisper, "Pssst, Flash." But when she turned around, she saw no one. Was her desire to see Swoosh so strong that she was imagining that she was hearing him?

"Psssssssst, Flash. Down here," and sitting at her feet was Swoosh holding a begging bowl and pretending to be a cripple. "I didn't think you'd ever come out of there. We've got work to do, and what have you been doing? Going around visiting friends and family like it's Yuletide. And another thing, you still think everything should be right in front of you when usually that's the last place it is."

"I am so sorry, Swoosh. Believe me, I am trying, but I do not have your life experiences."

Swoosh let out a huge sigh and then scratched his head. She was right. Actually, she was coming along rather nicely for a toff's daughter.

"Well, I've got some dirt to dish," he said, standing up. "I followed Piglet after he left Rick at the library. He went and talked to the lady what hangs out with your older sister. I think her name is Mrs. Clay, and I heard him say he was on his way to Sir Walter's to ask for your hand in marriage, and with your father on his side, there weren't no way you could get out of it."

"This is so unfair," she said, stamping her foot. "I spent eight years pining away for Captain Wentworth. Eight years! That's 2,920 days, if you do not count the leap years. And now, just as it seems that we are to be together, that, that, varmint is determined to ruin it all."

"Hey, Flash. Buck up! I came here with good news. Me and Rick are going to bust that petty, poisonous, pernicious piece of trash tonight."

"Did you come up with that string of pearls by yourself?" Anne asked, a smile now on her face because she knew it was Rick who had uttered that sentence.

"No, that's a quote from Rick. But here's what I got to say to you. All you got to do is to get through one more day with Piglet, and then we'll have the goods on him so you won't have to marry him. Rick's says you'll have enough evidence to get his sorry arse disinherited."

"You are right. I will buck up," Anne said with conviction. With Swoosh, Moves, and Rick in her corner, she knew that she could do it.

Chapter 22

As soon as Anne entered the townhouse, she was greeted by the family's butler of twenty plus years. In his service to the Elliot family, Mr. Allgood had seen it all. He had been a footman when Anne's mother had come to Kellynch Hall as the wife of the most handsome man in the county. He had shared in the joy of the births of their three daughters and in their sorrow for their stillborn son, and the great loss of Lady Elliot could still sadden him more than a dozen years after her death. With the Mistress of Kellynch gone, he knew how it would be, and he had watched as Sir Walter's vanity and spendthrift ways had caused the erosion of the family's fortunes until they were forced to leave Kellynch, his home since he was a lad of ten.

There were many nights when Allgood thought how easily it could have been avoided. He would think of all the money spent on carriages, livery, and matched pairs of horses. The finest wines and brandies. Clothes, boots, hats, and walking canes. Perfumes and pufferies. While servants, tenants, cottagers, and merchants watched anxiously as their fate was being decided in the great manor house, Sir Walter was ordering another shipment of Olympian Dew. What could be more important than making sure that the Master of Kellynch never had a liver spot?

But unsettling all the servants at Kellynch, uprooting the family, and the embarrassment caused by their self-inflicted poverty were nothing if Miss Anne could only be happy, but there was trouble afoot. Lady Russell, Sir Walter, and that pipsqueak, Mr. Elliot, were all in the drawing room waiting for the young lady whom he loved as dearly as if she were his own daughter. The last time such a convocation had met, the result had been the separation of Miss Anne and Captain Wentworth.

"Miss, your father wishes to see you immediately," Allgood informed Anne while helping her out of her pelisse.

"Does this have anything to do with Mr. Elliot?"

"That gentleman is in the drawing room as well." After hesitating for a moment, Allgood asked for permission to speak.

"Of course, Mr. Allgood, you need never ask."

"Please do not marry Mr. Elliot," he said, surprised to find that his voice was cracking. "He is unworthy of you."

"Mr. Allgood, never was a name so aptly bestowed," Anne said as she gently placed her hand on his arm. "I know that Mr. Elliot is unworthy of me, so please be assured that I may emerge from this meeting bloodied, but I will remain unbound." After Allgood opened the door, Anne went in to the drawing room to face her adversaries.

Mr. Elliot, who was preening like a peacock, bowed in greeting, while Lady Russell gestured for Anne to come and sit next to her.

"Do you know why Mr. Elliot is here?" her father asked as he returned a silver snuff box to the pocket of his waistcoat.

"I imagine he wanted to make sure that I got home safely from the library, and you can see that I have. But I am somewhat fatigued, so if you will excuse me, I think I will go upstairs and rest," but she had barely completed her pivot before her Papa called her back.

"Anne, don't be coy. You have been in Mr. Elliot's company enough to know why he has come and what he has asked and what I have answered." But something caught her father's eye, causing him to pause. "I am convinced that you have been going without your bonnet, Anne. You are positively brown. Are you using Olympian Dew every night?"

Anne knew that her father swam only in shallow water, but his advice for maintaining healthy skin and a glowing complexion was excellent.

"Yes, Papa. I wash my face every night with Pears soap and then use Olympian Dew as my moisturizer. In the morning, I apply Pears Liquid Bloom of Roses," and she rose and went over to her father, and knowing how much he disliked freckles, showed him that she had none.

"Excellent. There are few things more important than a good appearance. My daughters will never have freckles," he said to Mr. Elliot. "I will not allow it."

Mr. Elliot, seeing that the topic of his betrothal was at risk of being lost in a discussion of lotions and soaps, returned the conversation to its initial purpose: his marriage to Anne Elliot.

"Sir Walter, you may say that Anne is brown, but I see her as golden, like Diana the Huntress running through a meadow." And there was that gleaming smile that he used to reel the ladies in, but this fish would not be caught.

"Or King Midas's daughter," Anne responded.

That comment caused Lady Russell to frown, and she squeezed Anne's hand to let her know that her response was inappropriate.

"Miss Anne, surely my attentions have been too marked for you not to know why I am here."

"I certainly can guess. But before a possible union of the two Elliot branches of the family is discussed, I would like to suggest that we call a family council. After all, there might be some hard feelings left over from Mr. Elliot severing all ties with our family. I think it would be a healthy thing to do—get everything out in the open. Having a third party mediate might also be a good idea. We might call it a therapeutic session, one in which everyone has a chance to air their grievances."

Lady Russell's mouth dropped open at her statement, but quickly recovered, and gave a forced laugh as if Anne had just told a joke.

"Anne, you know very well that all has been forgiven," Lady Russell said, giving her a look that could have turned a person to stone.

"Yes, or so I am told. However, I think that these things need to be discussed. We would not want to have some resentment simmering under the surface because we did not deal with the particulars of this unpleasant matter."

"The particulars? There are no particulars," her father said too loudly. "Mr. Elliot has admitted that his actions were misguided. He has been forgiven That is all there is to it."

"But what about Elizabeth? At one point, she had anticipated an offer of marriage from the gentleman, but that did not happen. And she might want to know why he did not ask. It is probably the reason she is not here now, and, Papa, wouldn't you like to know why Elizabeth was passed over? After all, she is the prettiest Elliot."

"Beyond a doubt, she is the prettiest of you girls," her father said, nodding his head in agreement, and Anne could see that her suggestion was gaining traction.

"Another thing, Papa. Mr. Elliot might want to know why you never tried to contact him—to offer him an olive branch, so to speak."

"Not contact him? I wrote to him several times inviting him to Kellynch, and on at least two occasions, he wrote back to say that he would come, but he did not." A testy tone had entered Sir Walter's voice, which pleased Anne, but infuriated Lady Russell. What was Anne playing at? If she refused Mr. Elliot, she would never have another offer.

An annoyed and alarmed Mr. Elliot quickly stood up, and rather than address his comments to Anne, he chose to speak to the two people who, when all was said and done, would have the most say in the matter: Lady Russell and Sir Walter.

"Obviously, my behavior has left a residue of resentment. However, I must defend myself on one account, that of Miss Elliot. At the time of which we are speaking, I knew that I was not mature enough to take a wife, and that is why I did not make an offer to Elizabeth. I regret my actions, but it was never my intention to cause anyone pain."

"That was very thoughtful of you, Mr. Elliot," Anne quickly responded so that her father could not. "And speaking of wives, I think if we were to have a family therapeutic session before any formal plans were made for a courtship, it would be beneficial for you as well, as it would give you more time to deal with your feelings about Mrs. Elliot's passing. After all, you have only been widowed for eight months."

All kinds of red flags were going up in Elliot's brain. This was not the Anne Elliot who had translated the romantic Italian ballad for him, whispering "That's *amore*" in his ear, and where was the coquette who had given him the come-hither look when she had covered all but her eyes with her fan? More importantly, he wanted a return of the lady who had spanked his hand with her fan. That action had nearly brought him to his knees. Damn it! She had led him to believe that her staid exterior was merely a cover for a boiling hot interior. It appeared that this vixen was little more than a run-of-the-mill tease.

"I can assure you, Miss Anne, that I loved my wife dearly," and he managed to bring a tear to his eye. "As much as I suffered at the loss of my companion, you have become a part of the healing process for me. I know that it has been less than a year since my darling Phoebe left this world, but should I turn away from the love I feel for you, which is clearly a gift from heaven," and he crossed the room and addressed her. "I suspect that you are unaware of the magnitude of your charm and its irresistible pull, but let me assure you that my love is sincere. Yes, it is true that the time we have spent together is not long, but in that short span of time, you have claimed my heart."

"Yes, Mr. Elliot, it *has* been a short period of time," she answered, ignoring all the lying goop he was piling on, "and because of that, I think it is absolutely necessary for us to have a lengthy courtship."

At this Elliot blanched. A lengthy courtship? Impossible. His debts were numerous and mounting, and he was being pressed. An image of Willie McCoy, with his front teeth missing, appeared in his head. Elliot had entered Slim's Pool Hall with his pockets stuffed with cash, but he had walked out with nothing more than an IOU for £80. He had since learned that Slim settled his accounts with the thick end of a pool stick, and he started to break out into a sweat at the thought.

"I agree to all terms, Miss Anne," he said, smiling. However, it was his intention to shower her with gifts and perfumes and love letters and all the other crap that women needed before you could get them to go to bed with you. "As I have said, I am quite besotted, and perhaps you will change your mind about the length of the courtship."

"Oh, anything can happen, Mr. Elliot," and looking out the window, Anne thought, "I only hope that it will happen soon."

Chapter 23

By reminding Sir Walter Elliot, Baronet, that he and his beautiful Elizabeth had been snubbed by William Elliot, Anne had succeeded in reigniting her father's dislike of his heir. Sir Walter also did not like the fact that Mr. Elliot was already out of mourning. He had been in mourning for thirteen years and had no intention of ever remarrying because he knew that no one could replace his dear Betsy, or at least no one would be willing to put up with all his nonsense.

After all the details for the therapeutic session were worked out, Anne departed. However, instead of going upstairs for a rest, she retrieved her coat and headed for the Musgroves. The couple was delightful company, and any visitor was guaranteed to see a pair of smiling faces.

When she reached the Musgrove suite at the White Hart, she found all of the ladies were engaged in discussing their latest purchases in the parlor. The room was overflowing with fabric and flounces aplenty, ruffles and laces galore, and everyone had a story to tell. However, it was Mary who was the most eager to share hers. Not only had she been able to ease the discomfort of the Kale children and their little poxed bodies, she had found that Bath was overflowing with people afflicted with boils.

"Of course, that is why many people come to Bath, but I think the sores should be cleaned before they go into the waters, don't you?" Mary asked Anne.

Anne felt herself gagging. The treatment of a multitude of skin diseases was one of the reasons why people came to Bath, and it was also the main reason why she never went into the water. After a server had handed her a cup with his finger in it, she never again drank from the cups at the pump room. She believed that ingesting vast amounts of germs negated any possible health benefits derived from drinking the water.

With Charles beaming with pride at his own angel of mercy, Mary discussed abscesses, blains, boils, cankers, cysts, sores, ulcers, wheals, and welts. She was now an expert on any skin eruption that discharged, drained, or dripped, and there was nothing, no matter how disgusting, that she would not share.

While listening to Mary's description of lancing a boil, Mrs. Musgrove offered Anne a sandwich and a petit-four from a plate overflowing with them, but not surprisingly, Anne had no appetite. This kind lady, who was on the far side of two hundred pounds, was continuing to insist that she have just a little something when Captain Wentworth, along with Captain Harville, came into the parlor.

After greeting all the ladies and Mr. Musgrove, Rick turned his attention to Anne. "Miss Anne, it is good to see you again. I am here because I have been given a commission by my good friend Harville to have a miniature of Captain Benwick framed for Miss Musgrove."

"Oh, that is a happy task," she said beaming, and he indicated that he needed to write out the instructions for the framer, and while he did that, Anne went to speak with Captain Harville, who was staring out the window at nothing in particular.

"Look here, Miss Anne," and he showed her the miniature. "The painting was made for my sister, Fanny, by Captain Benwick, but I now have the charge of getting it set for another! But Wentworth undertakes it on my behalf," and with a quivering lip, he added, "Poor Fanny! She would not have forgotten him so soon. She doted on him."

"It would not be in the nature of any woman who truly loved. We certainly do not forget you as soon as you forget us."

"I will not allow it to be more a man's nature than a woman's to forget those they do love. I believe the reverse. Our bodies are stronger, but so are our feelings."

"Your feelings may be stronger, but ours are the more tender," she quickly retorted.

"Let me observe that all the histories are against you, all stories, prose and verse, songs and proverbs, all talk about a woman's fickleness."

"The writings you reference were all written by men and are therefore biased. I ask you what of Penelope, the faithful wife of Odysseus. She waited for twenty years, and in order to keep other suitors away, she wove and unwove a shroud for Laertes, day after day, week after week, month after month. Or shall we speak of Ariadne leading Theseus out of the labyrinth on Crete only to be abandoned by him once he reached the mainland." Warming to her subject, she continued, "And what of Ophelia, who loved Hamlet so much? He loved her; then loved her not. And in her grief, she climbed a tree, fell out, and drowned in a brook. Do you need other examples?"

"Miss Anne, you have completely won me over by your passionate defense of your sex. You are right. Men are swine."

"No, that is not the case at all. Generally speaking, most men are not swine; they just have more freedom than we do. We live at home, quiet, confined, and our feelings prey upon us. You have your profession that takes you back into the world and change soon weakens impressions. What I claim for my sex is that of loving longest when all hope is gone."

Anne could not say another word because her heart was so full, and Harville's attention was drawn to Captain Wentworth who was furiously making tracks across the paper.

"I always knew Wentworth to be a detail man," Harville said, "but my goodness, he is just giving the directions for the framing of a miniature, not the making of a watch."

Finally, Wentworth finished his letter, folded and sealed it, and put it in his inside pocket, over his heart. Before leaving with Harville, he looked into Anne's eyes and patted his pocket, and although she did not know why he thought she should care that he had written to the framer, she smiled nonetheless. She was still looking out the window when he returned to the parlor, pretending to have forgotten his gloves. He took the letter out of his pocket and placed it on the desk, and jerking his head in its direction, he let her know that the letter was for her.

Anne quickly gathered it up and excused herself and went into an adjacent room. Her hands were shaking as she tore open the seal, sending little bits of wax flying.

> *I can listen no longer in silence. I must speak to you by such means as are within my reach. You pierce my soul. I am half agony, half hope. I offer myself to you again with a heart even more your own than when you almost broke it, eight years and a half ago.*

He would bring that up, she thought, but continued.

> *Dare not say that man forgets sooner than woman, that his love has an earlier death. I have loved none but you. Unjust I may have been, weak and resentful I have been, but never inconstant.*

"Weak?" Never. "Unjust?" Possibly. "Resentful?" Definitely. "Never inconstant?" How sweet.

> *You alone have brought me to Bath. For you alone, I think and plan. Have you not seen this? Can you fail to have understood my wishes? I can hardly write. I am every instant hearing something which overpowers me. Too good, too excellent creature! You do us justice, indeed. You do believe that there is true attachment and constancy among men. Your most fervent and undeviating, Rick*

Anne fanned herself with the letter. Because of the circumstances of their parting, she had never had a love letter from him or from anyone else, for that matter, and this missive had nearly caused her to grow faint. She could feel her heart beating and her blood rushing, and a feeling that she was loved above all others coursed through her veins.

After running down the stairs, she rushed out into the street hoping to catch him before he returned to the Admiral's Club, but she could not find him, and her shoulders sank as she realized that she had missed him.

"Pssst. Hey Flash. Look behind you," and there in all his glory was Captain Frederick Wentworth, aka Rick, aka My One True Love. "Didn't Swoosh teach you to always look behind you?" he asked with a laugh in his voice.

Darn it! She needed to work on that, but not now, and taking his hands and with tears welling in her eyes, she asked, "Promise me that you will never leave me again."

"I never shall," and after taking hold of her hand, they hurried along to the Gravel Walk, a place of seclusion where the power of conversation would make the present hour a blessing indeed. After finding a suitable spot, Frederick opened his great coat to protect her against the evening's chill and pulled her to him. Nothing more was said as she laid her head on his chest and felt the beating of his heart.

Finally, when she was able to speak, she asked, "Did you mean everything in that letter?"

"Every word?"

"I pierce your soul?"

"You really do not want to know the agony I went through, the torment I experienced thinking you would never be mine. You had taught me how to love, but not how to stop loving. When I saw you at Uppercross, all my defenses gave way, and the love I had kept locked inside for all these years bubbled to the surface. I had neither the will nor the desire to fight it. I surrendered all."

He placed his hand under her chin and lifted her face to his, and when their lips met, she felt pulled into his very being. So that there would be no space between them, he put his hands on her hips and brought her forward, and as she felt his manhood rise, a bolt of lightning went through her.

"How I have longed for your kisses," he crooned.

"Only kisses, Rick?"

"My goodness, Anne! You will have me blushing once again."

"Well, if your imaginings are anything like mine, then you have been thinking about more than kisses."

With his big arms encircling her, he picked her up and hugged her. "If we were anywhere other than standing off a main street in Bath, I would certainly continue this conversation of what happens between a man and a woman."

"Then let us hail a cab, pay the driver to drive around town, and tell him not to stop until asked to do so."

"I would love to do just that, but I have to meet Swoosh about Piglet."

"Oh, I want to come," she said eagerly. She was certainly up to it. According to Swoosh, she had performed well when she had been in Tough Town. "If you will just give me ten minutes, I shall go change into my street clothes. I have a bonnet with the widest brim you have ever seen. With such a cover, Piglet would never recognize me."

"No, Anne, you cannot come," he said in a voice that indicated his regret that they must part.

"But you said that you would never leave me."

"After this, I never shall. But I have got a job to do. Tonight, Swoosh and I will go into the toughest part of Tough Town."

"And after that, what about us?"

"We will always have Lyme; if not Lyme, then Bath; if not Bath, then Kellynch. You must understand that if we don't take care of Piglet, we will regret it."

She knew that he was right. William Elliot was like an undiagnosed cancer growing in the belly of the family, and he needed to be removed.

"All right, Rick. But then you will never leave me?" she asked with a question in her voice.

"Of course not," but then he hesitated. "Well, actually that's not true either. I have been recalled by the navy and have been given a week to see to my personal affairs before reporting to Portsmouth where the *Laconia* is anchored. Napoleon continues his march to Paris, but I am not worried about the French because I know this time our forces will win."

With tears streaming down her cheeks, she said, "I just hope your ship does not get blown out of the water."

"That will not happen. There is virtually no French navy left. If anything, I will be on blockade duty."

"So I shall be like Penelope waiting for Odysseus to return, except I do not even have a shroud to weave," and she thought for a moment. "I could help Mary. She has come up with the idea of making and distributing what she is calling 'stickers,' little pieces of paper with glue on the back that are to be placed over everyone's kitchen sinks that say, 'Kill germs. Wash your hands often. If you ooze, you lose.' She really wants to emphasize sanitation."

"That is certainly a cause worthy of your time."

"And after that, you will never leave me?" Anne realized that she was being repetitive, but she wanted assurances that Rick would return to her.

"After Napoleon is defeated, my intention is to resign my commission. Not only is a peacetime navy boring, but it is unprofitable. I was thinking of leasing an estate in the country. I understand that one will shortly become available because a certain Admiral Croft is going stir-crazy at Kellynch. My brother-in-law has to be near the sea. He needs to smell the salt and see the masts and rigs. Besides, my wife must have a place in the country. She has recently taken up running, and since I intend to do the same, we shall need a large park for such an exercise."

"You have a wife?" Anne asked in a teasing voice.

"Do not toy with me on that subject, Anne, because hell will freeze over before I let you go again. But I must leave you now." And he gently kissed her before setting out to meet Swoosh.

Chapter 24

Knowing that Lady Russell would be lying in wait for her in the parlor, when Anne returned to Camden Place, she went through the servants' entrance. The looks she had given Anne all during her interrogation would have been comical if the situation had not been so serious. In her unhappiness with Anne, Lady Russell had raised her eyebrows, bugged out her eyes, tilted her head, coughed repeatedly, and one time, ran her hand back and forth across her throat to indicate that Anne had said enough.

Passing by Elizabeth's room, she could see her sister lying on her bed reading a magazine. She poked her head in, but did not know what to say. There had been a time when Elizabeth had thought she would marry her cousin, and now she knew that Mr. Elliot had preferred "plain old Anne" to her. That had to hurt.

"Are you to marry, Mr. Elliot?" Elizabeth asked as if she did not care one way or the other.

"No, I do not love him. When I marry, it will be because I am in love with my husband."

That statement caused Elizabeth to sit up. "So you will remain a spinster." As far as her sister was concerned, this was Anne's last chance to end up with a Mrs. in front of her name as she would never receive another offer of marriage.

"I shall not marry Mr. Elliot," she repeated.

"Why not?"

"I do not like him."

"Neither do I," she said, wrinkling her nose. "There is something lacking in his character, and it is not just because he snubbed me in favor of you, which obviously shows poor judgment. It is this feeling I have that he is not to be trusted. There is something sneaky about him. Honestly, I am beginning to think I shall never marry."

"Would that bother you?"

"No, I don't think so. I am too hard to please." No argument there. "There is no one who could possibly love me as much as Papa does, and we are so well suited to each other. We like the same things. How many men do you know who like to go shopping for fabric and baubles or who take such care with their appearance or who truly appreciate the finer things in life?"

"It is true that you enjoy each other's company very much, but you do not have the money for the finer things in life. That is why we are living in Bath and not at Kellynch."

"I know that," Elizabeth acknowledged. "But even with the economies we have already made, it is not enough to pay down our debts and pay the rent as well. The tailor is pressing father for payment and will not release his new coat, so he is going to sell the carriages and four of the horses."

"That is a good start," Anne said, nodding her head in approval, but saying nothing about the unnecessary expense of yet another coat. "The two of you like Bath very much, and you do not need a carriage here. Since you both share an interest in skin care and cosmetics, it is too bad that you cannot sell them, especially Olympian Dew, as a way of having some pocket money. You and Papa are walking advertisements for the lotion."

That was meant to be a joke—to cheer her up, but Elizabeth did not take it that way. "But how would we sell the lotion? Do you mean open a shop?"

Anne would have thought that Elizabeth would shudder at the idea of "earning a living," but she actually seemed to be interested. It was probably because of the word "shop."

"No, you cannot open a shop. You would have to pay rent, and you certainly cannot go door to door ringing doorbells: 'Ding, Dong: The Elliots calling.' Truthfully, I do not know how you would do such a thing. It was just a thought."

"But what if we invited friends to come to Camden Place. We could have an array of products set out, and they would order everything through us. If we purchased in bulk, we could get a discount and pass that on to our clients—or we could choose not to. Papa buys so much Olympian Dew that he already gets ten percent off. Their friends would tell their friends and so on. It would be like everyone getting together for a party."

"That sounds promising. I would suggest you begin by contacting the makers of Olympian Dew to see if an arrangement can be worked out."

"I would also contact Pears for their soaps, toilette water, and Milk of Roses. We would want to have an extensive product line in order to give the customer the most options," and Anne could see that the wheels were turning. "Thank you, Anne. You have given me something to think about. Are you playing cards tonight with Mrs. Little?"

"Her daughter is to marry Mr. Lamb, is she not?"

"Not if Mary can help it. She does not like him at all. He is fifteen years older than she is *and* has terrible skin." Elizabeth then pointed to spots all over her face where Mr. Lamb had scars from the pox.

"Well, at least he does not have freckles." Elizabeth, too, was freckle phobic. "But I shant be going. I promised to visit Mrs. Smith."

"Well, say hello for me. Even though I gave Miss Hamilton cause for aggravation, I did like her."

"I shall tell her you said that. She will appreciate it." She *would* appreciate it as soon as she got over the shock of receiving a compliment from Elizabeth Elliot.

Anne went to her room, and after kicking off her shoes, flopped down on the bed. She wanted to think about her time with Rick at the Gravel Walk, and the mere memory of his passionate kiss caused her temperature to rise. She had so many questions about relations between a man and a woman, but no one to ask. Perhaps, Mrs. Smith would be willing to share.

And while she was at Mrs. Smith's drinking coffee and eating tarts, Rick and Swoosh would be in Tough Town gathering evidence against Mr. Elliot. It did not seem fair. Just because she was a woman, she was going to be left out of something she had initiated, but because of Rick's objections, she would not be in on the kill. And then she bolted out of bed.

"Wait a minute. I am no man's wife. Rick cannot tell me where I can and cannot go. Not yet, anyway. I know he is concerned for my safety, but I have already walked through Tough Town, and I am here to tell the tale."

After writing a quick note to Mrs. Smith to inform her that she would not be visiting that evening, she got out the bonnet with the big brim and Patsy's dress and cloak. As she changed out of Anne Elliot's clothes into Flash's, she could feel the excitement building, and she felt empowered, and her chest expanded. "Yes! I am a woman! I am invincible! I am going into Tough Town—tonight."

* * *

After making sure that Rick had not yet left the Admiral's Club, Flash went across the street, and to pass the time, started to study all the people who were going about their business. Swoosh had pointed out how easy it was to identify people who were not where they belonged. While waiting for Rick, she had identified five pickpockets, four snake oil salesmen, three purse snatchers, two prostitutes, both of whom went into the Admiral's Club—no surprise there. But there *was* a surprise when a partridge, far from any field, landed in a nearby pear tree. As much as she was enjoying herself picking out the villains, as soon as Rick emerged, she was on the job.

It was a good thing that she was in shape because she really had to quicken her pace to keep up with his long strides, but as he drew closer to Tough Town, he slowed down, lowered his shoulders, and pulled his hat down over his ears in order not to draw attention to himself. The rendezvous point was outside Blackjack Cleaver's, and it seemed as if Moves was giving Rick a report. Since she needed to hear that report as well, she surreptitiously made her way across the street and sought cover behind a half dozen trees, dashing between them and hugging the trunks until she was sure she had not been seen. In doing so, she had been able to sneak up right behind them.

"Hey Rick. Hey, Swoosh. Don't you know that you are always supposed to look behind you?" Anne said, startling the group of conspirators.

When Rick turned around, his mouth dropped open. "Anne, what are you doing here? You cannot stay. It is not safe," and he stared at her in disapproval.

"I did just fine getting here, and I am not going home," she answered with her jaw jutting out.

Everyone was looking at Rick. Would an officer in the Royal Navy let his bird talk to him like that? In order to save Rick from any embarrassment, Swoosh chimed in. "Flash is all right. She's had the best trainer in Bath working with her and can handle herself," he said in an attempt to diffuse the situation. "She'll be fine. We'll keep her between us so no one pulls her off the street into an alley."

That statement caused Anne to gulp. She had not thought about what might happen to a woman walking alone in Tough Town.

Rick continued to try to stare her down, but Anne would not budge. "If anything happens to you, I will never forgive myself," he said, taking a step toward her.

"If you let anything happen to me, I will not forgive you either," and she took a step forward, and when she smiled, he melted and relented.

"Come on. Next thing you know, you'll be snogging," an impatient Swoosh said.

"Excuse me, Swoosh, but I do not know these three gentlemen," Anne said, indicating the two beanpoles and one dandy standing next to Swoosh. The two skinny men nearly died laughing at being called "gentlemen," and one said that he wasn't sure that was a compliment.

"This here is Arab, although he ain't," he said, pointing to a pasty white boy, and after patting the tallest boy on the back, Moves added, "and this here is Ice. He's the leader of the Wets. In Tough Town, it's the Wets what gets things done."

"The Wets?" Anne asked, totally confused.

"It's Bath—the Wets. Don't you get it?" Swoosh said elbowing her. "That's their name."

"Listen, Sister," Moves explained, "when you're a Wet and something bad's going down, you're never on your own. You've got family around."

"Don't mind my brother," Swoosh whispered in her ear. "He has very low toff tolerance."

"But what is he talking about?"

"Anne," the captain said, shaking his head at her complete lack of understanding of how boys, such as Swoosh, survived living on the streets, "they are a gang. They come together for protection."

"A gang? How stupid of me. I thought they only existed in large cities such as Bristol and London," and turning to Swoosh, she said, "You never told me you were in a gang."

"Swoosh ain't in no gang," Moves said, jumping in to defend his brother. Swoosh had a good deal going with Flash, and he didn't want to see it blow up because of any supposed connection to a gang. "And I'm only an honorary member, but I needed their help," and Moves explained why the two Wets were present.

"Piglet was all over the place, so I had to hire extra help because he was wearing me out, and a guy's got to eat and sleep. Ice here followed him out to a racetrack outside of town. Arab, although he ain't, stood next to him at a cockfight. In both places, he won tons of bread and honey. After that, I took over and followed him to Leroy Brown's. This toff is begging for it because Leroy is the badest man in the whole damn town, but since he don't dare go back to Willie McCoys's, Piglet went to Leroy's and dropped the whole bundle what he snatched up at the other two places."

Since he had left all his coins back at the Admiral's Club, Rick pulled two one-pound notes out of his pocket and handed it to the two Wets. If anyone had heard the sound of coins jingling, he would have been ambushed by the Toughs. The Wets went wide-eyed seeing all that nicker, and after taking off their caps as a sign of respect, the two departed, leaving only the dandy, who reeked of pomade.

"And who are you, sir, if I may ask?"

"You may indeed, Miss. I am Jimmy Whistler, at your service," he said, taking his hat off and bowing, and Rick laughed at his exaggerated gesture. It was just yesterday that he had told a lady to get her bottom off of his stool. "I am an artist in the employ of Captain Wentworth. I have been following Piglet around with either Swoosh or Moves and making sketches of his activities," and he produced nearly a dozen drawings of Mr. Elliot. "I did not go to the racetrack or the cockfight, but Ice and Arab did. By the way, Arab is actually a Welshman, but he thinks his exotic nickname creates an aura of menace, which serves his purpose as Ice's lieutenant. Both gave detailed descriptions of what took place."

Anne looked in horror at the picture of Mr. Elliot cheering wildly from the front row of a cockfight, with feathers flying, some of them in his hair, and blood splattered on his boots.

"Here we have Piglet meeting with One Eye Hatfield, the enforcer for Willie McCoy. I believe he is paying off some of his debts."

Anne was repulsed by Mr. Hatfield because One Eye really did have only one eye. There was nothing but skin where the other one should have been. He was an uncentered Cyclops.

With Rick looking over her shoulder, she saw sketches of Piglet paying a cover charge to gain entry into Leroy Brown's. Mr. Whistler was able to get in without paying the entry fee after promising to sketch Mr. and Mrs. Brown's lovely daughter. The drawings showed Elliot at the roulette table, the hazard table, the Pharo table, and signing IOUs at each one.

"He did not win anything," Mr. Whistler explained. "He can't even shoot marbles. Lost his shooter. He is terrible."

But it was the last sketch, showing Elliot with his arm around the waist of a well-dressed lady that caused Rick to gasp.

"He spends almost every afternoon with her," Whistler explained. "Of course, I couldn't sketch her right then and there, but I have a pictographic memory. But I did so as soon as an opportunity presented itself. I don't know her name, but..."

"I do," Rick said with anger in his voice. "That is Reddy Willing's wife, Ann Able. Captain Willing was my first officer on the *Laconia* before being awarded his own command. He is now serving in the West Indies. I am sure the pair of them met in Lyme. I saw Mrs. Willing with the wives of two other officers near the Cobb. They were having a lady's weekend, she explained to me." He banged his right fist into his other hand and cried out at the heavens, "Dear God! How fickle women are!"

In Anne's mind, Piglet was just as guilty as Mrs. Willing. After all, it took two to waltz. But they would have that conversation at a later date as Rick was much too upset now.

It was like taking a punch in the gut to find out that the wife of a fellow officer was servicing another man while her husband was serving his country half way across the world. Swoosh and Moves saw how affected Rick was.

"Listen, Rick. We've got the goods on him," Swoosh said. "Jimmy, here has made copies of all his sketches. As soon as Piglet sees them, he'll know we caught him with his britches down. No way he's getting out of this." Although Swoosh wasn't sure if Rick was listening, he continued, "You said you was looking for a case of moral turpingtood. Now, you've got it, so you don't have to follow him around no more. We'll stick with him." Moves nodded, indicating that he would remain on the job. "All you got to do is think about when and where you're going to show him all these sketches."

After taking one more look at the damning evidence, he said, "It will be my pleasure."

* * *

"Anne, we must walk quickly. It will soon be dark, and neither of us can remain in this part of town. It is not just our clothes or our words that will betray us, but the way we carry ourselves. We are at risk of being set upon by thieves. So let us put our training to good use and make haste, and they started jogging.

They soon found themselves outside Westgate Buildings where Mrs. Smith lived. The news about Mr. Elliot and Mrs. Willing had upset both of them, and they needed to go somewhere where they could talk. An understanding Mrs. Smith went into her bedroom, leaving the two lovers a place to talk in front of a fire. But because there were only chairs in the room, and since both needed to be in the other's embrace, they remained standing, holding tightly to each other.

"Oh, Anne, what wickedness there is in this world. I have fought in battles across the great oceans of the world, and I have taken blows and have been wounded. But nothing would have pierced me more than to learn that the woman I loved had been unfaithful to me." After gazing into her eyes, he told her, "But during all those missing years, you were here, back in England, with no ties to bind you to me, and yet, you remained unwavering in your devotion."

"No ties to bind me?" Anne said, touching his face. "You are wrong, Frederick. Granted, there were no papers signed nor vows exchanged before a clergyman, but we did not need them. You have remained faithful in your heart to me for eight years. As for my part, I would never have married anyone other than you. Is that not proof enough that we were bound together by a higher power?"

"Yes, you are right," he said hugging her even tighter. "When we marry, will you always be right or may I have the odd victory?"

"I will always be right, but on occasion, I will allow you to think that you have won the day."

"Fair enough." Rick sat down and pulled Anne onto his lap and whispered, "I love you more than life itself." While kissing her, he placed his hands where they had never been before, and she was glad they were sitting down, or her hands would have done the same.

Chapter 25

Rick held Anne tightly in his arms trying to keep his mind free of what awaited him once he took up his duties on the *Laconia,* but forces beyond England's borders were knocking on his door demanding his attention. All officers had been put on notice by the Admiralty that if Napoleon reached Paris, they were to return immediately to their ships to resume their commands. The only ones exempted were commanders of ships undergoing repairs, but the *Laconia* was not among them. She waited rigged and ready in Portsmouth harbor.

Anne was also thinking about how little time was left to them, and it was with great reluctance that she got off his lap. After straightening her dress and fixing her hair, she asked Rick what he thought their next step should be regarding her cousin. The idea of her family continuing to welcome such a detestable person into their home was unacceptable, and she wanted to move quickly to acquaint everyone with William Elliot's duplicity.

"If you are agreeable, I think it is I who should lay out all the facts for your father and sisters," Rick suggested. "Otherwise, you will have to explain how it is that you came to know of Elliot's comings and goings. To account for my involvement, I will say that you suspected that Elliot was up to something other than being the prodigal returning to his family, that you shared your suspicions with me, and that I took it from there. With the sketches to back me up, it will be difficult for anyone to believe that he is anything less than a person of the meanest character, a complete fraud, and someone who thinks of the Elliot family only in terms of the wealth it may bring him.

"After that, I will arrange to meet with Piglet. Once he sees the evidence we have compiled, he will know that your father has sufficient cause to disinherit him. He can fight your father in court and be exposed to the world, or he can relinquish all his rights and slink back into the hole he came out of with only the immediate family knowing of his unscrupulous behavior."

"And after we have exposed Elliot, what about Swoosh?"

"I have been thinking about him as well. Apparently, Ice is pressuring his brother and him to join the Wets. At the moment, everything he does is within the boundaries of the law—barely—but if he were in a gang..."

"I agree that we cannot leave him to his own devices or he will get in trouble. Are you saying that we should adopt him?"

Frederick smiled broadly. He had developed an affection for the feisty little half-pint. With guidance and education, Swoosh could easily leave the streets of Bath behind him and make something of himself, and the captain believed that Anne and he could provide the proper environment where he would be able to flourish.

"I would like to make him such an offer. But, Anne, you must keep in mind that he is an independent lad, and one who has been without adult supervision for so long. I just do not know what he would say to an arrangement where he must answer to an authority figure."

Even though it was likely that Swoosh would reject their proposal, both agreed that they would ask him before Rick returned to the *Laconia*. They also agreed that Anne would speak to her father in the morning requesting that he grant Captain Wentworth an interview. It was an absolute necessity that William Elliot be exposed.

The next morning, while dressing, Frederick decided that he would arrive at Camden Place dressed in his uniform and wearing, as Swoosh had put it, "the mother of all hats." There was something about an officer in His Majesty's Navy that commanded respect. His authority was less likely to be challenged if he looked as if he had just descended from Mt. Olympus.

When he went downstairs, in the sitting area, the hushed tones of numerous conversations were creating a buzzing sound that filled the room, and aides were moving quickly in and out of the Admiral's Club carrying baggage. He had little doubt that the topic of discussion was the events taking place in France, and when the clerk handed him a folded note with an Admiralty seal on it, he knew what it would say. The captain called out to an aide and ordered him to pack all his belongings and to make arrangements for him to leave by coach in the morning, and then he opened the note: *Napoleon is in Paris. You are to return to your ship post haste.*

He knew his duty, and he would do it. But his thoughts were now of Anne. To be engaged or married to a naval officer involved hardship and separation, but to be tested so soon after they had come together and after such a lengthy separation seemed cruel. After last night, when he had felt the heat of her kisses, the last thing he wanted was to leave her, and so he resolved to make the most of the day as the time they had together could now be measured in hours.

* * *

All the family, including Charles Musgrove, as well as Lady Russell, was assembled in the drawing room waiting for Captain Wentworth. When asked why such an audience was necessary, all Anne would say was that the subject of the meeting was the heir to Kellynch. The lack of information created an aura of mystery as if a murder had been committed at Camden Place and prompted a guessing game: Mr. Elliot in the drawing room with the poker.

Captain Wentworth was a man of action, and as soon as all the niceties were observed, he explained that he had been following Mr. Elliot's movements for a number of days. While Anne displayed the letter from Mr. Elliot to Mr. Smith, stating how he detested being an Elliot, Wentworth produced the sketches drawn by Mr. Whistler. As the drawings circulated around the room, gasps were heard, jaws dropped, and exclamations of disgust and anger were expressed. The tawdriness of the subject shocked all, but it was Elizabeth who spoke first. "I told Anne I did not like him. There was something about his eyes, which have a sharp, shrewish look, which I confess I did not like. His nose wants character, he has an overbite, and if he does not pay more attention to properly hydrating his skin, he will have premature aging."

After that opening, everyone had something to say. Mary, in her capacity as a Trained Angel of Mercy, thought there might be a medical reason for his behavior—possibly brain damage caused by a childhood infection. Charles revealed that he had found him to be much too forward when they had first met in Lyme—not the behavior of a gentleman at all, and worse than that, he did not hunt or shoot. Lady Russell reminded everyone that when she had learned that Mr. Elliot was seeking a reconciliation with the family that she had voiced her opinion that he should not be welcomed back into the fold. The only one who had nothing to say was the patriarch. Sir Walter sat staring at the letter in his hand. It was only when Elizabeth gently prodded him that he finally spoke.

"How could he? So cruel. So unfeeling. I killed the fatted calf for him," and he tilted his head back to catch the tears welling up in his eyes. "I treated him like a son, but did he merit such notice? No, he did not." His three daughters all went to comfort him, but he could not stop crying. After retrieving his spectacles, and with tears carving valleys through his face powder, he read aloud from the letter Mr. Elliot had written to a certain Mr. Smith.

> *Give me joy. I have got rid of Sir Walter and Miss Elizabeth. They are gone back to Kellynch, and almost made me swear to visit this summer...*

And he had to compose himself before he could go on and struggled over every word.

> *I wish I had any name but Elliot. I am sick of it. The name of Walter I can drop, thank God!*

But then the letter fell out of his hand, and Elizabeth had to finish it.

> *I desire you will never insult me with my second W. again, meaning, for the rest of my life, to be only yours truly. Wm Elliot*

Surprise turned to astonishment and astonishment to anger. How dare that weasel insult the name of Elliot? And a litany of pejoratives, blackguard, brute, heel, miscreant, profligate, rapscallion, reprobate, and scoundrel, fell from the lips of the offended parties. After using every abusive term they could think of in English, they switched to French: *villain, libertin, coquin, pollison, malfaiteur*.

Anne looked at Rick in complete bewilderment at her father's reaction. "I can hardly believe it. Piglet gambled away a fortune, associated with the lowest elements of society, attended blood sports, committed adultery, and so many other awful things, but what is Papa upset about? His feelings are hurt because the name of Elliot was disparaged. I thought there was nothing he could do that would surprise me, but I was wrong."

Rick took Anne by the hand, and they went into the hallway. "My love, you cannot teach an old dog new tricks. You may hope for a transformation in Elizabeth similar to that of Mary's change of heart, but as for your father, at his age, no major alteration is possible. In a few minutes, things will settle down, and then it is my intention to change the subject. But before I do that, is there some place we can go? I have something I want to ask you?"

They went to the room used by Mr. Allgood to keep the household accounts. There were two wooden chairs, a desk, and a bookcase all crammed into a small room that was not designed to hold so much furniture. But it was absolutely perfect for the two lovers, and they stood before each other holding hands and gazing into each other's eyes.

"Miss Anne Elliot, there have been poems and prose penned about great lovers throughout the ages, but the greatest love story of all is ours, and it is still being written. The middle and end will be determined by your response. I now ask if you will you consent to be my wife, and if you bestow this honor upon me, I will love you with every fiber of my being for all the days of my life."

Anne fell into his arms and cried tears of joy, and after she was finally able to compose herself, he took a box from his pocket and handed it to his bride-to-be.

When Anne opened it, she jumped for joy. "Oh, Rick. It is beautiful. How ever did you manage it?" It was a brand new stopwatch made especially for Anne Elliot by Mr. Chimes of the Worshipful Company of Clockmakers in London under the very specific directions of Captain Wentworth.

"It cannot keep track of time down to the second," Rick pointed out, "but it is accurate within a minute. I think that should be sufficient for your needs."

"Oh, yes. This is exactly what I wanted. No diamond or ruby would be more appreciated. Oh, Rick, I love it, and I love you," and she threw her arms around his neck and kissed him.

But there was another surprise, and Rick pointed out the material that the stopwatch was wrapped in that seemed to be of equal interest to him as the timepiece itself. Anne pulled out the square piece of spongy material, which was something she had never seen before.

"It is made mostly of rubber imported from South America," Rick explained. "After I left Mr. Chimes's shop, I went to speak to the bootmaker about having a pair of boots custom made for you so that you might run more comfortably. Mr. Hightop, whose assistant invented this material, intends to place a layer of the rubbery composition inside all of the boots he sells."

Anne could not decide which was the better gift: the stopwatch or the rubberized cushion. But after thinking of her sore feet soaking in a foot bath, she decided that it was the padding.

"The inventor," Rick continued, "hopes one day to attach a thicker and sturdier rubberized material to the bottom of the shoe."

"Wouldn't that make it more difficult for me to stay on the path? I can just picture myself bouncing all over the place. I might very well end up sitting in a tree."

"Well, that would be fine with me as I would come and rescue you," and Rick pulled her closer, "and you would certainly want to show your appreciation for my having done so." He began to kiss her, and his kisses were so forceful that he backed her up against the door. But even as he hungrily sought her mouth, he knew that they must stop. Mr. Allgood might try to open the door at any moment and wouldn't that be awkward? But before leaving, Anne took Rick's hand in hers and held it to her breast and whispered, "Beneath it lies my heart which beats only for you."

* * *

When the pair of lovers returned to the drawing room, they realized that they had not been missed nor had all of the anger of the injured parties been spent. When Anne heard the word, "*schurke*," she realized that all French synonyms for villain had been exhausted, and they were now venting their spleens in German.

In his booming baritone, the captain asked for everyone's attention. Not one to just dip his toe in the water, he dived in head long: "I wish to announce that I have asked Anne to marry me, and she has accepted my offer."

This news was as surprising to Mary, Elizabeth, and Lady Russell as the revelation of Mr. Elliot's character had been thirty minutes earlier, and they all sat there as still as statues.

"Will you not wish us joy?" Anne asked of everyone and anyone. Charles and Mary were the first to offer their congratulations. Now that Mary had dedicated her life to healing others, she wanted her sister to be happy as well, and Charles, knowing Wentworth to be a man of integrity, was as pleased as punch that one so deserving as Anne was now engaged to a man worthy of her love.

Elizabeth's felicitations were less effusive than the Musgroves, but her wishes for the happiness of the couple were sincere, especially when she thought of all those navy wives who might be interested in attending an Olympian Dew and Pears party.

Lady Russell offered her congratulations, but there was no joy in her voice. She recalled Anne saying how wrong she had been about Captain Wentworth's suitability as a husband, and she had predicted that her advice regarding Mr. Elliot would prove to be equally bad.

Embarrassed by her inability to take the true measure of a man, she quietly left.

But there was one more person to be heard from, and Sir Walter stepped into the middle of the celebration.

"Captain Wentworth, you have asked for Anne's hand before, have you not?"

"I have, sir, but you withheld your permission because you said that my future was too uncertain to take a wife. You also mentioned that since officers are exposed to every climate, we age prematurely and are not fit to be seen. But I think your main objection was that it brought persons of obscure birth into undue distinction." There was no mistaking that a good deal of resentment remained.

"I can see that the wound is still raw, and I do not blame you. But the reasons you gave for my opposing the match were secondary to the real reason. You see, Captain, Anne was so much like her mother, my dear Betsy, quiet, capable, reliable, a shoulder to lean on, a safe haven in a storm. I did not want Anne to marry because I did not want her to leave Kellynch. I thought I needed her more than you did, but knowing that you have loved her from afar and for so long, I now know that I was wrong. But I cannot change the past, and I am not one to dwell on unpleasant thoughts. It is how I am, and I have accepted it."

Anne sighed. Rick was right. Her father would never change. To his mind, he was imperfectly perfect and that was good enough for him.

Sir Walter then called out Allgood's name, and as always, the faithful servant was nearby. "Allgood, bring us a bottle of wine and several glasses. We have an engagement to celebrate."

Anne and Rick, who had been holding their breath for several minutes, were finally able to exhale. It was as it should have been eight years ago. They would be married with the blessings of all the family, and it filled Anne's heart with joy and Rick with relief because if Sir Walter had voiced any objections to the marriage, he had been prepared to take Anne by the hand and leave the lot of them behind. But that had not happened, and when Patsy, Mrs. Crocker, the cook, and her daughters joined them, they were inundated with well wishes and numerous toasts were made on behalf of the happy couple.

"What a life you will have, Anne," Charles said. "If you are like Wentworth's sister, Mrs. Croft, then you will be sailing the Seven Seas, and we will be receiving letters from distant ports and from every corner of the globe."

"Those things will not happen for a while," Anne said, cautioning her brother-in-law. "There is a certain Monsieur Napoleon who must be dealt with. Frederick will be leaving in a few days for Portsmouth where the *Laconia* is anchored to resume his command."

"But that is so little time for you to be together," Mary said. She liked long engagements because she was particularly fond of the word, *fiancée*. Sophisticated French versus Anglo Saxon—because once a lady married, she was merely a wife.

"Yes, that is true, but at least we still have a few days," and Anne turned to Rick. "Have you decided what day you will be leaving?" But her question was met by silence. "Frederick, when will you be returning to the *Laconia*?" she asked, an anxious note creeping into her voice.

"Anne, there was a message waiting for me this morning from the Admiralty."

"What did it say?" Anne could feel her stomach tightening.

"It said that I am to return to Portsmouth immediately."

The news knocked all of the air out of Anne, and she fell back on her heels into Rick's arms. Mary immediately rushed to her side and asked if she required medical attention.

"No, of course not. I was just caught off guard. I did not know the captain would have to leave so soon."

"Nor did I," he said, taking her hand, "but Napoleon is in Paris, and it seems that he will continue marching into the Low Countries. Therefore, all Atlantic and Channel ports must be blockaded to prevent any arms from reaching the French. The Americans are still unhappy with us since we burned their capital, and they might be inclined to lend their support to Napoleon."

"I understand that duty calls. Please forgive me. I guess I have a case of the blues, navy blue," Anne said, smiling weakly.

Elizabeth went to her side. "If Captain Wentworth is to leave in the morning, then why are you still standing here? You must make the most of every minute."

Rick offered Anne his arm. "Yes, let us go some place where we may talk. There are plans to be made because, when I return, you and I will be married the very next day, and after that, nothing will separate us ever again."

Anne nodded. She wanted to believe it. She needed to believe it. But for some reason, her gut told her that that was not what was going to happen.

Chapter 26

Before leaving Camden Place with Frederick, Anne returned to the drawing room to ask her father what the consequences of Mr. Elliot's actions would be. Without hesitation, Sir Walter indicated that William Elliot was no longer the heir to Kellynch and that he would be taking legal action to disinherit him as soon as he could meet with Mr. Shepherd. Knowing that the solicitor's daughter, Mrs. Clay, had some connection to Mr. Elliot, Anne suggested that a local attorney be used, and when she offered to pay the legal fees, her father handed the whole matter over to her.

"Anne, all I need to know is when and where the documents will be signed," and Sir Walter shooed his daughter in the direction of the door. "Captain Wentworth will be leaving shortly for parts unknown. These things can be discussed later."

After retrieving the sketches, Anne returned to the foyer and Rick.

"Moves has agreed to keep track of Piglet's movements throughout the day," Frederick informed her, and I will meet with Elliot tonight. But I do not wish to spend my last few hours with you talking about that scoundrel."

"I agree. But we need to find Swoosh," Anne said.

"That will not be very difficult. I passed him on the way here. He was following me. So I suspect if we start walking, he will find us."

They were admiring a necklace in William Bassnett's jewelry shop window when Swoosh came up behind them, and both acted as if they were surprised. Anne suggested that they go back to the kitchen at

Camden Place where they could talk and where Swoosh could get a decent meal.

"This is Mrs. Crocker, our cook, and her daughter, Betty, who does all the baking and makes the best tarts in the city, and her younger daughter, Hannah, who is a baker in training.

"Would you like something to eat, Master Swoosh?" Mrs. Crocker asked, and he answered that he wouldn't say 'no' to a sandwich.

While Mrs. Crocker prepared a plate for the little shaver, Anne politely insisted that Swoosh wash his hands, and she watched as a week's worth of dirt went down the drain. One cloth was insufficient to remove all the grime from his face, and Anne handed him a second one. It wasn't perfect, but at least he no longer looked like a chimney sweep.

When Betty put the raspberry tart in front of Swoosh, he just stared at it. "I ain't never seen one of them outside of a shop window," and he picked it up and finished it in two bites. "Damn! I mean darn! Actually, I meant to say, 'Oh my goodness! That's the best damn thing I ever ate in my life,'" and he winked at thirteen-year old Hannah. With crumbs sticking to his face, Anne handed him a napkin, and Swoosh took it and wiped his entire face and his neck for good measure.

Anne indicated to the Crockers that they would like to speak to Swoosh alone, and after they heard the kitchen door close, Anne and Rick sat across the table from their young friend. They had no idea how their offer would be received.

"Swoosh, your help has been critical in exposing Piglet's plans," Rick began, "and he will suffer the consequences for his actions. I intend to call on him tonight and give him the bad news that he will be disinherited."

Swoosh nodded his head in approval. "He'll get what's coming to him. He's a right bastard."

"I agree. But there is other news. I will be leaving for Portsmouth in the morning."

The easy-going Swoosh quickly disappeared, and the street-savvy boy who trusted no one replaced him. "Ain't no skin off my teeth. I knew you'd do a runner once you got what you wanted."

A pained expression appeared on Anne's face, but Rick shook his head indicating that she should say nothing. "I am not doing a runner. I have been recalled to active duty, and my ship, the *Laconia*, is anchored in Portsmouth harbor."

"You mean you're going to war? Are you going to kill some Frogs?" Swoosh was ambivalent about the war. Although his mother had never explained how she had managed to get knocked up by a Frenchie while living in Bath, she always insisted that his *pere* was French. He would hate to think that Rick might be shooting at his father.

"I hope I don't have to shoot at anyone. It is more likely my ship will be a part of a blockade, but I will do what is required. When I return, there will be some major changes in my life. I have made Miss Anne an offer of marriage, and she has accepted me. I will be retiring from the navy, and we will be looking for a place to live, possibly in the country, but we may end up living nearer to the coast."

Swoosh sat back in his chair and crossed his arms, acting as if he didn't care that both Anne and Rick would be leaving Bath—and him.

"We know that you are very independent and currently answer to no one, except possibly your brother," the captain continued. "However, we were wondering if, when we are settled, you would like to become a part of our family?"

Swoosh sat perfectly still, but when it finally sunk in what they were offering him, he was out of his chair in a flash and ran around the table. After wedging himself between the two, he put his arms around Rick and Anne's necks, "Mum, Pop," and he kissed the tops of their heads and hugged them tightly until their three faces were all scrunched together. “Maybe we could go sea bathing sometime.”

When Swoosh finally let go, he promised that he would be the best son anyone could ever want. He also assured Rick that he would take care of Anne while he was at sea. After enjoying another tart, he said that he was going to push off so that the two of them could have some time to themselves, and he winked at Rick before heading off.

“What do you think about that, Anne? We are not even married, and we already have a son.”

“Is it possible that the reason for our separation was so that we could provide Swoosh with a home?”

Rick nodded his head. “That is a possibility, but if the Fates decided that parenting Swoosh was sufficient reason to keep us apart for eight years, then I am really pissed at them.”

* * *

Anne and Rick walked to the park and found a bench nestled in a hedge, and it was there that they spoke of their future. Rick was surprised to learn that Anne did not want to live at Kellynch.

“I have a deep affection for Kellynch Manor and wonderful memories of my mother. However, that is where the old Anne Elliot lived. I am a new person, and I want a fresh start. You mentioned to Swoosh that we might have a place near the coast. I would find that most agreeable.”

After looking around to make sure no one was watching, Rick gave Anne a quick kiss, but it was not enough for her. With her arms around his neck, she pulled him back, and kissed him long and hard, and he felt his toes curling.

“Anne, we are in a public place.”

“Then let us find a private place. We can go to Mrs. Smith’s. I am sure she would be willing to leave us alone for an hour or two or three.”

“That is not a good idea,” but when Anne asked him why it was not, Rick answered, “because I would drag you into the bedroom and have my way with you.”

Anne voiced no opposition.

“Anne, I will not take you in some mindless explosion of passion. How do you think I managed all these years to remain faithful to you? It was because I would not give into passion alone. All those women waiting at the bottom of the gangplank calling ‘Freddie, over here.’ ‘Freddie, I have something you want,’ in every port and on every continent. I refuse to tarnish our love.”

“Then let us hire a cab and ride around Bath. In that way, we can at least be alone.”

“And what if someone sees us getting in a cab with no chaperone? It could do irreparable damage to your reputation.”

“Rick, that is easily solved. I shall get in at one place and have the driver pick you up at another.”

“No. Such close proximity would invite familiarity.”

“Really? Invite familiarity? Unlike the other night when you ran your hands…”

“Anne, do not say another word,” he warned, fearing that his manhood would put in an appearance at the mere suggestion of sexual intimacy.

“Rick, I know I am scandalizing you, but since you have come back, I think of little else.”

“All the more reason *not to get* in a cab.”

"All the more reason *to get* in a cab," she quickly responded. "We would just talk—nothing else. I could share with you a romantic scenario that I thought of when we were in Lyme. We are lying on the beach in each other's embrace..."

Rick put his finger to her lips, and his eyes pleaded with her to stop, and she nodded her agreement.

Dusk was soon upon them, and they walked back towards Camden Place. All of the family was in the drawing room playing cards, but Rick and Anne went into the small sitting room where they sat on the sofa. With his arms around her, Anne and he sat together in silence listening to the clock stealing minutes from their time together. When the clock chimed nine bells, Rick stood up, and after one last kiss and one final embrace, they went downstairs.

"Anne, although apart, you are always with me. I see you in every sunrise and sunset and in every passing cloud, and memories of our time together and your sweet kisses will sustain me until I return and call you wife." He ran his fingers along her face and brushed her lips with his and stepped out into the night.

Anne watched him until he disappeared into the darkness. When she went back inside, Elizabeth, Mary, and Sir Walter were waiting for her. With tears running down her face, she stood apart and alone, already sinking under the weight of their separation, but then her family formed a protective circle around her. All cried as they had not done since they had lost their mother and Sir Walter his life's companion, and Anne drew comfort from her family for the first time in thirteen years.

Chapter 27

Moves and Swoosh were waiting for the captain under the street lamp and reported that Piglet was still in his rooms in Marlborough Building, but the lanky teen expected him to appear momentarily because a high-stakes card game was scheduled to start at 10:00 at the residence of a certain Colonel DeTract, a friend of Colonel Wallis's. The captain thanked Moves, and after paying him the agreed-upon sum, he returned to Tough Town. However, Swoosh offered to stay behind until Piglet showed up.

"Thank you, Swoosh, but I am not waiting for him to come out. I plan to have a message delivered to his rooms to meet me at The Sitting Duck. I want to get this over with."

"Well, then it's goodbye. I'll make sure everything is aces for Miss Anne. No worries there. So take care of yourself, Cap'n," and Swoosh extended his hand, but then he hesitated. "There is one more thing. That big hat you got? I'd feel a whole lot better if you told me that you was going to wear something that didn't have a bull's eye on it. Remember what happened to Admiral Nelson. Maybe you could wear it when no one is shooting at you. It could be a half Nelson."

"As I explained before, the hat is necessary so that my men know where I am at all times, but I do not expect any engagements. The French navy is a mere shadow of the one that engaged Nelson at Trafalgar. No worries there," and he handed Swoosh a ten-pound note and told him to buy some clothes while he was gone. "Once you agreed to come live with Anne and me, you became a toff, and you will have to dress like one."

"Ah, crap. You didn't say nothing about that being part of the deal," he said smiling, and he pictured this slick cap he had seen in one of the shops on his head. "All right then, I'm off, and I'll see ya when I see ya."

"Stay out of trouble," Rick shouted after him as he was quickly swallowed up by the crowds. Then the captain turned around and went into Marlborough Buildings. The time for a showdown with Elliot had arrived.

* * *

William Elliot found Captain Wentworth at the rear of The Sitting Duck. He was pretty sure what this meeting was about. Wentworth wanted him to back away from Anne so that he could have her for himself. Well, he was in for a rude awakening. Elliot had already received permission to make Anne an offer from Sir Walter, and once he had endured that idiotic resolution session, he was going to announce their betrothal, have the banns published, and walk her down the aisle. After that, Anne, and all of her money, would be his. Believing that he had the upper hand, Elliot sat down prepared to crush the captain's hopes.

Piglet's smug look lasted all but a minute because Wentworth immediately produced Whistler's sketches.

"Where did you get these?" he asked, his face showing pure panic.

"Where or how I got them does not matter. It is what is in those drawings that matters."

Piglet looked at sketch after sketch, and each one told the same story. William Elliot, the heir to a baronetcy, was not a gentleman, but a nefarious fellow who consorted with criminals, thugs, and lowlifes.

Looking at the final sketch, he asked, "Who is this lady sitting in a rocking chair? I had nothing to do with her."

Rick grabbed the sketch. It was a picture of Whistler's mother that he had painted for her birthday.

"You had something to do with her," and he showed him the final drawing which captured the moment when Mrs. Willing and he had emerged from her residence after enjoying some afternoon delight.

If there had been any color left in Elliot's face from the time he had seen the first sketch, it was now gone. The gambling and blood sports might be overlooked because these behaviors were commonplace among the gentry and aristocracy, but adultery was another thing, especially with Sir Walter. Since their reconciliation, Elliot had learned that despite all of his faults and conceits, Sir Walter recognized that he had been united in marriage to a gracious lady with a kind heart, and he had remained faithful to her memory. If the baronet saw that sketch of Elliot with the wife of another man that would be the end of him.

"What do you want? If it is money, I will need time."

"Time? Do you mean a lifetime? You are so in debt, no one in his right mind would lend you a farthing."

"If you know I am broke, then what *do* you want?" and a picture began forming in Elliot's mind of what the captain's end game really was. He wanted to utterly destroy him. "Who else knows about these?"

"Only Sir Walter, Elizabeth, Anne, Mary, Charles Musgrove, and Lady Russell. At the moment, we are keeping it in the family as you are a complete embarrassment to them."

Elliot grabbed the pictures and tore them to pieces. "Now where is your proof?" he said with his jaw jutting out.

"In addition to be a swine, you really are stupid. Of course, we have duplicates of all of them. And I have some bad news for you: Sir Walter is disinheriting you. You have two options. You can sign the documents relinquishing all claims on the Kellynch estate, or Sir Walter will go before a judge, show him the drawings, and charge you with moral turpitude, which is specifically mentioned in the will as a cause for disinheriting an heir. My preference would be to haul your sorry ass before a judge. In that way, you will be exposed to the whole world, and you won't be able to marry some wealthy unsuspecting maiden or rich widow. However, I assume you will wish to have as few people as possible know what a real bastard you are."

Elliot was immune to insults. He had made his way in the world by stepping on or over anyone who got in his way. Being called a bastard didn't even sting. But he could not risk others learning of his true nature or it would take longer to recover, and recover he would. He always did.

"If I agree to sign away my rights, I want your assurances that I will get all copies of the drawings, including any black and white reproductions, and that no other copies exist which can be used against me at a later time."

"You will have all copies as soon as the judge sees them."

"I don't see that have I any choice, and, frankly, it is not that great of a loss. In the last few days, I have learned that the Kellynch estate is virtually bankrupt because of the gross mismanagement of the property by Sir Walter, and his problems continue to multiply. Because of the collapse of grain prices and the Army cancelling contracts for mutton and beef, the land can no longer produce sufficient income and is worth almost nothing. The current residents are not going to renew their lease, and no one will buy it."

"Well, you won't have to worry about any of that, now will you?"

"Before I leave, I want you to know that I do have one regret."

"I know what it is. You regret not getting your hands on Anne's money, and, yes, she knows all about you sniffing around her financial advisor to find out how wealthy she is."

"That was not what I was going to say. You may tell Anne that my affection for her was genuine, and that she is the only Elliot worth knowing. The other members of the family are worthless pieces of shit."

"It takes one to know one."

The last of the details addressing the legalities was discussed. Elliot would be notified when the documents were ready for his signature. After he had signed them, he was to have no further contact with any member of the Elliot family, most especially Anne.

"If I see you within a mile of her, I will snap you in half like a twig."

Elliot knew that the captain would follow through on his threat. But it would never happen because he didn't want anything to do with any of the Elliots. He had a fallback position. There was a rich widow in Bournemouth who had shown a fondness for him and had expressed an interest in moving to a move temperate climate, either the south of France or the Italian peninsula—a most agreeable prospect. He wouldn't be lonely for long.

"I believe that concludes our business," Elliot said, rising from his chair.

"No, there is one more thing," and Captain Wentworth punched Piglet hard in the gut. "That's for Captain Willing. We take care of our own."

Chapter 28

Anne was soon to experience what it was like to be the loved one of a naval officer. Rick's first letter did not arrive for three weeks, and in all that time, he had been in port trying to get a crew together. Not unexpectedly, some of his men did not heed the call to return to service, while others were scattered all over England. Some had left the country altogether, including his First Officer, who had emigrated to Australia. Benwick was to serve in his place because his ship was leaking like a sieve, and there was no other ship available for him to command.

Provisioning the ship turned out to be a nightmare. Because the Government had either cut back or had cancelled most of the contracts for just about everything, including food, cannonballs, and powder, the *Laconia* sat idle and would not set sail until sufficient provisions were on board, and when Rick's letters finally did arrive, they were filled with the frustrations of a man who was used to running a tight ship. Instead, chaos reigned. His vessel finally got under way nearly four weeks after he had left Anne in Bath.

By mid May, the *Laconia* was in position, and from numerous hints scattered throughout his letters, she was able to figure out that the *Laconia* was somewhere near the port of Ostend off the coast of the Low Countries. For a man of action, who had seen battle and who had taken numerous prize ships, blockade duty was excruciatingly boring. Since there was so little to write about, Rick filled his letters with stories about the eight years they had been apart. From them, Anne was able to piece together the life of Frederick Wentworth from 1806 until 1814, and she hoped that someday they would be able to share his adventures with their children.

There was one other topic of which Rick wrote extensively: Captain James Benwick. As he had once pined for his Fanny, now he longed for his Louisa. Wentworth would often find his friend staring off into the distance pretending that he could see England and his lady love and, finally, told him "to get a grip."

"Damn it, Benwick. I am newly engaged myself, but I don't mope about the deck depressing everyone else. You must accentuate the positive. For example, think how happy you will be once you are on shore and can see Miss Musgrove. I shall certainly be happy to have you on shore visiting the lady."

However, nothing could shake the man out of his melancholy, and when he thought Wentworth was not looking, he secretly started reading Byron and Shakespeare's tragedies. But when he was caught red-handed with *The Bride of Abydos*, he confessed all. He was immediately reassigned to the night watch, so that Frederick would not have to endure his poetic readings and exclamations about the genius who was Lord Byron. Besides, that poem was much too long. Wentworth was a couplet man himself.

Unlike Rick, who was bored to tears, Anne's days were overflowing with things to do. First order of business: Swoosh. After revealing to her father and sisters his pivotal role in trapping that poisonous spider, William Elliot, in his own web, they agreed to allow the boy to sleep on a cot in the kitchen, but only after he had been stripped down to his birthday suit and had his head shaved to get rid of any lice. Surprisingly, Swoosh did not object. He explained that he took shelter during the winter months at a Methodist mission hall and had to submit to the same procedures before the minister and his wife would take him in.

"At the Mission—that's where Moves took me after my mum did a runner—they feed us and gave us new clothes in exchange for going to church twice on Sunday and once on Wednesday. I know that's a high price to pay, but it keeps my arse warm and my belly full. But the first day of warm weather, Moves and me move into a squat where most of the Wets live near the River Avon, and we go back to the Mission around early November, depending on the weather."

"And they take you back every year?"

"It's their Christian duty is what Reverend Jack says, and his wife, Mrs. Sprat, says 'hope springs eternal.' She thinks they'll come a time when I'll *want* to read the Bible instead of being *forced* to read it. The Sprats are two of the best people I know—the most boring as well—but you have to take the good with the bad. That's what you done with me."

Then there was the subject of Swoosh's name. It would not be possible for him to keep his street name, but once again, there was no resistance.

"The Limeys have been fighting the Frogs the whole time I've been alive," Swoosh explained. "Because the French was our enemy, I took a lot of ribbing because of my name, Louie Renault. The Reverend said I should change the spelling from Renault to Reno so it would be less French, which I did, but then I realized that out of all my friends, only Ice knows how to read. Moves can do sums better than anyone I know, and he knows his letters. It's putting them together to make words what gives him trouble, but he's getting better."

"Do you have a name in mind?" Anne asked.

"Can I take one of the captain's names? He's got more than he can use." So the pint-sized twelve-year old chose Alexander because he had once read a book about Alexander the Great given to him by Mrs. Sprat.

"Mum, you give me a chance here to make something of myself, and I'm not gonna disappoint you. I'm expecting to do great things."

"And I am expecting great things from you," Anne said, smiling. "The sky's the limit."

Anne was shortly to meet the Sprats. When Mary learned of Alexander's history, she immediately visited the Mission to offer her services as a Trained Angel of Mercy and offered to host a free health-care clinic. Mary sent word to her assistants, Miss Nightingale and Miss Barton, asking that they come to Bath to assist her, and Dr. Gurgling came as well. Everyone agreed to pitch in, except Sir Walter, who feared that someone might show up with a skin eruption or lesion, but even Elizabeth volunteered for one day and sold Mrs. Sprat and Mary's trained angels bottles of Olympian Dew.

The Rev. Sprat was as tall as his wife was wide, but they were a wonderful couple, who were committed to doing good among Bath's poor. When the day arrived for the clinic, there were lines circling the Mission. The Sprats had got the word out, and mothers dragged their children kicking and screaming into the clinic. Alexander proved invaluable. He moved easily among the children reassuring them that there was nothing to be afraid of. In fact, they would be given a sweet at the end of the line.

The two-day event was repeated the following weekend with two local doctors offering their services. It was on the second Saturday that Anne noticed that Mary was wearing a plaid tam o' shanter.

"Mary, we do not have a drop of Scottish blood in us. Why are you wearing a tam?"

"I have adopted it as a symbol. I needed to stand out from all those who are not trained as I am. Everyone can easily find me now because of the tam."

"But why a tam?"

"Because I am a Trained Angel of Mercy or T.A.M."

In addition to Mary, only Miss Nightingale and Miss Barton were allowed to don tams, and the instruction, "to look for a lady with a plaid cap," became a common refrain throughout the days the clinic was in operation.

Anne was in awe of Mary's abilities. Her sister had studied every textbook and medical tract that she could get her hands on with special emphasis being placed on diseases of the skin and how to prevent infection. She became a crusader for maintaining a sterile environment during all medical procedures and insisted that her two assistants observe the strict protocol she had established. It was with great reluctance that she left Bath, but her boys were home from school, and she needed to be with them.

While Mary and Anne had been busy at the clinic, Elizabeth was hosting Olympian Dew parties with her first recruits, Mrs. Smith and Mrs. Rooke. Class rank was strictly observed, and her first party was for Miss Carteret and her friends with Lady Russell sending her regrets. Fortunately, Lady Dalrymple chose not to attend. After years of wearing heavy face makeup laced with lead, her skin was past the point of rescue. One of Elizabeth's selling points was that all her products were lead and mercury free, and because of that promise, she had to drop Gowland's from her line of products.

Even though Olympian Dew and Pears Liquid Bloom of Roses were readily available in Bath, Elizabeth sold *beaucoup* amounts of both. The secret for her success was the party format. Women liked to get together to exchange beauty secrets, discuss the latest fashions coming out of London, and to share gossip.

Anne sat in on the second party, which was made up of the wives and daughters of merchants and trades people and watched Elizabeth in action.

"I shall introduce myself. I am Miss Elliot, the daughter of Sir Walter Elliot, Baronet. Because you are not of my rank, I shall rely on my assistants, Mrs. Smith and Mrs. Rooke, to interact with you. However, in order to get you to leave your shops and to come here, Mrs. Smith thought it would be a good idea to have a drawing for a prize of some sort."

Elizabeth held up a near empty bottle of French perfume, and she explained that it was very expensive and so far out their reach, that even a quarter of bottle was more than they could ever afford. A murmur arose among the ladies as they discussed this development, and all agreed that it was generous of Miss Elliot to give them *any* of her perfume, no matter how small the quantity.

"I have one more thing to say before turning this over to my assistants," Elizabeth continued. "Skin care must become a top priority for all of you. Your shops and children will always be there, but your skin changes every day. I know that none of you could possibly guess my age, and I shall not reveal it. But I am sure most of you look much older than you actually are. However, with my line of products, you will be able to slow down the aging process, so that you do not look like hags when you are in your forties."

There were oohs and aahs at this statement because none of them wanted to look more like a hag than they already did, and their appreciation for Miss Elliot knew no bounds. It was Mrs. Kale, the greengrocer's wife, who suggested that she pick a name for her business. The name of the river cutting through Bath was suggested, and when a vote was taken, Avon River Products won handily.

With Elizabeth raking in the money, Sir Walter decided to jump in and host an all-male party. Since he had never promised lead-free products, he included Gowland's in his line, feeling that most men would be dead from excessive eating and drinking and lack of exercise before the lead and mercury could cause any brain damage.

Camden Place became a happy place, and when Elizabeth and Sir Walter were happy, everyone else was happy, including the servants. Their happiness was important because their assistance was needed in order to have successful parties. Mrs. Crocker outdid herself with the *hors d'oeuvres*, and Betty's cakes were so popular that she would shortly open a bakery with her sister with seed money from Anne.

However, there was one person missing from the happy household: Mrs. Clay. After learning of Mr. Elliot's unsavory behavior, Mrs. Clay revealed all to Elizabeth. She confessed that Mr. Elliot had used her to find out what was being said about him by the family. She shed copious amounts of tears of true regret. A month earlier, Elizabeth and her father would have shown her the door with baggage to follow. But both were now entrepreneurs, and instead of being upset, they saw an opportunity. Mrs. Clay returned to her father and the village near Kellynch as a distributor of Avon River Products.

With everyone busy and content, Anne decided to accept Mrs. Croft's offer to join her in Folkstone where she was leasing a cottage with a view of the Channel, and Alexander and she set out for the seaside town in Sussex after a very difficult parting from Moves. He understood that this was a golden opportunity for his little brother. All he asked was that when they returned to Bath that they look him up. He could always be reached by leaving a message with Mr. Strop who owned the leather shop right outside of Toff Town.

Once the pair arrived in Folkstone, there wasn't anything Alexander would not do for the two ladies, but after completing his daily chores around the small seaside cottage, he took off for the beach where he would hang around the fishermen and help them repair their nets. When he was with them, he was Swoosh, but as soon as he crossed Mrs. Croft's threshold, he became Alexander Wentworth.

Before leaving Bath, Rick had encouraged Anne to visit Mr. Hightop in London to get fitted for a pair of running boots, and Alexander, who had taken to running with Anne in the early morning hours, was also to be measured for a pair of boots as well. With the new boots and the rubber inserts, Anne felt as if she was walking on air and that she could outrun Nike.

The two running partners returned to Folkstone from London on June 15th, the same day Napoleon crossed the Belgian frontier and engaged the Allied Armies. Early reports coming from the battlefield were grim. Marshall Ney had crushed the Prussians, allies of the British, at the Battle of Ligny. Now, it was up to Wellington to defeat the Armies of France, and in preparation for the attack, he had moved his regiments into a defensive position on the low ridge of Mont St. Jean ten miles south of Brussels near the village of Waterloo.

From the *Laconia*, Captain Wentworth could hear the roar of the guns from the battlefield, and he longed to be in the thick of it and to strike a blow against the man who had kept Europe in a perpetual state of war for nearly a quarter of a century. Instead, he was sidelined, reduced to using his spyglass to scan the horizon for any ships attempting to run the blockade, but Wentworth had seen nothing and done little.

Because of the fog of war, news of Wellington's victory was slow in coming. The casualties on both sides were horrendous, and when Wentworth's services were finally required, it was to transport the wounded back to England. He would have loved to have anchored his ship off Folkstone so that he might see Anne, but his position in the Channel determined that the wounded taken aboard the *Laconia* would be delivered to Great Yarmouth. The separation continued.

Chapter 29

It was on the morning of June 18th that Alexander returned to the Croft cottage to report that he had seen an unusual number of ships at anchor, and Anne and Sophie decided to have a look for themselves. Having been married to a naval officer for sixteen years, Sophie immediately recognized what was happening.

"Those are the wounded coming back from the Continent," and turning to Anne, she said, "There are too many of them. They will quickly be overwhelmed."

"Then we must help," and both women and Alexander returned to the house, changed their clothes, grabbed every bandage in the medical cupboard, and went in search of someone who could tell them how they could be of assistance.

Their offer was quickly accepted, and they were told to report to Dr. Home, who, after minimal instruction and no oversight, put them to work. Most of the men were ambulatory. The worst of the injured had been kept in hospitals near Brussels because it would have meant their deaths to have moved them. Even so, Anne was overwhelmed by the sheer numbers of casualties. After hours at a makeshift hospital, she returned home and quickly dashed off a letter to Mary asking that she come immediately and, if possible, with her assistants, and sent the letter by express rider. Three days later, Mary, Miss Nightingale, and Miss Barton arrived in a wagon driven by Charles Musgrove loaded down with medical supplies. And a miracle followed. Out of the darkness and chaos came light and order, all brought about by three women wearing plaid tams.

Anne's every waking hour was spent at the hospital, and fearing that her assistants would collapse from exhaustion, Mary had set up a schedule alternating physically demanding work with light duty, followed by time off. Rather than go home, Anne usually spent her downtime with the wounded who had little to do other than shoot the breeze. As with any military encampment, rumors spread like wild fire, but Anne usually paid them no heed. However, there was one circulating about a ship that had suffered extensive damage when a powder magazine had exploded, killing dozens on board, and so she had asked if anyone knew the name of the ship that had been damaged.

"If I hear the name, I'll know it," one of the sailors said.

"Was it the *Laconia*?" Anne asked while biting her lower lip.

"That be the one," the man answered, and Anne felt her stomach lurch into her chest.

"No, man, it was the *Ansonia*, not the *Laconia*."

"Yer both wrong," a third man said. "It was the *Harmonia* what blew up."

"There ain't no such ship as the *Harmonia*."

"There is too," and the three men began to argue.

"Shame on all of you," Anne said, interrupting them. "You don't really know. You are just guessing. You should not say such things unless you really know the truth. I have a loved one on the *Laconia*."

"Sorry, Miss. It's just that we be bored. Nothin' to do. If only we could have some music in here to liven things up a bit."

Anne immediately thought of Louisa. "Would you enjoy listening to someone play the harp."

"Ain't that what the angels play?" one asked. "I don't think it would be fitting in a place where you have a pretty good chance of getting to listen to one of them in person."

"What are ye talking about? Ye ain't going to heaven, you old cus," one of the sailors shot back.

"I take that to be a 'no,'" Anne said, interrupting the three tars before another argument could get started.

"I'd rather listen to dead people's music than none at all," the older and wiser sailor said.

"I shall see what I can do," and Anne turned around to find a handsome man, who had been listening to the exchange, staring at her.

"It was the *Dulwich*," he said. "The magazine that blew up was on the *Dulwich*. It was in today's newspaper."

"Thank you, sir, for that information, and who are you, if I may ask?"

"Merely a visitor to these parts. My father recently died, and I am in Folkstone settling his estate. When I saw all the tents, I made inquiries and found out that they were makeshift hospitals. I thought I might be able to provide some assistance."

"Do you have a wagon?"

"No, but I can hire one. May I ask for what purpose?"

"To transport a harpist and her harp from Uppercross. Can you do that?"

"Consider it done."

Chapter 30

When Anne had finished at the hospital, she invited the visitor back to the house. Alexander was clearly unhappy with the idea of any man, other than Rick, being in the cottage and slouched in his chair with a sour look on his face. But from his clothes, accent, and demeanor, Anne knew that the stranger was a gentleman, which caused her to question his ability to drive a wagon and transport so large an object as a harp.

Once he was in possession of a cup of tea, the man introduced himself as Mr. John Branford Goode of Surrey. As he had mentioned earlier, he had come to Folkstone to settle the estate of his father, but had lingered because the seascape had called to him.

"It called to you?" Swoosh asked. "What did it say?"

"Alexander, please go into the kitchen and see if there are any tea cakes left from last evening?" Alexander did as he was told, but Swoosh looked over his shoulder and gave Mr. Johnny B. Goode of Surrey the eye to let him know he was being watched.

"Your son is suspicious of my motives, but I can assure you that they are honorable. Even though I am a gentleman, I like to be useful."

Anne smiled at the remark, and visions of her idle father and the hours he spent looking in the mirror popped into her head.

"I do not question your motives, Mr. Goode. However, how do you plan to get to Uppercross, and do you really know how to drive a wagon?"

"I shall go to Uppercross by horseback as I keep a road horse stabled here in Folkstone. Once there, I will hire a wagon. Now, to put your mind at ease as to whether or not I know how to drive a wagon, I can assure you that I do. I am a breeder of poodles."

"No way," Swoosh said, returning from the kitchen. "That's a dame's dog. I seen the ladies carrying them around Bath, kissing their noses and feeding them sweets. All poodles do is yap, yelp, and crap."

Mr. Goode had to put his teacup down because his hands were shaking from laughter. "That is largely true, young man, of the toy poodles, at least. However, I also breed a standard poodle, and they hunt truffles."

"I might be more impressed if I knew what a truffle was."

"Alexander, I think I shall continue this conversation without you. You may return to the kitchen."

Anne gave her visitor a brief summary of how Swoosh had come to be with her. "He no longer lives on the street, but there is plenty of the street left in him. He is a work in progress, but we love him dearly."

"You say 'we' love him dearly. I heard you mention a loved one on the *Laconia*. Is that Alexander's father?"

"Alexander's adopted father is Captain Frederick Wentworth. We are not yet married, but plan to do so as soon as he is released from duty. However, we have no way of knowing when that will be."

"In his absence, I would consider it an honor to be of some assistance. If you will provide me with the directions to Uppercross and all necessary instructions to complete my assignment, I shall leave in the morning."

The next day, Mr. Goode arrived at the cottage exactly at the agreed-upon time. However, Anne had decided that having such a cumbersome instrument as a harp in a makeshift hospital was not a good idea. If Louisa would agree to come, she should bring her lute and lap harp.

"We have too much to do at the hospital to be moving a harp around, and Miss Musgrove is proficient on both instruments."

As Mr. Goode made his way down the road, Swoosh made himself ridiculous by jumping up and down and waving goodbye in an exaggerated fashion to the departing Good Samaritan.

"I'm glad to see the back of him. Let him go sit his arse down in someone else's parlor."

"Alexander, you and I need to talk," his mother said in her sternest voice.

When Anne had finished outlining the basic tenets of being a gentleman, Alexander agreed to work on those areas most in need of improvement, which was basically everything, but most especially talking back to adults and swearing. But as for his behavior to Mr. Goode, there was no contrition whatsoever. While his father was at sea, Alexander was the man of the house, and he intended to live up to his role as protector. Every night, he placed a chair in front of the main entry to the house and slept on a cot in the kitchen near the back door. One night, while Alexander lay asleep, Anne had tiptoed into the kitchen. Instead of seeing a lad sleeping contentedly without a care in the world, she had observed a boy who was wrapped up as tight as a coil ready to jump at anyone lurking nearby. Because he had lived so many years on the street, she wondered if change was possible or if a part of him would forever remain Swoosh.

* * *

After her talk with Alexander, Anne immediately set out for the hospital to relieve Frederick's sister, who was nearing the point of exhaustion. She had been assigned to the tent that housed those with the most serious wounds and required her constant attention. When she arrived, she found Mrs. Croft in tears.

"I can hardly stand I am so tired. But that evil man will give me no rest, and nothing I do pleases."

"What evil man?" Anne asked, but she already knew who she was talking about.

"Dr. Home. He is cruelty personified. No naval surgeon would act in such a manner. I blame it on the Army."

"What did he tell you to do?"

That question opened a floodgate, and Mrs. Croft listed an endless series of physically-demanding tasks that he had assigned her, and no sooner had she finished one, then she was sent to do another. It was not that she was being singled out. He was an equal opportunity abuser, waving his cane at everyone, and scaring the tar out of the orderlies.

"You should have heard what he said to one soldier's family," Sophia continued, after dabbing her eyes with an offered handkerchief. "Private Ryan's parents and sister had come all the way from Cheshire, and at great expense, to see him, and after days of sitting by his side, his sister said, 'He's looking better today, isn't he, Dr. Home?' And that awful man answered, 'You and I must be looking at different patients.'

"And when I told him I was ready to drop from exhaustion, do you know what he said? He said," sniffle, sniffle, "He said, 'You must be confusing me with someone who cares,' and walked off."

Anne went to retrieve Mrs. Croft's cloak. If she were to recite all the horrible things that Dr. Home said, they would be there the better part of a day, and no work would get done.

After sending Frederick's sister on her way, she sought out Mary to talk to her about Dr. Home, and not just on behalf of Sophia. Anne had been on the receiving end of one of his insults as well. He had asked her if she had a brain, and if she did, would she mind if he borrowed it since she didn't seem to be using it. The expected results, tears streaming down her face, seemed to please him.

"Why isn't a senior officer taking him to task for being so cruel to the staff?" Anne asked. "We are volunteers, not soldiers."

“Because he has been an Army surgeon since the Norman Conquest and has seen it all. I know he is as nasty as they come, but he gets the men the care they need, including saving Private Ryan. Even minor wounds put the men at grave risk for gangrene, which greatly increases the need for amputations. Very often amputations are the same as being condemned to a slow death. His patients have less mortality than any others. We, all of us, must endure him.”

Anne could see how exhausted her sister was. The three TAMS had been working so hard, much harder than Anne or Mrs. Croft for that matter, and so she said no more, changing the subject to Mr. Goode going to Uppercross.

“I did not ask Charles to go with Mr. Goode because he has been running errands for Dr. Johns and Dr. Hopkins,” Mary explained. “When Mr. Goode offered his services, it seemed foolish not to take him up on his offer, and it was a very good idea that you had about sending for Louisa. There is actually reason to hope that the worst is over. It appears that Portsmouth and the other ports with real hospitals will be able to handle the casualties still coming over from the Low Countries. Those with less serious injuries will be kept here until discharged. But in the meantime, the natives are restless, and the grumbling has increased considerably.” After sitting down and rubbing her tired eyes, she added, “We are all in need of entertainment. I just hope Louisa does not pass out when she gets here. She can be very dramatic,” so said the former drama queen.

* * *

Louisa did not pass out, but she did gag from the smell. After tying a lace cachet of posies around her neck, she did better. At Mr. Goode’s suggestion, she had stopped at a shop in town where she bought some sheet music for some livelier tunes, but because she was so pretty and bubbly, her mere presence made a big difference with the soldiers and now the sailors from the *Dulwich*.

Mr. Goode continued to make himself available for any errand, and, eventually, he took over Charles’s duties so that he might go home to his boys. After some initial instruction from Mary, he was assigned to Anne, which he was very glad of because the head TAM had been a tough taskmaster.

It was a rare evening when Mrs. Croft, Alexander, and Anne were all at home together. After they ate dinner, Anne was looking forward to spending some quiet time reading, but as soon as she sat down, Alexander asked to speak with her.

"You need to tell Mr. Goode to go home to Surrey. He done his part, and now he can go back to his poodles."

"Alexander, Mr. Goode is a volunteer, as are we all, and he will decide when his services are no longer required. I have nothing more to say on the matter."

Out of the corner of her eye, Anne could see Alexander looking at Mrs. Croft and pointing in her direction with repeated jerks of his head, and after Sophia gave him a nod, he left the room. The two of them were in cahoots. But about what?

"Anne, you need to be careful around Mr. Goode," Sophia began. After hesitating, she took the plunge, "He is openly flirting with you, and people are talking about it."

After putting down her book, Anne responded. "I disagree with you, but even if Mr. Goode was flirting with me, do you think me capable of transferring my affections to him? Do you question the depth of my love for your brother," and now talking in the direction of the kitchen where Alexander had his ear to the door, "and of my love for your father?"

"Absolutely not," Sophie quickly said. "It is just so obvious to everyone how much he wants to be near you."

"The gentleman is in need of a lot of direction. All of his knowledge is canine based. I swear sometimes he thinks of arms as if they were a third or fourth leg. Humans do not bend in the same way as dogs do."

"I just wanted you to be aware," Sophie answered in a softer voice.

"Sophia, our acquaintance has been short, and you have only recently learned of my history with Frederick. But I have waited eight years for your brother, and I will wait another eight years if that is what is required. I have never loved anyone other than him, and I shall go to my grave as Mrs. Frederick Wentworth or as Miss Anne Elliot. I shall bear no other name," and Anne picked up her book and went to her room.

Chapter 31

With the families of the wounded soldiers and sailors crowding into every inn and private residence in Folkstone, Mary, Louisa, and the volunteer TAMS were staying at Mr. Goode's house. When schedules permitted, they would dine together, and the gentleman would spend the evening with his female guests. But when it came time for everyone to retire, he went to a neighbor's house and slept in the attic. Although Anne continued to hold him in the highest regard, she did notice that he was often near her, and in order to avoid giving the gossips something to talk about, she started to distance herself from him. She was thinking about asking Mary to reassign him to another tent when Mr. Goode approached her. After hemming and hawing and twiddling and twitching, he finally got after it.

"Miss Elliot, if I may, I would like to have a few moments of your time." After all his kindnesses, what could Anne do but listen, and she reluctantly agreed.

"I am a widower, my wife having died nearly two years ago. Lenora was the best of women, and the dearest part of my life. We were married for eight years. That is a long time."

"Yes, I know how long eight years is."

"When she died, I never thought that I would love again, but I have met someone who has touched me deeply."

"Mr. Goode, you should be very careful here and not rush into anything. After such a loss, one can imagine oneself to be in love when it is something much closer to friendship."

"Is that how she regards me? As a friend?" he asked anxiously.

"How *she* regards you? I am not one-hundred percent certain." Who, pray tell, was *she*?

"I have seen the passing of thirty-three summers, so I know that an age difference of twelve years is considerable."

Anne quickly did the math: thirty-three minus twenty-seven equals five. He was not talking about her, so who was he talking about?

"I could hardly believe how moved I was the moment her fingers touched the strings of her harp. It was like angel's music. And on the carriage ride here, we talked all the way, and when we arrived in Folkstone, Louisa told me that was the first time she had been in a carriage when she had not needed to stop to empty her stomach."

"Mr. Goode, that is quite a compliment," Anne said greatly relieved. "Louisa has always suffered from carriage sickness. Apparently, she has found a cure in you, but are your feelings for her reciprocated?"

"I think so, but she is hesitant to say anything because of Captain Benwick."

"Oh, I had forgotten about him," and a vision of the captain, with his basset hound face, looking out across the Channel toward England and his lady love appeared before her. "Truthfully, I have not had any time to speak with Louisa since they became engaged. It all happened so fast and under the strangest of circumstances."

"Will you speak to her now?" he asked with pleading eyes. "I need to know. I must know. Surely, you have noticed how often I have attempted to bring up this subject with you?"

"Yes, I did and I am glad you finally spoke up, and I shall speak to Miss Musgrove at the earliest possible moment. As soon as I have her response, I shall let you know. I can tell you from personal experience that there are few things worse than uncertainty."

* * *

Louisa Musgrove. The last time Anne had seen her she had resembled a propped up rag doll, and it had taken every ounce of her Christian charity not to shake her silly for jumping off the steps on the Cobb and, perhaps, ruining forever any chance of happiness she might have had with Frederick. But that Louisa was a child who had done a childish thing. She needed to know if the knock on her noggin had been a life-changing event. Was she mature enough to marry, not just Mr. Goode or Captain Benwick, but anyone?

The next day, Anne invited Louisa to supper. At the conclusion of the meal, she suggested a walk on the Strand. After complimenting Louisa on her role in providing entertainment for the troops, Anne asked her in a very matter-of-fact way if Captain Benwick was a faithful correspondent.

"Oh, yes. He writes every day. Of course, I do not get them every day. They come in bunches. Mostly, he copies out poetry." This was said with a decided lack of enthusiasm, and Louisa began to bite her lower lip.

"You seem distressed. Separation can certainly do that. Unless, of course, there is another reason for you to be unhappy."

"Oh, my goodness, I am so transparent!" Louisa said, grabbing Anne by her arm. "You have guessed. I know you have. I wear my heart on my sleeve. Of course, he does not know how I feel. I cannot give any hint of my attachment because I am engaged to another."

"Let me be sure we are speaking of the same person. Are you in love with Mr. Goode?"

"Oh, I do so love to hear his name: Goode," Louisa said sighing. "He does good. He is good. I feel good when I am around him."

"And what of Captain Benwick?"

Apparently, Louisa's visit to Deal to meet Benwick's relations had gone badly. James's father had died when he was quite young, and he had been raised by his mother and three older sisters, none of whom had ever married. It seemed as if the ladies of the house were of one mind with their brother when it came to their choice of depressing literature and poetry. As a result, the captain had suffered a Byronic relapse.

"Do you know what his mother's favorite Shakespearean character is? Lady Macbeth. That is not normal," Louisa said, shaking her head. "For entertainment, they act out Shakespeare's tragedies. While I was there, newly engaged to their brother, the sisters chose *Othello*—a story where an enraged husband smothers his wife in her bed while she is sleeping. They wanted James to be Othello and for me to play the part of Desdemona, but I would have none of it. And my refusal to play so bleak a role brought on accusations of my being uncooperative. They are acting out a truly depressing play, and I am the party pooper! I think not. But as for James and me, what is done, cannot be undone."

"Why ever not? You walked away from Captain Wentworth without so much as a look back. Why are you hesitating with James?"

"Because Captain Wentworth never loved me. Although my injuries were no one's fault but my own, he felt responsible for my fall on the Cobb. But I would never have married him. There was a sadness about him that was heart-wrenching. I did not know whom he loved, but I did know that he loved another. Now that I have met Mr. Goode, I know that I never loved either captain. I just wanted to be married because I knew that my sister would soon be Henrietta Hayter. I was older than she was, and so I thought it should not be so. What a stupid girl I was."

Anne counseled Louisa that she should not marry Captain Benwick. Two wrongs did not make a right. After that, Anne felt comfortable in acquainting the young Miss Musgrove with the discussion she had had with Mr. Goode, and Louisa was ecstatic.

"However, in all fairness to Captain Benwick, you must write to him. He cannot return to England thinking that he will shortly be married."

"Oh please, Anne, can you not write to him? You are the only one who ever made him smile."

"No, I cannot. It must be in your hand and with your own words. I wouldn't worry about it too much. You were together for such a short time, and he will get over it. Besides, he has his memories with Fanny Harville as a fallback."

Anne hoped that Captain Benwick would recover quickly because she knew that she would never have got over Frederick no matter how long she lived.

* * *

Mary was correct. There was light at the end of the tunnel. It was now known that although the battle of Waterloo was, in the words of Wellington, "a near run thing," Napoleon's forces had been defeated, and the Emperor of France had been taken aboard the *HMS Northumberland* with a one-way ticket to the island of St. Helena in the Atlantic.

But there was still so much to do. It had been decided to transfer all remaining patients into two buildings separated by a garden path, which required moving all the medical supplies needed for their care. With Dr. Home riding roughshod over the staff, Anne was so busy that when Alexander handed her a letter from Rick, she stuffed it in her pocket. If it was like all the others, he would have little to say that she was not already experiencing herself. While he transported the wounded, she cared for them, and there simply were not enough hours in the day to do all that needed to be done.

When Anne finally went to the cottage, she collapsed in the chair, and while doing so, she heard the crinkling sound of Rick's letter. After reading it, all color drained from her face, and an alarmed Sophie and Alexander asked her what was wrong.

"Mum, what's it about? What did Pop say?" Alexander asked again, but Anne remained silent, staring at the letter.

"Frederick. Something has happened to Frederick," Sophie said, nearly choking on her words.

"No. Nothing has happened to him. He is fine. It is just... It is just that he has received new orders. He is to proceed immediately…," and Anne looked at them with a face filled with pain. "The *Laconia* is to go directly to the West Indies from blockade duty. Frederick will not be returning to England."

Chapter 32

Anne wanted to cry, scream, pull her hair out, kick the furniture, and throw a flower pot across the room. But she dare not do any of those things because Alexander was looking right at her, and he was on the verge of tears. For a tough kid to break down and cry in front of two women would be humiliating, so instead of hurling a geranium through space, she handed the letter to him.

Dearest Anne,

I can only write a few lines because the mail boat is leaving, and I wanted you to know that the ***Laconia*** *has been ordered to proceed to the West Indies directly from Ostend. Once there, I shall immediately inform the Admiralty representative of my intention to resign from the Navy. With the defeat of Napoleon, the Navy has too many captains, and I believe my resignation will be accepted. As soon as I am discharged, I shall be on the first ship back to England. I must go now, but know this: through these trials and separations, your love sustains me. Give my regards to all, especially to our son. Yours always, Rick*

Alexander handed the letter back to Anne. “It ain’t—it isn’t right what they’re doing. A boy my age needs his father,” and he ran into the kitchen and out the back door.

Sophia did not know what to say to Anne, especially since she had received a letter from her husband, in which he had informed her that he was being forced into retirement and would soon be home. Although he was one of the Royal Navy’s most experienced officers, now that the wars with France were over, the Admiralty wanted these old warriors to get out of the way in order to make room for a new generation of officers who would command ships in a very different world from what the aging Admiral Croft had known. The irony, of course, was that her husband wished to remain in the navy, while Frederick wanted to leave it.

"Sophia, I can see that you are struggling to find the right words to say to me, but there is nothing to say. Frederick was ordered to the West Indies, and that's that. All I can do is hope that the navy will accept his resignation and that he will return to me as soon as possible. I imagine it will take a minimum of three months for him to get to the Caribbean and back, so in the meantime, I have work to do at the hospital."

For Anne, the next two days were a blur. She cried; she slept. She cried; she ate. She cried; she worked. And Alexander did the same. Sophia, recognizing their unhappiness, suggested to Anne that they go to Kellynch to recover from all their exertions at the earliest possible time. A bucolic setting would soothe frazzled nerves.

"Alexander and you will be able to run in the country, and you may visit with all your friends and the tenants who love you. Every time I passed by Mr. Goodenough's farm, he asked after you, and the servants, God bless them, they miss you terribly."

"Kellynch," Anne said, sighing. "Oh, how I would love to be in the country again, but before I do that, I need to take Alexander to London. He needs all new clothes as he has grown three inches this summer, and he wants another pair of boots."

"But his boots are brand new."

"Yes, I know, but they are already too tight, and he wants to have a pair made to his exact specifications. He has it all drawn out. The boots will have a white star embossed on the ankles, and all the stitching will be white as well. And he has the money to do it. All those errands he has been running for the soldiers and their families? Well, almost every one of them pressed a coin into his palm, and so he's got plenty of bread and honey to spend."

"Bread and honey?"

"It is a joke that Alexander and I share," and Anne smiled at the memory of their first meeting. The wise street urchin and the naïve fine lady. Swoosh and Flash. What a pair they had made!

* * *

With each passing day, more soldiers and sailors were going home, and rumors were circulating that the site would be shut down and the patients moved to Great Yarmouth. Miss Nightingale and Miss Barton had already returned to Somerset, and Mary was getting everything in order so that she might do the same as she missed Charles and the boys very much.

"Oh, there you are, Anne. I have been looking for you," Mary said. "I need some of the bandages we use for wrapping ankles from the other building."

"But I just brought a box of them to you yesterday."

"I know that, but I need more."

Anne looked around and saw no new patients. "But I have already changed all of the bandages, and there are at least a dozen in the cupboard."

"Anne, we have spoken before about your arguing with me. You are not a TAM, but a subordinate. I am really surprised by how much you struggle with authority. Now, do you know where the bandages are kept?"

"Of course, I do. I was just there yesterday," she said in an exasperated voice. She wanted to say more, but Mary was right. When they were within the four walls of the hospital, Mary was her supervisor. But now that the patient load had dropped, it seemed as if she was just ordering Anne around because she could. She staged a minor protest by stamping her foot, but said nothing else. Instead, she turned on her heel and went out onto the garden path that connected the two buildings, but once in the garden, she came to an abrupt halt.

Standing before her in all his awesomeness was Captain Frederick Wentworth.

"Hello, Anne," he said in that soft deep voice that caused her knees to buckle. Quite overwhelmed by his sudden appearance, she remained rooted to the earth and said nothing. "Is this your idea of a warm welcome for a sailor who has come home to you from the sea?"

Anne ran down the path into his open arms, and he drew her to him and kissed her. This prompted a round of huzzahs, and Anne turned around to see Mary, Sophia, the hospital staff, and all those patients who were ambulatory, clapping and cheering. And then there was Alexander with his broad grin and a sparkle in his big blue eyes. With one arm around Anne's waist, Rick used the other to embrace his son, and Alexander buried his head into his father's coat because he did not want anyone to see him cry.

But soon Anne stepped away from Rick and poked her finger in his chest. "I should be very angry with you. What a cruel joke you have played on your family, Captain Wentworth."

"I can assure you that my letter was no joke. I will explain all, but is that what you want to do right at this moment? Have a conversation about how I came to retire from the Royal Navy?" and the group shouted, "No."

Rick turned and faced the crowd. "So what shall we do?"

"Get a room, Cap'n," a sailor shouted.

"We are not married, sir," he said, laughing.

"Then *get* married," the old tar answered. "What are you waiting for?"

"Yes, Anne what are we waiting for? Have you done all that I asked? Have you obtained the license? Have you had the banns published here in Folkstone? Have you a wedding dress?"

"Yes, yes, and yes. Everything is ready. But do you think your brother will be unhappy when he learns that he will not be marrying us?"

"I don't care. I am not traveling over two hundred miles to get married. I told you when I came home that we would marry the next day, and that is what I intend to do."

* * *

That evening, Rick explained to Anne, Sophie, and Alexander all that had happened since he had written the letter telling of his posting to the far side of the Atlantic.

"All officers went ashore at Ostend for a meeting so that we might receive our new orders. I had made my superior officers aware that I wished to retire, but, apparently, that news had not reached Admiral Schooner, which was why the orders for the West Indies had been issued. For the next few days, everyone tried to get an interview with the Admiral as many were unhappy with the changes, including Admiral Croft, who was made to retire," he said, looking at Sophie, and his sister nodded, indicating that she already knew of the change in her husband's status.

"When my turn came, Schooner was in a foul mood and said that if I was unhappy with my orders that I should get out of the navy. I told him that was exactly what I wanted to do. 'So you can sit on your arse and collect half pay,' he said. 'No, I want to be paid off,' I replied. Because I am a young man, he was shocked that I would desire such a thing, but he told me that too many things needed to be sorted before he could consider such a request and that I should prepare to sail for Nassau.

"I had no sooner sent off my letter to you with the mail boat when I received a message from Schooner accepting my resignation. Apparently, the navy wants to avoid putting anyone on half pay if it can be avoided, so I was practically kicked off the *Laconia* to make way for the new captain."

"Who is the new captain?" Anne asked.

"Benwick.

"James Benwick?" Anne said stunned. She could hardly believe that a man who brooded and sulked like a child, and who lacked Frederick's assertiveness and confidence, would assume the command of the *Laconia.* It was a good thing that the wars with France were over.

"And speaking of Captain Benwick, my dearest Anne, I have a bone to pick with you. Why did you encourage Louisa to break their engagement while he was still under my command? As soon as he read the letter, the man started weeping and wailing, but crying did not prevent him from reciting Shakespeare. Nothing keeps him from reciting something."

"What did he say?"

Come, bitter conduct, come, unsavory guide!
Thou desperate pilot, now at once run on
The dashing rocks thy seasick weary bark!
Here's to my love.

"Oh, my goodness! That is from *Romeo and Juliet* where Romeo takes the poison because he thinks Juliet is dead."

"Yes, I know. Do you want to hear Juliet's lines as well because he recited them to me and everyone else in the mess?"

"No, thank you. I know the captain well enough, so that I can easily picture the scene. The poor man."

"The poor man! I am the one to be pitied. I had to listen to it. But when I had finally had enough, I told him that he was one of those people who is not truly happy unless he is unhappy. And you know what? He did not disagree with me. He moped around until he learned that he was to take command of the *Laconia*. But why are we speaking of Benwick? We should be speaking about our wedding. Alexander, will you stand up with me?" he asked, turning to his son.

"You bet, sir. Mum bought me a new suit when we was in London that makes me look like a real toff."

"Then I suggest that we all go to bed because we are to be at the church by 9:00 and are to be married by the navy chaplain. After that, we will have a wedding breakfast in the garden near the hospital. I am told that Mary and Sophia are seeing to all the preparations."

Alexander and Sophia said good night, and for the first time since Rick had gone away, their son slept in his own bed.

"And where are we to go after the wedding breakfast?" Anne asked.

"On the way here, I stopped and made arrangements at a cottage about three miles east of Folkestone called The Hidden Nest, and that is what I want to do—build a nest and hide away from everyone. Other than taking nourishment, I want the two of us to stay in our room and make up for eight, nearly nine, years of lost time."

"If we are going to be in the room that much, shall I bring my knitting?"

"If you wish to see it floating in the Channel, you may bring it."

"What about cribbage or a chess board?"

"Only if you want to see how far I can throw them."

"If you are determined to reject my suggestions, then you must take responsibility for our amusement."

"Gladly. If you will come here, I will give you a preview."

"No, sir, I shall not as you have a lean and hungry look, and so I am to bed," and Anne started walking backwards up the stairs.

"You may go, Miss Anne Elliot, but tonight is the last night I shall call you Miss."

* * *

Anne lay on her bed staring at the ceiling, remembering every moment of the day from the time she had first seen Rick standing in the garden. In the short time they were alone together at the cottage, Rick had practically devoured her. He had picked her up, put her on the kitchen table, and wrapped her legs around him. It was a good thing that they were to marry on the morrow.

With the darkness closing in around her, she thought about what her wedding night would be like. Because of her work in the hospital, she had seen a man's member in all its incarnations: furled, unfurled, half mast, and full mast, but she decided not to think about the captain's cannon, but of the wedding itself.

When she had gone up to London, she had bought a lovely dress that she had seen in a shop window. The satin was of the palest yellow and complimented her bronze skin, and it was beautiful in its simplicity. But Alexander insisted that lace be added to the bodice and little tassels to the sleeves. "Mum, it's your wedding day. Even you have to get dressed up for that!"

While Alexander had been at the bootmaker's, she had returned to the shop to buy a silk nightgown that laced in the back. At the time, she could not imagine looking at a man while he undressed her, but now she was thinking that she should have got the one that laced in the front. Oh, well, they would have a lifetime to do such things, and she rolled over and went to sleep, knowing that, at long last, Rick and she would be together.

Chapter 33

Captain Wentworth fidgeted at the altar, and it was his thirteen-year old son who had to keep his father calm.

"She is late," Wentworth said, looking at his pocket watch. Alexander took out his brand new pocket watch that the captain had bought for him in Ostend and told him that his mum wasn't due at the church for another fifteen minutes. "I think your watch is running fast."

"She can't be early? Is that a rule? When I am ready to sail, I pull up anchor and go."

"But, Pop, she ain't—she isn't a ship. She's a woman what's—she's a woman who's getting ready for the most important day of her life."

Alexander hated the English grammar lessons he had agreed to take as part of the arrangement for him to come live with Anne and Rick. Did people really care if you said "what" instead of "who?" According to Anne, they did. "It is a sign that you have been educated. Some people, such as lawyers, preachers, and writers, make their livings by words."

"That's 'cause they can't get real jobs," he had answered.

The captain would only have to pace for a few more minutes because Anne was en route. When she arrived, the church was packed, mostly with patients and staff from the hospital, because there had been no time to get word to Sir Walter, Elizabeth, the Musgroves, or Edward Wentworth. But Sophie and Louisa were there, and Mary was her sister's matron of honor.

When Anne appeared at the rear of the church, she looked radiant in her yellow dress with yellow ribbons woven into her brown hair, and she was wearing the dangling earrings and a rope of pearls given to her by Sophie. Upon looking at his lovely Anne, Rick had to fight back tears. Over the years, during their separation, he had often imagined them as man and wife, raising a brood of children, but then a veil of darkness would descend. In his despair, he believed that they would never marry. But there she was—his beautiful bride. The veil had been lifted, and they would never again be separated.

When Rick slipped the ring on her finger, Anne's hands were steady, and looking at her husband, she knew that it had been their destiny to be together all along. All the heartache and pain she had suffered in order to reach this day would soon be forgotten in the joy of being Mrs. Frederick Wentworth.

At the wedding breakfast, the couple walked around the garden greeting their well-wishers. All the patients praised Anne's wonderful nursing, and the doctors lauded her tireless efforts on behalf of the wounded. But her devotion to those in need was not news to Rick. He would have expected no less from someone with such a generous heart. A few navy men were present, most of whom were either grumbling because of their new postings or elated because they were on shore at half pay while the navy tried to figure out what to do with them. Seeing Louisa and Mr. Goode, Anne said that she would like Rick to meet the gentleman. She related all that she knew of Mr. Goode, but Rick was not impressed.

"Poodles? That is a woman's dog. All they do is yap and crap."

But when she mentioned that Mr. Goode had offered them his carriage for their wedding journey, he was all praise for his efforts on behalf of patients and poodles.

"He has been standing next to Louisa since we arrived. Why is that?" Rick asked.

Anne hesitated. What would Rick say when he learned that Louisa was romantically involved with Mr. Goode? After all, just a few weeks earlier, she had been betrothed to his First Officer.

“Mr. Goode has asked permission of the Musgroves to court Louisa.”

“Good Lord! Are you serious? Three weeks ago, she was engaged to Benwick.”

Anne explained how it was that they had come to be together. “Rick, they are well suited for each other, both having easy and joyful dispositions. He is a far cry from Captain Benwick.”

“Well, my advice to Mr. Goode is to remain by her side around the clock. If a single man happens to walk by and he is not there, she might go off with him.”

“Oh, stop it. This is a tender subject with you because she threw you over for Benwick.”

“Well, I have an answer for that. Louisa and I were together longer than she was engaged to Benwick.”

“But that is only because she was unconscious when you two were a couple. Once she woke up, she immediately transferred her affection to James, probably because you have such strong opinions and are not afraid to voice them.”

Putting his arm around her waist, he drew his wife near to him. “I have a very strong opinion about you. Would you like to hear it,” and she nodded. “I have visited every part of the globe, and I can say, without qualification, that there is no one on earth like you and that I am the luckiest man alive.”

“Then are you agreeable to saying goodbye to our guests so that we may go to The Hidden Nest where you can show me just how much you love me?”

Rick stepped away from her, and in a booming voice, announced to all that they had to leave so that they might arrive at their destination before dark.

"Thank you for coming. Enjoy the food. Stay as long as you like. Hopefully, we won't be seeing you any time soon," and everyone laughed. After saying goodbye to Alexander, who had tied his first pair of running shoes to the back of Goode's conveyance, they climbed into the carriage and headed off on their honeymoon.

* * *

The Hidden Nest really was a secluded retreat, concealed behind towering hedges which served as a buffer against the winds coming in off the Channel. It was now September, and the crowds had started to thin, so they were able to get one of the best rooms with a view of the rocky shore and breaking surf. As soon as they went into their room, Anne lit a candle, and it cast a soft glow on everything. Neither was hungry, except for each other.

Rick sat in a chair and took off his boots, and Anne watched as he removed his jacket and pulled off his shirt. As he stepped out of his breeches, Anne could almost hear a drum roll in the background. When he stood before her as naked as Adam, an "Oh, my goodness" escaped from her lips. Apparently, his awesomeness extended to every part of his body. "All I can say, Frederick, is that you are truly blessed."

"I know," and he went over and took hold of her hands, but she made no move to get ready for bed.

"Anne, I am a graduate of the Royal Naval Academy, and after years serving in the navy, I have no modesty left, so standing before you stark naked is not embarrassing to me. However, I do feel the cold just like everyone else. So may I unbutton your dress and, perhaps, untie the laces of your stays so that we may retire?"

"I stopped wearing stays when I started running," she said. But her thoughts were not of under garments, but of what awaited her.

"Good. One less thing to undo," and he turned her around so that he might unbutton her dress, and he helped her to step out it.

She went to get her nightgown from her valise, but then she stopped, and returned to Rick. She removed her shoes, took off her stockings, and pulled the chemise over her head, and she stood before him as naked as Eve in the Garden.

Looking at her in her natural state, he said, "I don't know what to say to you, except that I love you and that I want to be the best husband in the world."

Because they had not bothered with a fire, the room was chilly, and so they burrowed under the covers. Once they were comfortable, Anne placed her head upon Rick's chest and waited for some direction. There was no need for her to try to arouse him, as he had an erection that could have easily poked a hole in the cover, and so she whispered, "I don't know what to do."

"All you have to do is love me."

When their passion was spent, he drew her to him, and they were soon asleep in each other's arms.

* * *

For the next few days, Rick and Anne made love with an intensity that caused both of them to remark that it was as if they were trying to make up for lost time, but neither was complaining. When they did leave their room, they walked along the shore and spoke of Rick's adventures on the high seas and the changes in Anne's life since she had started jogging. But on the fourth day, a storm forced them indoors, and they turned their attention from the past to their future life together. Where would they live? What would Rick do now that he had retired? And most importantly, what of Alexander? He was a bright boy on the verge of becoming a man, and he needed to be educated so that he could make the most of his God-given talent. These plans were gone over at length and in great detail, and much of what they had discussed that week at The Hidden Nest came off as planned—something entirely new to their experience.

On the last night of their honeymoon, as her husband lay sleeping beside her, Anne looked out the window and saw a sliver of a waxing moon shining in the darkness of the Milky Way, and she thought of the wedding vows Frederick and she had exchanged earlier in the week: "For this cause shall a man leave his father and mother and shall be joined unto his wife." And so it was in the year of Our Lord, 1815, that Anne Elliot and Frederick Wentworth finally became one.

Epilogue

And they lived happily ever after? Of course, they did. Considering all of the heartache Anne and Rick had experienced during their lengthy separation and because of their inherent goodness, they had earned such an ending. But more about them later.

Mary Musgrove continued her work as a Trained Angel of Mercy, but because she would give birth to two daughters, she limited her efforts to the villagers and farmers near Uppercross and left the professional nursing to Miss Barton and Miss Nightingale. However, one of her most prized possessions was her red cross pin, which she wore every day. Charles was now a happy man. Despite the collapse of agricultural prices following the end of the Napoleonic Wars, he was content to live on a lesser income with fewer guns and not as many dogs because his wife was no longer a whiner and party pooper. Of equal importance was the fact that he was now admitted into his wife's bedroom at least once a week, usually on a Saturday night, thus accounting for the daughters. Both of their sons, Charles, Jr. and the other one, became doctors.

Elizabeth and Sir Walter Elliot developed their own line of lotions and cosmetics and reorganized as Advanced Avon River Products. AARP specialized in a product line of creams for women over forty that was hugely successful, making the pair very wealthy. The Elliots eventually sold their business to an American company and retired to the south of France where they shopped until they dropped—dead—literally. It was exactly how they had always hoped it would be.

By the time old man Winthrop died, Henrietta had grown accustomed to the name of Hayter, and so the Hayters they remained. Because Henrietta's reproductive system could only produce twins, Charles and Henrietta had a very large family, and even after four sets of twins, they never gave up the dream of having a single child.

Louisa and Mr. Goode's children were their poodles. While Mr. Goode concentrated on breeding a better truffle-sniffing standard poodle, Louisa threw herself wholeheartedly into the breeding of toy poodles—the smaller the better. She eventually bred a poodle that was so tiny that it could fit into a teacup, and Goode's teacup poodles became all the rage among the ladies of the *ton*.

After getting the boot from the widow in Bournemouth, William Elliot moved to Naples. In Napoli, he encountered the now widowed Signora Culogrande and became her boy toy. Even as her beauty faded and her girth expanded, he remained with her because he had been led to believe that he would inherit the fortune she had made touring the Continent as a much sought-after coloratura soprano. When she died and her will was probated, Elliot learned that she had left everything to the perpetual care of her sixteen cats. After leaving the door open so that all the cats could get out, he departed Italy and was last seen smoking a hookah in Constantinople.

Mrs. Smith was able to sell her property in the West Indies for an amount sufficient to buy an Advanced Avon River Products distributorship from the Elliots for Bath and its environs, and she hired Mrs. Rooke as her administrative assistant.

Lady Russell's tenure as the *grand dame* of matchmaking came to an end when she suggested that Elizabeth Elliot marry the heir to a barony, the future Lord Knox-Seema. When it was discovered that Lady Russell had failed to take into account that the gentleman regularly experienced skin eruptions, all of her credibility with Elizabeth and Sir Walter was lost. When Lady Dalrymple died, she became a companion to Miss Carteret, who spent the next six years of her life worrying about the possibility of Napoleon escaping from St. Helena and invading England. She was greatly relieved to hear news of his death.

* * *

And now for our hero and heroine. As soon as the Kellynch property became available, the Wentworths moved there from Folkstone because they wanted Alexander to grow up in the country. Shortly after their arrival, they decided that the estate was too large for just the three of them, and Anne and Rick contacted Reverend Sprat and requested that he send their way any boy or girl who showed an aptitude for academics. All were educated by tutors from England's great universities at the Wentworths' expense. Upon reaching the age of twelve years, most of the boys went on to attend public schools, while the girls went to seminary or to Uppercross for training as TAMS under Mary Musgrove's supervision.

Anne was delivered of her first child one year after their marriage. Betsy would be followed by Frederick, Jr., Thomas, and Maria. A running track was built on the property that connected to a series of paths that equaled the length of a marathon. The two boys became outstanding runners and excelled at that exercise at Winchester College and Cambridge, and it was a joke within the neighborhood that the two Wentworth daughters would never marry because no man would ever be able to catch them.

Having experienced so much heartache before they had wed, Anne and Frederick were heartache-free in their marriage. There was nothing they enjoyed more than having all the family and boarders together in the parlor playing cards or charades or going to the theater room where the children would stage plays with Alexander directing. When the children married and moved away, Anne and Frederick enjoyed walking around their property, arm in arm, and they would go to a favorite spot on the estate. It was there that Frederick had first seen Anne as she had emerged from shade into sunlight. From that moment, he believed that they were destined to be together, and, of course, he was right.

* * *

And so the tale is told, except for Alexander, and we shall allow him to tell his story in his own voice.

"From the day I met my mother, my life improved, and when she married my father, it got even better. Mum and Pop wanted the very best for me, and they insisted that the only way for me to make my way in the world was by getting a good education. To say the least, I was rough at the edges and was not ready to attend a public school, so they sent me to live with Edward and Margaret Wentworth.

I went, but I was not happy about it. However, that lasted only a short time as Aunt and Uncle Wentworth reminded me of Mr. and Mrs. Sprat. The age of Uncle's congregation has already been mentioned, and the collected wisdom of the members of that parish equaled a public school education. I received instruction in the physical sciences, mathematics, geography, and history, and I learned to read Latin from my uncle and to speak French with my aunt.

But it was not all work, and no play. Every Friday night, the over-the-hill gang assembled at the parsonage for Bible charades, and with the exception of some of the most obscure figures, I can act out any character from either the Old or New Testament. Particular favorites of mine were David, so that I might slay the giant, and the Roman Centurion because I got to carry a spear. I was also introduced to the King James's Bible—not just as a religious work, but as a classic in the English language. It proved helpful in my career to be able to quote Scripture.

My school terms were broken into six-week intervals. After that, Pop would come and fetch me, and we would return to Kellynch. On that second return visit, Pop said that they had a surprise for me, and I saw what it was as soon as I entered the great hall. Mum had a baby bump, and the thought of having a brother or sister filled me with joy, and I would become the adored big brother to them all.

That is how my life went for the next several years, but after the members of Uncle Wentworth's parish had taught me all that they knew, it was time to move on to a university education or an apprenticeship. My parents were very patient with me as I tried to make a decision as to which direction I should go, but at that point, I only knew what I *didn't* want to do. And I did not want to go into the navy. After seeing how much my mother had missed my father during his months on blockade duty, I could not do that to my family, and my experience at the hospital left no doubt that I was not cut out for the medical profession. As far as taking holy orders, I would have made the worst curate in the history of the Church of England. I could just imagine some of the topics for my sermons: "Stop Whining and Do Something about It" or "He Never Promised You a Rose Garden." So what was I going to do?

Although Pop had retired from the navy, his interest in ships never waned. When he received a letter from a former fellow officer, now the captain of a merchant vessel, stating that he was in London, we went down to the docks. By this time, I had been aboard just about every type of ship there was, and so I asked if I might stay behind and observe all the activity taking place on the docks, including watching the Thames River Police in action. The policemen were pretty good, but if I could spot them, it meant that there was room for improvement. I had found my profession.

For the next fifteen years, I worked from a base at Wapping High Street, and there wasn't a disguise I didn't use to infiltrate the ranks of those who made their living by thievery. I drew extensively on my experiences as a youth in Bath. I could talk the talk and walk the walk. I went back to wearing clothes that were too short, too tight, and very dirty, and I blackened my teeth so they looked like everyone else's. In truth, I enjoyed being the reincarnated Swoosh. But when I went undercover so that I might arrest those on the receiving end of the stolen goods, thanks to the Reverend Wentworth, his parishioners, and my parents, I could be the son of a lord or a Bible-quoting clergyman. It was dangerous work, but I was good at my job. There was only one person who came near to me in the quality of my policing and that was my brother, Moves, who had been taught to read by my mother.

In 1839, the Thames River Police became a part of the newly-created Metropolitan Police Services, and I left the docks forever. By that time, I had married Hannah Crocker, Betty's younger sister, and a superb baker in her own right, and had started a family of my own. I eventually rose through the ranks to become a Commander, a rank my two sons surpassed.

And what of Kellynch? After William Elliot was disinherited, an agreement was made that the oldest son of the oldest child would inherit the estate and title, and since Elizabeth never married, by default it fell to Frederick and Anne's son, Frederick, Jr. Unlike his grandfather, the younger Rick had little interest in sitting home and reading the *Baronetage*. Instead, he was elected to Parliament and became one of the most prominent voices championing the expansion of the franchise to vote, which finally bore fruit in the Second Reform Act of 1867.

Now that I am retired, I have the time to write an autobiography which will begin with my experiences as a street urchin in Bath. I can still remember, as if it were yesterday, the first conversation I had with Miss Anne Elliot:

"I been tailing you for the last ten minutes, and if that toff had looked back but one time, he would have made you out," I had told her.

"Do you mean that he would have known that I was following him?"

"If he didn't know, he'd be the only one."

"But now I have lost him."

"No you ain't. I know where he's going, but I ain't in the habit of giving anything away for free," and Anne had placed a coin in my hand.

"That coin better have a friend or I'm out of here."

While Anne searched for another coin, she had asked, "What is your name?"

"Swoosh."

And although I have become a respectable member of society, there will always be a part of me that remains forever Swoosh.

The End

Correcting the Record

Florence Nightingale, an Englishwoman, noted for her nursing during the Crimean War (1853-56), and Clara Barton, founder of the American Red Cross, who worked miracles during the American Civil War (1861-65), were not alive when the original story took place. They were born one year apart (1820 and 1821), and both died in their nineties.

Napoleon's official surrender following the Battle of Waterloo was made to Captain Frederick Maitland on the British frigate *Bellerophon* on July 15, 1815. He was then transferred to *HMS Northumberland.* After ten weeks aboard ship, the former Emperor was introduced to his new home, St. Helena, a small, windswept island in the North Atlantic under the control of the British. He died in 1821.

The use of rubber in shoes did not come about until 1853, when Hiram Hutchinson of Britain invented the vulcanization process and applied it to footwear. He moved to France where he established A l'aigle (To the Eagle).

The Swiss company Tag Heuer claims to have had the first stopwatch patent, which was registered in 1869. Being Swiss, they would know.

Avon Products, Inc. was founded in 1886 by 28-year-old David McConnell, who sold books door-to-door and gave out perfume to entice women to buy his books. In 1954, their trademark advertising campaign, "Avon Calling," was introduced.

According to Wikipedia, Betty Crocker is a brand name and trademark of General Mills. The name was first developed by the Washburn Crosby Company in 1921 as a way to give a personalized response to consumer product questions. The name Betty was selected because it was viewed as a cheery, All-American name. It was paired with the last name Crocker, in honor of William Crocker, a Washburn Crosby Company director.

The hospital in Folkstone is entirely made up. During the Napoleonic wars, there were hospitals in Portsmouth, Greenwich,

Plymouth, and Great Yarmouth. However, casualties at the Battle of Waterloo were so horrendous that five British hospitals were established in Belgium where, in an area of two square miles, there were 40,000 dead or wounded. It seems likely that some of these casualties would be sent back to England—just not to my imaginary hospital in Folkstone.

Because of a quarter century of fighting wars, the French were more experienced in dealing with casualties and had "flying ambulances" in the field and had an established casualty evacuation system which got the wounded to a field hospital much quicker than the Allied (Prussian and British) forces. The French also made faster decisions than the British as to when to amputate a limb. As a result, the British fatality rate was much higher than that of the French. After 1815, the British pretty much copied the French system. It would not be needed until the Crimean War in the 1850s.

The reason I chose Folkestone was because of its later importance. During World War I, the wounded from France were placed on hospital ships traveling between Boulogne and Folkestone. While on board ship, the men would be asked "Where in Blighty do you live?" Once in port, they would be put on the boat train and sent to hospitals nearest to their homes.

Because Captain Wentworth was not on active duty while he was in Bath, he would not have been wearing his uniform and his awe-inspiring hat. Uniforms could not be used for the purposes of strutting about or for picking up the ladies. However, since I cannot imagine Rick, in all his awesomeness, without the hat and white breeches, I have sacrificed accuracy for comedic effect.

The Rev. Jack Sprat and his wife are real.

A final note: Although Jane Austen had two brothers who were Admirals in the Royal Navy during the Napoleonic Wars, *Persuasion* is the only novel in which that conflict has a role. She preferred to write about what she knew best: the intricate personalities and social mores of a country neighborhood. She left the wars to the historians.

About the Author

Mary Lydon Simonsen combines her love of history and the novels of Jane Austen in writing re-imaginings of Miss Austen's work. This is her first novel inspired by Austen's *Persuasion.* She is also the author of *Searching for Pemberley* which is now available in bookstores and on line. Her second *Pride and Prejudice* inspired novel, *The Perfect Bride for Mr. Darcy*, will be available in December 2010 and a third, *A Wife for Mr. Darcy*, has a release date of July 2010. Also available, exclusively on-line, is her modern novel, *The Second Date, Love Italian-American Style*. The author lives in Arizona.

COMING IN DECEMBER 2010

THE PERFECT BRIDE FOR MR. DARCY

(To win Elizabeth Bennet's heart, Mr. Darcy needs the help of a matchmaker…or two)

BY

MARY LYDON SIMONSEN

PUBLISHED BY SOURCEBOOKS

Praise for Searching for Pemberley*
By Mary Lydon Simonsen

"Simonsen is clever and evenhanded, maintaining an unhurried pace in both the Austen adventure and Maggie's love life. Fans of historical fiction and Austen should savor this leisurely read." (*Publisher's Weekly*)

"Written with respect for Jane Austen and a passion for history, Simonsen has combined two genres into a bittersweet war-time drama." (Laurel Ann Nattress, *AustenProse*)

"*Searching for Pemberley* grabbed me from the first page. Simonsen did an admirable job moving between the Regency, Great War, and World War II settings." (Anna Horner, *Diary of an Eccentric)*

"*Searching for Pemberley* is without a doubt a must read for any fan of *Pride and Prejudice* or simply a fan of people finding one another, beating the odds, and falling in love." (Cholla, *The Long and Short of It)*

"An exceptional Austen-inspired novel that combines history, romance, war, and *Pride and Prejudice."* (Meredith Esparza, *Austenesque Reviews)*

"I lost myself reading this story and empathized with each and every character along with their trials and tribulations. I just wanted to make them all a cup of tea." (Jennifer Ritter, *Jenny Loves to Read*)

"In this sweet and nostalgic novel, Simonsen borrows from *Pride and Prejudice* to create her own post-World War II love story." (Amanda Woytus, *The Romantic Times)*

"This was such a sweet, lovely read, with such rich characters, and it was with much regret that it had to end." (Bella McGuire, *A Bibliophile's Bookshelf)*

"Unlike any other Jane Austen sequel I have ever read. I thoroughly enjoyed every minute of it." (Grace Lociano, *Books Like Breathing*)

"Well done and rich in emotional and physical detail, showing Simonsen's deft research and keen eye." (Serena Agusto-Cox, *Savvy Verse & Wit*)

Searching for Pemberley is published by Sourcebooks Landmark
www.sourcebooks.com. For more information please visit:
www.marysimonsenfanfiction.blogspot.com.

*previously published as Pemberley Remembered

CPSIA information can be obtained at www.ICGtesting.com
Printed in the USA
244390LV00001B/140/P